**"Who are you?" she asked,
putting her paintbrush down.**

She bent to scoop up a piece of the fired clay and he quickly joined her, getting down on one knee.

"Here . . . let me help you." He tossed his hat onto the nearby table, narrowly missing the wet paints, and then set to picking up the remains of the mug. She couldn't help but be aware of the fresh pine scent that clung to him and frowned at herself for even noticing.

"*Danki.* . . ." she said when he'd made a small pile of the pieces on the table. "Now, who are—"

He looked up at her with startling blue eyes framed by thick lashes. "I'm . . . the answer to your ad."

"My ad. . . ."

He blinked and she was once more struck by the unusually intense color of his eyes.

"*Jah,* the ad—for the *Amisch* mail-order groom. I'm the one."

She rose to her feet and he hastily got up off his knee. "But . . . I don't understand," she said.

"You did write the ad? I—thought I'd respond in person."

She gazed up into his handsome face and shook her head slightly. "But . . . he's already here."

"Who?"

"The *Amisch* mail-order groom. He arrived this morning. . . ."

THE AMISH MAIL-ORDER GROOMS

Courting
Caleb

KELLY
LONG

NATIONAL BESTSELLING AUTHOR

ZEBRA BOOKS
KENSINGTON PUBLISHING CORP.
www.kensingtonbooks.com

Prologue

WANTED: An Amish Mail-Order Groom. Age 20-30. Must understand that courting will follow the marriage ceremony in *gut* order. Seeking one who is reserved, quiet, and bookish. Must cherish a woman as the vessel of *Gott*'s making. Bride would prefer groom to write poetry and have a cultured reading voice. Reply to: Abigail Mast, Blackberry Falls . . .

Twenty-five-year-old Caleb King read the ad in the *Renova Record* for the fifth time, then shook his head. He eased his black hat back from his forehead and leaned against the warm side of his horse, Tommy. He felt safe with the horse . . . *no questions* . . . *no demands*. . . .

He glanced up as someone slid the barn door open, and he squinted in the sudden wintery sunshine. When Caleb turned and saw that it was his *fater*, he had the childish desire to hide the newspaper behind his back and probably would have if the situation hadn't been so deadly serious.

Still, he was unprepared for the brutal backhand his *fater* calmly delivered.

"Why did you do it?" His *fater*'s straight yellowed teeth looked like an animal's, and Caleb struggled to focus for a moment as he licked blood from the side of his mouth.

"Every other suitor within a fifty-mile radius was at her *fater*'s funeral except for you. But it's you Charity Miller wants, and I swear that it's you she'll have."

Caleb resisted the urge to close his eyes against the memory of the last encounter he'd had with Charity Miller. He'd caught her kicking a stray dog with a well-shod foot, and when he'd picked the animal up and out of harm's way, the girl had merely shrugged at him with menacing eyes. "What difference does a stray *hund* make?" she'd sneered. "Besides, sometimes it feels *gut* to let others know who's in charge. Don't you think?"

Caleb had felt vaguely like throwing up or giving her a taste of her own medicine. He'd shuddered to think that his *daed* wanted a union between Charity and himself. A marriage to join their adjacent farmlands to create King's Acres—the largest farm in the whole of Elk County.

Now Caleb snapped back to the moment and looked into his *fater*'s angry face; then he squared his shoulders. "*Nee, Fater.* I will not marry Charity Miller. I have another . . . engagement."

"What? Where?" the older man bit out in red-faced fury.

Caleb smiled and clutched the newspaper tighter. "In a place called Blackberry Falls. . . ."

Chapter One

It was a cold, late-November afternoon as Abigail Mast, the potter of Blackberry Falls, gently lifted a paintbrush and touched it to the dab of pink paint that she'd made from juiced mulberries. She brushed the color onto the mug she held in her opposite hand and steadily shaped the first petal of a rose. The action was calming, and she needed peace—especially today. She shivered as a gust of wintery air blew in through the open door and swirled past her ankles. She liked the door open to catch the air even on the most intemperate of days.

"Abigail Mast?"

The mug fell from her hand and smashed on the hardwood floor of her cabin. She glanced up to the open doorway and frowned at the stranger who stood there. He was big and broad shouldered and *Amisch*, based on his clothing. The afternoon light glinted on his overly long blond hair. *At least he has his hat in his hands,* she mused. *He can't be all that threatening.* She was used to living alone on the fringe of the community and she preferred it that way.

"Who are you?" she asked, putting her paintbrush

down. She bent to scoop up a piece of the fired clay and he quickly joined her, getting down on one knee.

"Here . . . let me help you." He tossed his hat onto the nearby table, narrowly missing the wet paints, and then set to picking up the remnants of the mug. She couldn't help but be aware of the fresh pine scent that clung to him and frowned at herself for even noticing.

"*Danki*," she said when he'd made a small pile of the pieces on the table. "Now, who are—"

He looked up at her with startling blue eyes framed by thick lashes. "I'm . . . the answer to your ad."

"My ad . . ."

He blinked, and she was once more struck by the unusually intense color of his eyes.

"*Jah*, the ad—for the *Amisch* mail-order groom. I'm the one."

She rose to her feet and he hastily got up off his knee. "But . . . I don't understand," she said.

"You did write the ad? I—thought I'd respond in person."

She gazed up into his handsome face and shook her head slightly. "But . . . he's already here."

"Who?"

"The *Amisch* mail-order groom. He arrived this morning. . . ."

Caleb felt a sinking in his stomach as he came to grips with the words she spoke. *Idiot . . . Of course another man is here already. I should have written. . . .*

"Where have you come from?" Abigail asked with a frown, as if searching for a way out of the dilemma.

"Renova," he said absently. "My *bruder* Matthew married someone from here a few months back."

"*Ach*, you mean my *gut* friend, Tabitha Stolfus."

He looked at her, taking in the sheen of her brown hair, which was nicely parted and mostly covered by her *kapp*. She was tall and held herself erect with perfect posture, yet the top of her head barely came to his chin.

"Does Matthew know that you're here?"

Caleb sighed to himself and shook his head. "*Nee*—I came rather suddenly." He watched her wet her lips. "I suppose—"

"Great walleyed catfish and pork bellies! Who do we have here?"

Caleb turned to see a spry, elderly *Amischer* with a thick gray beard standing behind him.

"I'm Caleb King. . . . I came to see Abigail because—"

"Because, uh, he's Matthew King's *bruder*. He wondered if I knew the way to Tabitha and Matthew's," Abigail replied quickly.

Caleb turned back to watch as a flush stained the fine features of the woman before him. Clearly, lying didn't come easily to her and the thought made him strangely glad. He wasn't about to betray her to the *auld* man.

"*Jah*, my *bruder* Matthew . . ."

Caleb paused and Abigail hurried on. "Uh, *sei se gut*, excuse me, Caleb. This is Bishop Kore."

Caleb shook hands as he rapidly considered the circumstances. *Lying to the bishop. . . . It was enough to get a body shunned, but still, she risked it. Was it possible that she had not sought permission to write the ad?*

"Bishop, sir, perhaps you would show me to my *bruder*'s. I've got my horse and dog out back here."

"*Jah*." The bishop nodded. "MoonPies and Popsicles! Let's *geh*!"

Caleb resisted the urge to study Bishop Kore's bald pate, wondering what ailed the *auld* man's mind, but then, Abigail Mast was acting as if such talk was normal. Caleb followed the bishop out of the cabin and briefly turned back to look at her. *There's something about her that makes me think of swimming in deep water.* But then he shook his head and walked out into the sunshine of the wintry day.

"I cannot believe that this has happened! Two of them! What are you going to do?" Mercy knew her voice rose an octave as she stared at her younger sister. Abigail looked as serious and thoughtful as usual, and this only irritated Mercy more. She could never fully understand Abigail's calm yet closed personality.

"They say still water runs deep," Mercy muttered.

Then she straightened and glared at her sister once more. "Abigail—I'm serious. What are you going to do?"

"Perhaps marry Phillip Miller. He got here first. . . ."

Mercy put her hands on her hips, pinching her ample curves to calm her temper. "I don't know why you have to marry either one of them. What kind of thing is it to send in the mail for a husband? Your life is full enough at the pottery, isn't it? Why do you—"

Mercy stopped speaking abruptly as her fourteen-year-old *sohn*, Joshua, entered the cabin with a blast of cold air. Mercy sighed to herself as she considered her *buwe*'s tall frame and shock of wheat-colored hair. He was every inch his father and Mercy had to admit to herself and to *Gott* that she wished Joshua resembled her instead of the shiftless *Englischer* whom she had thought loved her.

"I got the goats done, Mamm. Can I head out to do some ice fishing now?"

Mercy frowned. "With Tad?"

Tad Stolfus was a troublemaker if she'd ever seen one. The *buwe* had been in and out of mischief since the day he'd turned ten and rode Grossmuder Mildred's pet hog, Henrietta, through the cemetery and burial service of *auld* man Tucker.

"*Jah*," Joshua confirmed. "With Tad. Okay?"

She nodded reluctantly. "But be back by supper and make sure you've got a few trout to put on the table."

"Sure will, Mamm. *Danki*. Goodbye, Aenti Abigail."

Mercy watched her younger sister embrace Joshua and wondered once more how she was going to help Abigail out of her mess with men.

"You don't need to worry about this, Mercy. I'll figure things out," Abigail said briskly once Joshua had closed the door behind him.

"How?"

"Well," Abigail mused, "*Gott* says that He is working things out for good in our lives if we love Him, so maybe there were meant to be two mail-order grooms."

"You cannot marry two men!"

Abigail gave her a sudden smile. "*Nee*, but perhaps I can court two. I hadn't wanted the bishop to know about the ad, but now I think it will be all right. I'm going to talk with him this very minute."

"Court? Two? Wait! Let me *geh* with you."

Mercy snatched up her black cloak and followed Abigail outside even as she muttered to herself about the burdens of being an *aulder* sister.

Chapter Two

Phillip Miller never thought he'd be bathing in a water-fall, in fresh falling snow, to get ready for his marriage ceremony. In fact, he'd never imagined being married at all. He was a farmer, through and through—the very earth was his mistress. And even in the winter, he thought of heirloom seeds, plant catalogs, and the design and layout of next year's gardens. But as he lathered his jet-black hair with a chunk of gritty homemade soap, he mused that a man had to have support on a farm at times. A wife—not just a hired girl—and *sohns*, he supposed. To help till the ground. He thought briefly of his soon-to-be wife's rather solemn but pretty face and he wondered how he'd ever bridge the gap between that seriousness and making *sohns* with her. . . .

He'd just flicked suds out of his eyes when he caught the sound of cheerful whistling coming through the deluge of icy cold water around him.

He squinted at the bank where he'd left his clothes and glasses atop his coat and made out the blurry shapes of what he thought were two *buwes*. Better safe than sorry, though. . . . He had no desire to wade out of the creek and frighten a woman with his nakedness. . . .

"Uh . . . *buwes*?" he called over the rush of water.

"*Jah?*" two youthful voices responded, and Phillip felt safe to move. He slogged over the icy and slippery rocks of the full creek and climbed the bank. He eyed the *buwes* for a moment while he got his glasses on, then hastily drew on his pants and wrangled his blue shirt over his wet back. Boots, suspenders, coat, and hat followed in due order, and then Phillip cleared his throat as he struggled to keep his shivering to a minimum.

"Ice fishing, are you? What are you using for bait? I'm Phillip Miller, by the way." He held out his hand and had it wrung in succession by the two *buwes*.

"I'm Tad," the shorter, dark-haired *buwe* said with a laugh in his voice. Phillip smiled good-naturedly because he could see the merry trouble brewing in Tad's brown eyes, and he reminded himself to keep an eye out for the *buwe* in any questionable circumstance.

"I'm Joshua." The second youth's voice was carefully polite, and he seemed bashful. "We're using grubs to fish."

Phillip nodded. *Here then is the faithful friend, the sometime victim and usually unknowing accomplice to Tad's scheming. . . .* Phillip understood the role, having grown up with a Tad of his own. . . . He quickly turned his thoughts from his boyhood and pulled on his black gloves. "All right, *buwes*. Hope you'll have *gut* fishing. I have to *geh*—I'm late for my wedding."

* * *

Caleb was struck by the quality of the craftsmanship that he saw as he stood in his *bruder*'s home. The main room of the cabin seemed full of intricate wood carving, from the arched beams of the ceiling to the detailed rungs on the ladder that led to the loft.

"All courtesy of my gifted *frau*," Matthew said with a smile, and Caleb felt himself pulled close to his *aulder bruder* for a quick hug.

Caleb felt tears sting at the backs of his eyes. *It has been so long since someone has touched me with kindness. . . .* He knew he could have sought out many girls back home—both *Amisch* and *Englisch*—who would have eagerly satisfied his normal need for human contact, but somehow, a hug from the *bruder* he admired touched him more at the moment.

"It's *gut* to see you," Caleb managed; then he bent to embrace his petite sister-in-law, Tabitha. He was struck by her physical beauty as he imagined any man would be, but there was also a confidence about her and an air of purpose. Still, he couldn't stop the image of Abigail the potter from leaping into his mind. Something about her seriousness drew him . . . but it was all for naught now that the true mail-order groom had arrived in Blackberry Falls.

Caleb noticed that Bishop Kore, who had been genially standing to the side in the rush of greetings, now hopped on one foot to open the door and ushered in Abigail and another woman. There was a flurry of laughter and snowflakes that seemed to bubble around Caleb, making him wish that he might join this seemingly happy community.

Then he heard a strong knock at the door.

"Ladles and soup meat! We've got the last beaver to the party!" The bishop opened the door once more and a tall man with damp black hair entered. He seemed to gravitate toward Abigail.

Caleb knew at once that this was the groom who had answered the ad properly.

"Well, now," Bishop Kore suddenly thundered in a voice loud enough to cause Caleb to blink. "Claw-foot tables and onion baths! We have got a situation here. . . ."

Caleb felt the strange desire to say something— anything—because he knew instinctively that Abigail the potter had been found out. But the *auld* bishop was on a roll. . . .

"Abigail, is there something you'd like to discuss?"

Caleb watched Abigail's pretty face flush, but her mouth was set with visible determination.

"*Jah*, Bishop Kore. I must confess to all here involved that I decided to send an ad to the *Renova Record* for a mail-order groom."

"Aha!" The bishop punctuated his exclamation with a slight tapping of his toes. "And you had multiple replies, right?"

Caleb found his voice. "*Nee*, sir. I was not . . . did not write a reply. I came without an invitation, so Abigail has only one prospective bridegroom. I should *geh* out and put up my horse in the barn and leave you all to celebrate a wedding together."

He nodded briefly and was about to leave the pleasantly warm room when the bishop roared at him.

"*Nee, buwe!* You'll stay right here! Now, is it my understanding that both you and you"—he waved a hand in the dark-haired man's direction after pointing a stubby finger in Caleb's chest—"want to marry Miss Abigail? Is that right?"

Caleb nodded and the other man did likewise.

"All right," Bishop Kore continued. "I say that Abigail needs to court both of you—not to end in two marriages, of course. But rather, to work with what *Derr Herr* has provided. Now let's see, it's nearly December. . . . We'll give you until Valentine's to make a proper decision as to who to marry and, in the meanwhile, you, Caleb, will reside with Birchbark up on the far side of Blackberry Falls."

Caleb thought maybe that he'd imagined it, but there was a faint, collective groan from those gathered. But he had no time to hash it out in his mind before his opponent—so to speak—was ordered to stay with someone called Grossmuder Mildred for the duration of the double courting.

"Now—" Bishop Kore gave everyone a genial smile, apparently back to acting like a mild but *narrisch auld mon* instead of a thundering preacher. "I think this should be *gut*. You'll have to work out your own times for the courting and, *buwes*, I expect you both to contribute to the community here in some manner. No questions? *Gut* again. I'll see you *buwes* to your respective hosts."

Caleb felt dazed as he nodded in Abigail's direction and followed the bishop outside. It had started to snow seriously now, and he was glad for the familiarity of his horse and his dog. But, he wondered, with a vague unease, what good could possibly come from living with someone called Birchbark. . . .

Chapter Three

Abigail watched the men troop outdoors and felt un-expected laughter bubble up inside her chest so that it was difficult to keep a straight face. She longed to hug her arms around herself but didn't like to show such obvious emotion. Besides, Mercy was working herself up into a frenzy now that the bishop had gone.

"This is absurd!" her sister declared.

"*Ach*, I don't know," Matthew offered with a smile as he pulled his petite wife into the circle of his outstretched arm. "My *bruder* would never allow himself to be roped into the absurd. The strange, maybe. But never the absurd."

Abigail smiled at Tabitha and Matthew. She knew that her best friend's husband loved to tease, but Mercy clearly wasn't in the mood. In fact, her sister gave another huff of disapproval, then excused herself from the cabin.

"All right, ladies," Matthew said lightly. "I think that's my cue to take myself out to do some chores. I know you want to discuss this strange idea of mail-order grooms." He bent to kiss Tabitha, winked at Abigail, then pulled on his coat and hat and left the cabin.

"Now"—Tabitha laughed—"before I head down to

the mill, tell me how you managed to hook two men with one ad."

Abigail shook her head. "I'm not sure. . . . How is the mill, by the way?"

Tabitha had recently been given leadership of her *fater*'s mill, an unusual role for an *Amisch* woman, even though many *Amisch* women ran businesses of their own. But Abigail could tell that Tabitha was not to be led away from the point at hand.

"You're going to court two men, and only Bishop Kore can imagine how that might work. Do you have any inclination toward one or the other?"

Abigail drew a deep breath. "*Nee*, how could I?"

"Hmmm . . . Well, I suppose you'll have to pray for the right choice. I guess I was blessed that there was and is only one Matthew King."

"Your own mail-order groom," Abigail agreed, rising to her feet. Her practical nature told her that she would somehow manage the unusual courtships set before her, and she followed her friend out the door into the frosty air.

The snow began to fall in heavy, wet, flakes, and Phillip found himself hopelessly lost. The bishop's vague pointing toward Grossmuder Mildred's cabin had been meaningless in the storm, turning his surroundings to a blur of white. He finally bumped into a solid wall and realized he had at least found shelter of some sort. He felt his way along to what appeared to be the main doorframe and tried the latch; it gave, and he half fell inside.

"What do you think you're doing?"

The feminine voice was shrill, and he groaned faintly

to himself—if this was Grossmuder Mildred, then he might be in for a long few months. He rose, took off his hat, and straightened to his full height. Then he removed his fogged glasses. He could make out the cheerful brightness of a fire in the grate and the smell of something warm and sweet that reminded him of childhood.

"Here."

A white tea towel was thrust under his nose and he took it and began to clean his glasses with his hat under his right arm. Then he slipped the lenses on and was surprised to see the redheaded woman—Abigail's sister,—standing with her hands on her curved hips.

"Hello." He rubbed the towel through his damp bangs, then gave her a half smile. "I'm sorry. The bishop pointed in this direction when he told me to *geh* to Grossmuder Mildred's and then the snow really started to come down—"

"And you got lost." It was a statement more than a question, and he could hear the doubt in her voice.

"I can *geh*," he answered evenly. "If you'll just point me—"

"You'll never find it in this snow and you've already dripped all over my clean floor. You might as well wait a few minutes. I'm Mercy, by the way. Abigail's *aulder* sister."

"Okaaay." He stood, shivering and uncomfortable in his wet, black wool coat. "I'm Phillip Miller." She gave him a stiff nod, then turned back to the stove. Clearly, Mercy did not mean to give him a proverbial *Amisch* welcome. He watched as she opened the cookstove and slid out a pan of sticky buns. She put them on top of the stove trivet then gave him a wry glance.

"I suppose you're hungry?" she asked with a frown.

"Not a bit. I detest fresh sticky rolls and cinnamon buns of all kinds."

She gave him a wry smile. "Fine. Hang your coat up and *kumme* have a bun and one cup of coffee."

"*Ach*, I'd never ask for more than one." He slipped his coat off and found the wooden peg to the left of the door. An assortment of smaller *buwes'* coats hung on several pegs, but he didn't see a man's coat.

He turned back to face the cheery kitchen and stepped out of his sopping boots, then made his way to the table, where Mercy had thumped down a heavy coffee mug. He sat down on a chair, which creaked alarmingly under his weight, and glanced up at his reluctant hostess as she served him.

He guessed that she was in her late twenties, but he quickly dropped his gaze to his plate when a flush colored her cheeks. He didn't want to offend her, especially as she was Abigail's sister. He told himself that he was simply curious, and information from Abigail's older sister might give him insight into his potential future *frau*. So, he sank the fork into the treat she'd given him and had the first bite lifted partway to his mouth when she snapped at him, her green eyes flashing.

"I don't approve of you."

He put his fork down. "Somehow I guessed that."

"Did you? Did you also guess that I think it's *narrisch* for my sister to do—this mail-order groom thing? Did you guess that I'll never see her hurt, by you or the other man, or anyone else who happens to come plodding up to Blackberry Falls? Abigail is out of her mind to marry a complete stranger. . . . *Ach*, and did you guess that I'm thirty-four, because you wondered, didn't you?" She banged the coffeepot on the stove.

Phillip had the distinct feeling that she would have continued if the front door of the cabin hadn't burst open, sending snow flying and ushering in the two teens he'd met at the falls that afternoon.

Mercy swallowed the words she was going to heap on the mail-order whatever-he-was and focused on Joshua and Tad.

"Hang up your things, *buwes*. I've got hot sticky buns." She tried to keep her voice neutral, having no desire to let her temper get the best of her again around Phillip Miller.

But instead of her *sohn* and his friend hanging up their snowy coats, they clumped across the floor, dragging a string of frozen trout, and began to talk to the man at the table in excited tones.

Mercy felt herself frowning. "*Buwes*, look at the floor!"

Phillip put down his fork and rose from the table. "*Geh* on, *buwes*. Take off your things and help me dry the floor for your *mamm*." He turned to look at her. "We met earlier at the falls. Is Josh your *sohn*?"

"Joshua," she bit out. "And yes, he's mine." She swallowed hard and was amazed to feel tears prick at her eyes as the man and *buwes* got dishcloths from the nearby sink to tidy the floor.

Mercy wanted to find fault with the way they were working, but nothing came to her lips. She could only swipe hastily at her eyes and move to cut two more buns from the pan. *Why en der weldt am I crying?* She decided it was because of her concern over Abigail and her strange ad.

She set about cleaning the fish, trying to ignore the cheerful male chatter behind her. The talk was something that she was not familiar with, and she realized that Joshua rarely sounded so happy. She supposed that her rather stern love for her *sohn* was not good enough, in some ways, especially when it came to trying to be both *fater* and *mamm* to the *buwe*. She sighed faintly, knowing she was simply feeling sorry for herself and that *Gott* was *Fater* to all.

She'd turned with the plate of expertly filleted fish, intent on getting to the frying pan, when she ran full tilt into Phillip's broad chest. She looked up and gave him a shaky smile as he caught the plate of fish.

At the rate the snow was falling, Caleb expected the bishop to come into the cabin with him, but instead, the *auld* man waved him on to the barn, then disappeared into the curtain of snow. Caleb entered the warm confines of the barn and turned up a lantern he found hanging on the wall. He wiped Tommy down, then settled him with food and a comfortable bed of hay for the *nacht*. He scooped up Fred, the faithful yellow Lab that he'd rescued from Charity Miller's kick, and struggled from the barn to the nearby cabin.

Caleb pounded on the door with as much force as he could but realized that he probably wasn't going to be heard over the wind of the storm. He hiked Fred up higher on his shoulder and tried the latch, which gave so easily that he stumbled in the door.

He was met with cheerful warmth from the burning embers of a stone fireplace and decided that his host had not been gone long. He lowered Fred to the floor, where the dog scuttled to the hearth. Caleb decided he'd do the same. He slipped off his black coat and hat, hung them up, then made for an oversized bentwood rocker near the fireplace. He let his gaze travel up the log walls around him and decided that he'd enjoy living in a cabin instead of the austere farmhouse he'd grown up in. He closed his eyes for a minute, lulled by the fire, only to jump from his chair moments later as the cabin door banged open.

A mammoth man, covered in snow and heavy furs, pushed the door back against the wind and Caleb noted that the stranger didn't appear to be surprised by his presence.

The thickly bearded *Amisch* man drew his large hands from his fur mittens and nodded at Caleb.

"Name's Birchbark. What ya see is what ya git. . . ."

Caleb had to hide a smile. *If only everybody went around with a life slogan like that. . . . Caleb King . . . no idea what I'm doing. . . .* He shook hands with Birchbark, then stood rather awkwardly until his host cracked his large back and gave a prodigious yawn.

"I heard you'll be stayin' awhile."

Caleb nodded. "If that's all right."

"Right as rain. Can get kinda lonesome up here. What's yer dog's name?"

"Fred."

Birchbark gave a low growl of approval and bent to stroke Fred's yellow coat. "Says ya rescued him from some screwy *Amisch* girl—full of money and hate. Says she kicked him before you came along."

Caleb blinked, then rubbed his hand across his eyes. *Am I hearing things or did Birchbark just have a conversation with my dog?*

"*Nah, buwe,* ya ain't *narrisch.* It's a gift *Derr Herr* give me. I talk much better ta animals than ta people."

"All right." Caleb nodded. At this point in the emotionally exhausting day, he'd believe just about anything, so a hairy mountain man who talked to Fred seemed to be the least of his concerns—because, somehow, he had to win the potter's heart.

Chapter Four

The storm passed and by daybreak, the snow and ice had transformed Blackberry Falls into a wintery delight, with gumdrop bushes and laden branches bending as if curtseying to the day.

Abigail looked on the scene with a feeling of deep contentment. During her morning prayers, she had felt led to study the Bible verse that read "For I know the plans I have for you—plans to prosper you and not to harm you, plans to give you hope and a future. . . ." She believed that *Gott* was speaking to her through His Word and that there was change coming into her otherwise quiet life. She leaned against the deep windowsill of the cabin's sitting room and smiled softly to herself. She was to have the pleasure of courting with two men; it was a heady thought.

She pressed her forehead to the cold, ice-etched window and prayed that *Derr Herr* would help her to choose the right man. And when she lifted her head to look out upon the day once more, she nearly jumped as Phillip crossed the line of her vision and gave her a cheerful wave.

She waved back, taking in his dark good looks, then hurried over to open the door for him.

"*Gut* morning," he said, sweeping off his hat and giving her an infectious grin. "I've brought some seed catalogs over. They're not new, but they're pretty to look at."

He held out a brown wrapped parcel and she took it with a smile.

"*Sei se gut, kumme* in." She widened the door to accommodate his large frame and she found that he carried the scent of fresh snow with him.

"Your hair's wet," she muttered, just catching herself in time to keep from scolding about wet hair and cold air—she didn't want to sound like a *mamm*.

"*Jah*, the falls were freezing this morning."

Abigail's mind flashed with a sudden image of him bare-chested, standing in the icy water. She swallowed hard and squeezed the seed catalog package hard. *Wherever did that thought come from?* Still, she realized that it was perfectly normal to feel attraction for a handsome *mon*—especially one who'd *kumme* to court her.

"*Sei se gut*, sit down at the table. I've got some hot chocolate heating."

"That sounds great!"

There was a brief awkward pause while Abigail joined him and opened the first seed catalog. Then Phillip spoke abruptly.

"I met your sister last *nacht*."

"*Ach* . . ." Abigail murmured, knowing Mercy's moods. "How was she?"

She could tell by the way his jaw worked that he was struggling not to say what he thought. Abigail laughed. "Don't worry, Phillip. I know Mercy!"

He laughed then too. "What is her story? And I met Joshua and Tad as well. They both seem like great *kinner*. Does Mercy's husband work away from home?"

"Mercy isn't married." Abigail spoke the words calmly, waiting for the normal surprised reaction. Of course, there were other women like Mercy in the *Amisch* community— women who'd conceived and never married, but their circumstances were difficult. Abigail knew her sister felt that she was always being judged, and that hurt.

But Phillip merely nodded his dark head and opened another seed catalog, and Abigail was pleased by his silence.

Caleb woke with a pounding headache. The shifting air pressure of the mountain made his sinus cavities throb. He wanted to lie in bed, but once he turned and nearly rolled into Birchbark's armpit, he decided getting up was better. And he knew that tonight he'd sleep on the floor, no matter how cold it might be.

He fed Fred some rehydrated jerky that he'd had in his pack, then quietly opened the cabin door to reveal the beautiful scenery outside. He stepped out onto the snow-encrusted porch, then reached up to snap off a low-hanging icicle. He sucked at the tip of the ice reflectively, wondering what the day might bring and when his headache would subside.

"Ya got the door open, *buwe*!"

"Sorry." Caleb stepped back inside and closed the door behind him. Birchbark's brownish hair stood on end and Caleb could now see some gray strands in the mess.

"Are ya gonna stand there and stare at a *mon* or git ta makin' breakfast?"

Caleb blinked as his head pounded at the *aulder* man's subdued roar. "Breakfast," he mumbled, the icicle between his teeth. He was hoping that the burning cold would distract him from his headache as he stepped over Fred and lifted a massive cast-iron skillet to the cookstove top.

He was a dab hand at cooking, mostly because of the necessity of eating back home. As the youngest, he'd often been stuck with what his *fater* called "the woman's work." So, it was with minimal fuss that he whipped up scrambled eggs, pancakes, and slab bacon, as well as hot coffee. He was aware of Birchbark moving behind him, and heard the mountain man give an appreciative sniff. Then Caleb plated the food, grabbed a maple syrup tin from a nearby open shelf, and joined his host at the small hickory wood table at the side of the stove.

For several long minutes, there was no sound but Birchbark chewing. Then he gave a long belch and slapped his huge hand down on the table, making the salt and pepper shakers jump.

"By all that's *gut, buwe*! Ya can cook!"

"*Danki*." Caleb nodded, swallowing his own food.

"Don't let yer woman know."

"Hmmm?"

Birchbark sighed and burped again—a sound so prolonged that it seemed to come from some dark pit. "Don't let her know right off. Surprise her with yer cookin'."

Caleb got to his feet, then scraped the remains of his breakfast into a bowl for Fred. "Well, I don't, er, have a woman, Birchbark, but your idea is *gut*. A great meal served by lantern light might make for an interesting evening of courting."

Birchbark grunted then looked down at Fred. "He wants two more eggs, sunny-side up."

Caleb got up and cracked the eggs with mute resignation, wondering what else his dog would want.

"Well, I best git on. I'll be gone overnight," Birchbark announced.

Caleb turned. "You're going to work? Uh, what do you do? Won't the snow hold you up? I imagine you'll have a hard time getting through."

"Ha! Love waits fer no man."

Caleb tried to follow the trail of the conversation as he watched Birchbark swipe back a green curtain to reveal one of the most abundantly stocked pantries he'd ever seen. A towering shelf was chock-full of preserves, and jams, and pickles, and canned tomatoes, as well as potatoes and sacks of sugar and flour.

Caleb watched as Birchbark pulled a large, wood-framed backpack from a corner, then turned back to the shelf and ran his work-hardened hands over the various jars and supplies with surprising care. He seemed to be making a very purposeful selection of items to add to his pack.

"What do you mean about love not waiting?" Caleb asked once the pack was nearly full.

"Jest what I said, *buwe*. You'll find out fer yerself someday." Birchbark added a final quart mason jar of blackberry preserves, then set about pulling on his long fur coat. He hefted the pack onto his back and nodded at Caleb. "Open the door, *buwe*. I'll be back tomorrow sometime. And Fred wants ta remind ya not ta burn the cabin down."

"You can count on me," Caleb said drily as he opened the front door. He watched Birchbark make his way off the front porch and out into the knee-high snow; then Caleb went back into the cabin. He caught sight of the lantern Birchbark had left on the table and hurried to take it outside.

But when he stood on the front porch, he realized that Birchbark was gone. "Odd," Caleb muttered to himself. The *aulder mon* must have been moving amazingly fast to have already cleared the slope and disappeared into the tree line. Caleb went back inside and looked down at Fred, wondering what the dog was thinking. . . .

Mercy fed the goats, then trudged through the snow, feeling rather exhilarated despite the sodden condition of her skirts. She'd always loved the snow. She'd prepared a kettle of sweet baked beans and bacon and wanted to make sure that Abigail had some for lunch. She worried that her younger sister didn't eat enough or even take the time to eat while she was involved with her pottery. And now, with this *narrisch* courting scheme, who knew when Abigail would find time to eat properly?

She supposed she might have sent Joshua over, but the *buwe* already was busy with his chores and she'd promised to let him *geh* sledding with Tad, though visions of broken arms and legs danced behind her eyes. But still, Joshua deserved some fun. She deliberately pushed aside thoughts of her *sohn*'s excited talk with Phillip Miller the evening before; she didn't trust the *mon* one bit. . . .

She finally reached Abigail's cabin and struggled briefly with the latch before plowing inside. She stopped cold, feeling her face flame, as Phillip Miller rose from the small kitchen table to *kumme* forward and help steady her.

"I'm fine," she snapped, and he moved away with the small-handled kettle that she reluctantly gave over.

"It's barely ten o'clock in the morning," Mercy hissed at Abigail. "What is he doing courting at this hour?" But she got nothing but a shushing smile from Abigail, which only served to make Mercy feel more frustrated.

Abigail was helping her with her wraps and cloak and sopping bonnet. "I don't need to stay. I—"

"Mmmm . . . baked beans with brown sugar and bacon. These smell delicious."

Mercy turned with her sister to look at Phillip, who'd set the kettle on the table and lifted the lid.

"They're for Abigail," she huffed.

Phillip replaced the lid. "Sorry."

Mercy watched as Abigail calmly hung up her wet things. *She felt foolish somehow—and it surely was all Phillip Miller's fault . . .*

Phillip felt vaguely sorry for Mercy but knew instinctively that she wouldn't appreciate the sentiment. And, although she was quite pretty, he'd never met a more cantankerous woman . . . Abigail's sister or not.

He sat back down, then caught Abigail's eye. "Perhaps you need some extra firewood cut? It would give you ladies time to visit."

"*Jah*," Mercy snapped. "*Geh* cut two cords full."

He frowned, thinking he had better leave the two sisters alone, but Abigail laughed a bit and waved him back into his chair.

"Mercy, come and sit and have some cocoa. I think that you need to get used to Herr Miller. After all, he may become your *bruder*-in-law one day."

Phillip waited for the retort he'd expected from Mercy and hid a smile when she sat down opposite him at the small table, blatantly glaring. *She might be feisty, but I like her willingness to defend her sister at any cost. . . .*

Abigail served them the hot cocoa in large, blue glazed mugs.

"Some of your own work?" Phillip asked, indicating his mug with a smile.

He watched Abigail give a modest smile. "*Jah*."

"They're beau—"

"Beautiful?" Mercy queried in a saccharine tone. "Of course they are. Abigail is the most talented potter in the mountains. What about making a toast to her eyebrows and telling her they're beautiful too—which they most certainly are. . . . You'll have to do more than pass compliments to win my sister's heart."

"Mercy, let him be," Abigail admonished.

"*Nee*." Phillip chuckled. "I rather like your sister's temper. It matches her hair."

Abigail groaned faintly and Phillip raised a quizzical brow while Mercy looked as if she was choking with temper.

Abigail glanced at him with a faint smile. "Mercy positively hates when anyone comments on her—well, hair. Don't you, Mercy? Now if it had been russet, or strawberry blond . . ."

Phillip flashed Mercy a commiserating smile. "*Ach*, vanity! And in an *Amisch* woman at that. At least it's not purple, you know? Though dyeing it some outrageous color might lift your spirits a bit or at least calm that fiery temp—"

"That's it!" Mercy slammed her hands flat on the table, then got to her feet. "I am not going to sit in my sister's *haus* and be baited like—"

"A hungry trout?" Phillip supplied, keeping a look of innocence on his face. It was simply too much fun to tease Mercy, but he was surprised at his own persistence.

Mercy flounced to the door and Phillip smothered a laugh. He decided that apologizing to Abigail might be worth it since he loved to tease, but then he realized he'd have to apologize to Mercy as well, and that thought gave him regretful pause. . . .

Chapter Five

Abigail spent the rest of the day in her pottery shop, which was really nothing more than a large back room in her cabin. She was finishing a set of large cereal bowls for Tabitha and Matthew, who were still growing their supply of dishes.

As she worked, she reflected on the visit she'd had from Phillip Miller. Certainly, it might have ended with some more interesting conversation if Mercy had not left in a huff. Phillip, too, seemed to have abandoned his seed catalogs and bid her *gut* day.

He had promised to come back the following day though, and of this, she was glad. She found him quiet and companionable, even though his interest in the seed catalogs seemed intense. But she knew how she got when there was a book on pottery around. She smiled as she turned the clay. She was usually very quiet as she worked, the motion of her hands bringing her great peace.

She'd learned from her *fater* the Word of *Derr Herr* about a "peace that passes understanding." She let her mind move back through time with the fluidity of the clay she touched. For a moment, she was a child again, never afraid when she accidentally broke a piece on the dusty floor of the pottery.

Her *fater* would chuckle reassuringly and pull her close for a hug. "Never mind, my *maedel*. We will make a new thing."

Abigail came back to the moment when she heard a knock on her door. She grabbed a rag and tried to dry off the clay, opening the door latch with both her elbow and hand. She couldn't help but wonder who might be calling so late.

Caleb took his hat off and stepped through the potter's door.

"Hiya." He nodded at her. "*Danki* for letting me in. I know it's late." He tried to hold Fred's inquisitive nose and wriggling frame back with his leg.

"I'm always up late," she admitted, and he watched her pretty face flush becomingly. "You and your pup are welcome to *kumme* in. I just need to wash my hands quick."

He entered the kitchen of her neat home and Abigail soon returned briskly from washing her hands. "Here, let me have your coat, *sei se gut*."

He slipped out of the thick, damp wool and then waited in awkward silence as she hung it up and smoothed its folds absently with her slender hands. He shivered, feeling a tingling warmth across his shoulders, almost as though she were touching him instead of the coat.

He was grateful that she misunderstood his shiver and urged him inside, out of the cold.

"I'm in the back room, finishing some glazing," she said.

He and Fred followed her trim form into another

room of her neat cabin. Here, it was ordered chaos—with potter's tools, clay, and ceramic pieces in various stages of completion surrounding the wheel. He stopped to touch a teapot with a gentle finger, marveling at the perfection of the curved spout. There was something inherently sensual in the flow of the design that made him think of slim arms tangled about his neck. He cleared his throat.

"You're a talented artist," he said softly as Fred settled under the table.

"*Danki*, but I still learn new things every day from the clay and the wheel."

He nodded. "It's *gut* to keep learning in life, though I can't see how you'd improve on this teapot, no matter how you might try." He glanced over at her where she stood, haloed by rich lantern light, and he remembered that he was here for their first courting.

"Tell me how you learned all of this work." He gestured to the room at large. "I've never been inside a pottery."

She smiled, revealing a slight gap between her two front teeth, then started to show him around. "First, there's the treadle wheel—it looks like a kick wheel but makes a much more rhythmic sound when you move it with your feet."

He watched her hands run lovingly across the surface of the wheel. "So, no electric wheels?" he teased suddenly.

"*Nee*. Though I long to try one. . . ."

She bit her lip at the admission, and he shoved away the irreverent thought of what it would be like to kiss her with passion. Then she moved, gesturing to the right side of the room.

"Here's the kiln—the flue runs outside. The ventilation is more than adequate, and I can open the transom windows if needed."

He gestured to the arranged glaze buckets and the unfamiliar tools on the workbench. "How did you learn all of this?"

She shrugged. "My *fater* taught me."

He sensed that she would try to deflect attention from herself, but he wanted to get to know her. Before he could frame a response though, she took a step closer and spoke in soft tones.

"What did your *fater* teach you?"

The quiet question threw him, as much as if someone had punched him in the gut, and he struggled for a moment to *kumme* up with a suitable reply.

"Farming—chores, things like that."

She tilted her head a bit and he felt the weight of her gaze. "Mmm-hmm. So, you're a farmer then?"

"No," he admitted. "I guess I'm more of a handyman. I can get along by fixing most things."

"There's always a need for a *gut* handyman."

He nodded and reached to pick up a pea-sized piece of clay. He rolled it gently between his thumb and forefinger.

She laughed, an even, melodious sound that struck him as something unusual and fine.

"What's funny?" he asked, looking at her.

"I was remembering—throwing pea balls of clay at *Fater* and Mercy when I was five or so. My sister never wanted to be here and my *daed* was always consumed by his artwork, so I'd get their attention by pelting them with clay."

"So, you had fun with your family?"

"*Jah*, though we worked hard too."

He nodded. "What else did your *daed* teach you about the clay?" He waited for a response, hoping to skitter away from any mention of his own *fater*.

"He talked a lot about the truth that *Gott* is the Master Potter, as it says in His Word."

"That's hard to remember sometimes when we would like things our own way."

She smiled at him, a faraway expression on her pretty face.

Acting on impulse, Caleb threw the heat-softened clay from his fingers to land directly on her cheek.

"You've picked the wrong target, Herr King." She grabbed some damp clay and pelted him with ball after ball until he threw his arms up in mock surrender.

"I give up." He chuckled, beginning to pluck the clay from his face and shirt.

"Here. Let me help you. I'm afraid that wasn't quite fair."

He let her help him remove the bits and watched her dark eyes sparkle as she stretched to pull a piece from his forehead. But then she stopped and ran her free hand down through the length of his hair. He stilled, unsure of what she was thinking.

He knew it was an intimate thing—touching his hair—but then she was an artist and maybe she needed to touch to experience things better. In any case, he waited until he heard his own heartbeat in his ears.

* * *

Abigail looked up into his blue eyes as she stroked the fall of his blond hair. She marveled at herself, making so free with his person. Then she swallowed hard. *What am I doing? Just because he's a mail-order groom doesn't make him mine to . . . examine.* She stepped away, leaving him visibly frozen in place.

"I—forgive me, Herr King. I was admiring your hair—an artist's eyes and all that." She felt herself flush.

He moved a bit, shifting his weight from one long leg to the other. "That's what I thought—you being an artist. Touch must matter. . . ."

His voice was hoarse, and she nodded, telling herself it was her own imagination that his gaze had skittered across her bosom. She was thinking how she could change the subject when there was a loud knock on the front cabin door.

She had almost left the pottery when Caleb spoke. "*Sei se gut*—let me answer. It's late and you never know who—"

"Might *kumme* courting?" she asked with a smile.

She watched his blue eyes dance in response. "You're right, Abigail. Perhaps it's time I was formally introduced to my rival."

She was conscious of his nearness as they walked to the door, and she turned to smile over her shoulder at him. "Actually, I don't think it's a suitor."

She opened the door to the dark *nacht*, and a slightly built *Amisch* man crossed the threshold of the door followed by a passel of snow-dusted hounds. She bent to greet each dog in turn, then rose to make introductions.

"Caleb King, please meet Pork Chop Lulu or Herr Lapp, if you prefer."

"Herr Pork Chop," Caleb responded after a moment, extending his hand.

Abigail hid a smile. "Pork Chop works late in Farwell, the nearest *Englisch* town, and it's a long hike back to Blackberry Falls. I've got an order ready for him. I'll be right back."

She hurried to the shop, listening to the low rumble of the men's voices. She liked Caleb's manners. And his hair, her mind whispered naughtily. She frowned, suppressing the thought, then carefully lifted Pork Chop's platter from a high shelf.

She shined it with the elbow of her dress, pleased at how the pattern had turned out, then went back to the kitchen. The two men were sitting at the kitchen table, but both quickly rose to their feet when they saw her.

She nodded and then held the platter out to Pork Chop. She was conscious of Caleb looking on over her shoulder and wondered what he thought. The platter was a gift from Pork Chop to his aunt—Grossmuder Mildred. Abigail had carefully painted red roses and ferns in the center of the white platter before it was glazed and then fired.

"It's beautiful, Abigail." The short man smiled, showing two front teeth missing. "What do I owe you?"

"No charge for the painting. And twenty even for the platter."

The cheerful *Amischer* handed her two twenties and spoke in a low aside to Caleb. "Never charges enough, she don't." He took the platter and whistled to his dogs, then set out into the *nacht* with a tip of his black hat.

"Pork Chop?" Caleb asked when the door had closed.

"You'll find that a lot of *Amischers* around here have nicknames. It's really kind of a way to know you're home—having an odd name."

Caleb smiled, and she was once more drawn to his height and shape. She told herself that she was being ridiculous. *Of course, he's good-looking, but I don't want to press him in clay.* . . . Then she blinked when she realized that she'd absolutely love to shape his body in her art.

She felt warmth in her cheeks when she glanced up at him, but he seemed flushed as well. *Almost as though he caught fire from the heat of my thoughts.* . . .

"It's late," he said. "I'd best be going. But . . . *danki*, Abigail, for our first *nacht*'s courting."

She held her breath for a few moments, wondering impulsively if he might kiss her goodbye, but he simply swung on his heavy coat and headed out into the *nacht*. . . .

Caleb dug his fisted hands deeper into the pockets of his coat and thought about the evening with Abigail. He was glad for the bite of the cold; it did much to drive away the pleasurable lassitude that had built up inside of him in the potter's presence.

There was her general air of kindness and her pleasant speaking voice, which made him consider her ad in the Renova paper—that the mail-order groom might write poetry. In truth, the only poetry he knew was an inappropriate little rhyme about a girl named Sue . . . but still, he could try his hand at writing and remember to cut his hair less often as Abigail enjoyed touching it.

As he made his way through deep drifts of snow, he considered the fact that she had taken the time to show him her pottery room. It seemed a warm and intimate thing, and his mind flashed through the tools, lantern light, and the clay in quick succession. He'd enjoyed their play with the dabs of clay and discovering that part of her was a free spirit though she dressed plain, and her posture was carefully erect. He had a sudden vision of holding her, kissing her, and imagined what it would be like to feel the lithe movement of her body. He was enjoying the fantasy when he fell far into a drift and ended up face-down in the snow.

"Well, that's what I get," he muttered to himself aloud. "For thinking about a woman when I should be watching my footing." He retrieved his hat and floundered out of the drift, determined to keep his mind on the snow and not the potter of Blackberry Falls. . . . Besides, he knew that Birchbark would somehow get the whole story out of Fred. . . .

Chapter Six

The next morning, Phillip brought in an armload of firewood for Grossmuder Mildred, then sat down to listen to the elderly, blind woman who was his host until Valentine's Day or perhaps his wedding day—if he could ever get past Mercy's defenses so he could talk to her sister.

"I sure enjoy havin' ya here, *buwe*. Gets a mite lonely at times. Tho' dontcha *geh* spreadin' that around none. Folks have enuff doin' fer me as it 'tis."

"Well, I'm glad to be here. I've heard that the other—um, mail-order groom had to hike up past the falls."

"Sure did. He's stayin' with Birchbark, but I think ya got the better deal." She laughed, and Phillip couldn't resist giving in to laughter as well. He admired the *auld* woman. True, she had no sight in her raisin-black eyes, but he had the feeling that she could see in other ways.

"So, what do ya plan ta do to help out in the community like I heard Bishop Kore said you ought?"

Phillip sighed. "I'm a farmer, and though there's plenty of small jobs I can do in winter, there's not a lot—"

"Seeds!" Grossmuder Mildred clapped her hands.

"What?"

"Heirloom seeds! 'Round here everybody got their own idea of how ta preserve seeds best, but I betcha can teach 'em how ta do it right proper. And after the Christmas holidays, we have a community seed swap—makes the days seem shorter ta plantin'—*Derr Herr* willin', that is."

"I'd be glad to help," Phillip said, feeling relieved that there was something he could do that would produce a future crop in Blackberry Falls. He pushed aside the thought that he and Abigail might one day grow a crop of their own. . . .

He was shaken from his thoughts by the sound of a gun cocking. Grossmuder Mildred stood beside the table, a shotgun balanced perfectly in her *auld* arms.

"Shhh," she whispered. "Now *geh* on and open the door real quick."

Phillip rose to his feet and tried to decide what would be worse—dying while wrestling a gun from an *auld* woman or getting shot by her poor aim. He opted to open the door, but first leaned over to whisper in the blind *frau*'s ear, "Don't you think we should ask who it is before we shoot?"

"*Nee—ach*, well, all right. Ask who it is, just for fun."

He cleared his throat. "Who is—"

The roar of the shotgun seemed to shake the small cabin's foundations, and Phillip doubted he'd be able to hear right for a week. Worse still, was the peppering of shot that let in numerous points of morning light. Phillip rushed to open the door, afraid of what he'd find on the other side.

To his great surprise, Mercy Mast stood back from the door. Her pale skin was flushed red on her cheeks and he noticed that her crossed arms bore no sign of shot.

"Mercy?" he exclaimed. "Are you all right?" He was surprised at the tightness in his throat as he asked the question.

She glared up at him, her bonnet slightly askew. "Of course, I'm all right, you—you . . ."

"Mail-order groom," he said with a smile, relief that she wasn't hurt washing over him.

He turned back to look inside the door and saw Grossmuder Mildred standing with the gun at her side.

"Mercy! Why, I forgot that ya wuz comin'. Hurry inside now, or you'll catch yer death of cold."

"It would be better than being shot to death," Phillip said in a low undertone to Mercy. He caught the scent of her skin as he spoke—something like vanilla—warm and homelike, then he shook himself mentally.

"You're rude!" Mercy snapped hotly.

He found himself nodding in agreement.

"What's goin' on?" Grossmuder Mildred called. "Best hurry or the oatmeal will get cold in the kettle."

Phillip had to resist the urge to help Mercy up the slight slope to the door. Instead, he beat a hasty retreat. "I'll go get some wood and try to mend this door. *Gut* morning, ladies!"

Mercy muttered to herself as she entered the spare bedroom in Grossmuder Mildred's cabin. It, of course, had to be her day to help Grossmuder Mildred when Phillip was about. She put down her bucket and scrub brush on the wooden floor and stared at the tangled bedsheets on the big rope bed.

She marched forward to grab the end of a sheet and, against her will, images of Phillip Miller in various states of undress and repose flickered through her mind. The fact that his bed bore the manly scent of fresh cedar soap only added to her discomfiture.

"Stupid *mon*," she said aloud as she bundled the linen sheets in her arms. For some reason though, as she held her light burden to her breast, she felt tears prick her eyes. She couldn't understand why.

She felt things falling backward in her mind, and she remembered Joshua being born—the intense pain, the squalling of her *sohn*, and then, the incredible loneliness that had swamped her.

Mercy sighed aloud when she heard Grossmuder Mildred call and decided she'd better stop her silly notions and get working before Phillip Miller returned.

Herr Troyer
Miss Smucker
Anke Mast
John Stolfus
Aenti Fern

Caleb read the list out loud, then glanced up at Birchbark. The mountain man had returned that morning, his large pack noticeably empty.

"*Jah*." Caleb nodded. "It's a list. What do I do with it?"

"Heard ye're a handyman of sorts—well, these folks need yer handiness. So, git movin'."

"Wait, I only just told Abigail last *nacht* that—"

Birchbark's fierce eyebrows arched like two caterpillars dancing. "That ye're handy? Well, word gets 'round, *buwe*! My toolbox is out in the shed. You might as well walk until the drifts settle down. Then we'll git your horse, Tommy, hooked up to the sleigh. I'll stay here and doze a bit with Fred—who's bored, he says."

"Uh-huh," Caleb muttered, pulling on his coat and hat and trying to avoid Fred's baleful gaze. "I'll be back."

He trudged out of the cabin, squinting in the snow glare, and made his way to a shed that looked like it might collapse at any moment. It was odd that there were no tracks to walk in, he thought. Birchbark should have left prints in the snow as big as a bear's. . . .

Caleb managed to get the gray woodshed door open and pulled out an old-fashioned toolbox. Then he started down the mountain. He had no true idea of where he was going. Someone named Herr Troyer was at the top of his list. He did know pretty much where the pottery was and thought about asking Abigail to give him more formal directions. But he decided that he'd bide his time and wait to visit her at *nacht* unless, of course, the other mail-order groom got there first.

He eventually saw what appeared to be the general store and decided to ask for directions there. A hand-painted sign over the white door read CUBBY'S and he entered with the heavy toolbox in hand.

The place was surprisingly quiet and didn't seem to have the bustle and aromas he'd *kumme* to associate with bulk stores back at home. It seemed to lack a woman's touch, especially in the arrangement of the goods. After all, they were coming up on the days of Christmas in a matter of weeks.

"Can I help ya?"

Caleb identified the storekeeper by his white apron and walked to the back of the place to offer his hand in greeting.

"Caleb King," he said with a smile that was returned only briefly. "I'm one of the mail-order grooms traipsing to Blackberry Falls these days."

"Uh-huh. Sam Fisher. So, what can I do for ya?"

Caleb ignored the storekeeper's lack of sociability. "I'm staying with Birchbark and—"

"Birchbark, huh? Not exactly the sharpest tool in the shed, if you ask me."

Caleb felt an unexpected surge of anger on behalf of his host up the mountain. And he wasn't used to *Amischers* being uncharitable. *Unless it's my* fater *we're talking about*. . . . Caleb frowned and held out his list. "Do you know where these folks live?"

Sam Fisher gave brief directions, and Caleb left the store, not even willing to buy some licorice if it meant giving the man who insulted Birchbark any cash in the till.

He walked along the fresh tracks of a runner sled and smiled to hear the voices of children sledding down a nearby hill. He continued on his way and soon reached what he hoped was Herr Troyer's cabin.

He mounted the clean-swept steps of the neat cabin and was about to knock when the door was yanked open from inside. A frazzled-looking *Amisch* man stood there with a screaming toddler hanging on each pant leg.

"*Ach*, thank *Derr Herr* you've *kumme*. I know Aenti

Fern got word to Birchbark that she would be away today, and we never expected . . . I mean we expected—but you know what I mean." The stranger walked as he babbled, and Caleb followed him into the chaos of the kitchen. In addition to the two toddlers screeching, a puppy gamboled around the table, sweeping up scrambled eggs with an eager mouth. Caleb could smell burnt bacon grease, and something else seemed to be burning on the cookstove.

"Uh, Birchbark said you needed—"

"Help! Dear *Gott* in Heaven, *jah*! *Ach*, you brought a toolbox; that's funny!" He tugged Caleb's coat off. "Okay, here's the bedroom door. *Gut* luck!"

"Wait, but I—" Caleb was pushed into the room, and the door slammed summarily closed behind him. He considered going back out, but the poor *Amischer* seemed so shaken that surely Caleb could try to fix whatever was broken in the bedroom. He scanned the lamplit room and nearly jumped a foot when a low, keening wail came from the bump of quilts on the bed.

"Uh . . . hiya . . ." he choked out. "Do you want me to get—"

"Henry? *Neeeeee*—he faints dead at the sight of blood, even so much as a drop."

"Okaaay." Caleb cautiously lowered the toolbox to the floor. "So . . ."

"*Sei se gut*, jest *kumme* and git on with it! I'm sorry for fussin' but it huuurrrts."

"Right." Caleb felt himself propelled forward by the intensity of the woman's cry. He rounded the bed and cautiously lifted the top quilt to reveal a tousled mass of dark blond hair. Her blue eyes were filled with pain as she lay on her side and clutched her protruding belly. A shapeless cotton *nacht*gown covered her.

"I'm Nan," she panted.

"Uh—Caleb King." He felt his heart begin to pound.

She nodded, turning her perspiring face into the pillow for a moment then looking back up at him. "Hadn't ya better wash up? The bowl and pitcher's over there." She gestured with her chin, and Caleb, propelled by the urgency in her voice, rolled up his sleeves and set about washing well.

When he turned back to the bed, Nan had moved onto her back and her cries competed with the children's screeches outside the door. Caleb felt as if he was trapped in some *Englisch* horror film and shuddered even as he moved to stand awkwardly next to the laboring *frau*.

"Praise *Derr Herr* it's not breech," Nan gasped. "I can tell because one of the twins wuz. *Ach*, I think it's time ta push!"

"Dear *Gott*," Caleb mumbled.

"*Jah*," she said, nodding. "Prayin' will help. But I bet yer experience will be even more useful."

"My exper—"

"Now!" Nan screamed and Caleb moved instinctively.

The next half hour passed in a stress-filled blur until finally, Caleb was able to step back and admire the baby girl that snuggled at her *mamm*'s breast.

Nan smiled at him. "*Danki*, Dr. King. We couldn't have done it without ya."

"Doctor? But I'm just an average—" He paused as the bedroom door eased open a crack.

Herr Troyer peered in with a worried eye. "Nan . . . the uh . . . doctor's here from Farwell."

"Ha!" his wife retorted. "Tell him Dr. King beat him ta it."

Caleb tried once more to explain but then gave up. He passed the dandy-suited doctor in the chaotic kitchen and accepted a smoked ham as payment for his services— such as they had been. He bid everyone a brisk *gut*bye, then started on to the next name on the list—a Miss Smucker. "Dear *Gott*, let her not be pregnant," he muttered as he lugged the twenty-pound ham through the snow. *Wait until I get hold of Birchbark. A handyman's list, my eye . . .*

Chapter Seven

Abigail closed the pottery up after deciding that she needed a few more ingredients for some of the dishes she planned to make for the community dinner that Herr Stolfus, Tabitha's *fater*, was hosting in his sprawling carved wood cabin. While it was unusual in a Mountain *Amisch* community for such a vast cabin to exist, Herr Stolfus had dedicated the place to *Derr Herr*, to be a community gathering location even though church services rotated from barn to barn.

Engaged in her thoughts, Abigail almost missed the strange sight of Caleb King crossing her path with a brown-paper-wrapped ham. "Caleb? Is that a ham?"

He gave her a wry smile from his handsome mouth, and she fell into step with him.

"Yep. Smoked ham, it is."

She felt the absurd urge to giggle—something she hadn't done in years. "Are you giving it to someone?"

"Now that's a *gut* idea! Do you know Miss Smucker? Could she use a ham?"

"Well, I—"

He leaned in closer to her. "She's not pregnant, is she?"

"Caleb!"

"You can never be too sure."

She shook her head. "Why do you have to see Lilly Smucker?"

"Birchbark gave me a list of folks who need a handyman. She's second on the list."

"Who was first?" she asked curiously.

"It doesn't bear repeating. Hey, would you like to *kumme* with me to Lilly Smucker's place? You never know when a woman might be necessary to a situation."

Abigail swung her empty shopping basket and considered. On one hand, she didn't want to appear too eager but, on the other, she would be glad to spend time with Caleb—there was no use denying it. "*Jah*, I'll *kumme* to Lilly's. I don't really know her well. She only moved here this past autumn. She had some distant family here, but there was a shooting and a murder—"

He stopped abruptly and she would have fallen into the snow if he hadn't caught her by the arm. "Wait—a murder?"

She nodded. "Didn't Matthew tell you that Tabitha was kidnapped?"

"I clearly need to have more conversations with my older *bruder*! *Nee*, he didn't."

"Well, in any case, we need to see Lilly Smucker for who she is, not for her unsavory relative." She gestured to a cabin to the right of the path that had a small plume of smoke curling gently in the air. "Here we are."

Abigail knocked and smiled at the snow-dusted holly wreath on the cabin door. It was a reminder that Christmas was not far away. . . .

Lilly Smucker opened the door only a few inches. "*Jah?*"

"Hiya, Lilly. It's Abigail Mast and Caleb King—Birchbark sent Caleb to be a handyman for you."

"*Ach, jah.*" The petite middle-aged *Amisch* woman nodded and widened the door. "I have a *spuk haus.*"

Abigail listened to Caleb's muffled groan and wondered if he was superstitious. "A haunted *haus*, Lilly?" Abigail asked as she took off her cloak. "Why do you think so?"

"The noises at *nacht*, things squeaking. . . . I think maybe it wasn't a *gut* idea for me to *kumme* to Blackberry Falls."

Abigail glanced back at Caleb and was pleased to see a serious look on his face. So many people would have dismissed Lilly's claims, but clearly, Caleb had empathy for the older woman.

He took off his coat and hat and swiped his hair out of his crystalline-blue eyes. "Do you have a broom?"

Lilly nodded and lifted her chin as if to say, "What *gut Amisch haus*keeper doesn't have a broom?" She repaired to the kitchen and was back in seconds with an old-fashioned twig broom, which she handed to Caleb.

Abigail watched as his lean fingers stroked the broom handle in an almost meditative motion. Then he snapped to attention. "I'll have to see the attic. We must sweep the *spuks* downward and out the door."

Lilly nodded as if his strange suggestion made sense, and Abigail found herself intrigued as well.

Caleb put a kind hand on Lilly's shoulder and steered her into a chair. "Now, you stay here, Miss Lilly, and Abigail and I shall settle this matter of the *spuk haus.*"

He grabbed a lantern, and Abigail followed him to the loft ladder, where he gestured for her to *geh* up first. "It's better if you're first—then I can catch you if you stumble."

Abigail nodded. What he said was true, though she felt slightly embarrassed to be showing the backside of her skirts to his penetrating blue eyes. Still, she climbed up into a low space that ran the length of the cabin. The place held old-fashioned trunks and some small pieces of furniture. It was also particularly warm, and Abigail scooted backward on her knees to make room for Caleb and the broom.

"Do you really believe in sweeping *spuks*?" she whispered.

He smiled at her in the lantern light. "*Nee*, but I figure I'd better do something or Birchbark is likely to make me deliver—uh—*kumme* here again."

He crouched along then poked with the tip of the broom handle at the ceiling. "All right, here's the crawl space. I'd better *geh* up and have a look. It's probably squirrels running around and dropping nuts in the walls."

Abigail tugged at the collar of her blouse, which suddenly seemed tight in the confined space.

"Undo a few pins," he suggested amicably, but Abigail clenched her hands in her lap in sudden embarrassment.

"I—I'm fine."

"Okay. Here I go."

She watched him ease his broad shoulders and part of his chest through the upper crawl space door. Then she heard him sneeze three times in quick succession.

"Bless you," she whispered, unsure whether he could hear her. But then there was the distinct sound of him knocking his head on a rafter, and he dropped back beside her, hastily pulling the crawl space panel in place.

"What's wrong?" she asked, having to resist the urge to pull away a cobweb that was marring the sheen of his hair in the lantern light.

"Nothing. Everything's *gut*. Let's get going."

"Caleb—what's up there?"

He gave her a grim look, then shook his head. "Nothing."

"Squirrels? Opossums? How about raccoons?"

"*Nee.*"

"*Spuks?*" she teased.

"Worse."

She moved closer to him at the horrified sound of his voice. Then, somehow, he caught her in his arms. She was completely encircled by him—the brush of his hair on her cheek, his scent, and the folds of his blue shirt. She felt skittish but was also intrigued by his touch. "Caleb, *sei se gut*. Tell me what you saw."

He groaned and turned his mouth into her hair. "Bats," he muttered hoarsely. "Lots and lots of bats."

"*Ach*," she exclaimed softly. "I find bats beautiful, but you obviously do not." She reached up with tentative fingers and touched his cheek. "Why?"

She felt him draw a shuddering breath. "Let's say it's a childhood fear."

"Do you want to tell me?" she asked, because despite the heat and the improper way he held her, she had a desire to know him . . . intimately. And the mind seemed to her to be the most intimate of all places. . . .

He thumbed at the damp pieces of hair that had escaped her *kapp*, and she was spellbound by his touch.

Then he began to speak. "My *fater* treated me as though I wore the skirts in our *haus*, so the woman's chores were left for me . . . except when it came time to clean the chimney. Then I was *buwe* enough to just fit up the flue with the long black brushes. I remember that one time it started to storm and somehow I got stuck. The thunder must have stirred up the bats because they were wild."

He paused and pulled a pin from the neckline of her dress. She would have started, had she not been caught up in his story, but, as it was, she welcomed the coolness his movement brought to her skin.

"So, you were trapped—alone, with the bats."

"*Jah*. My *aulder bruder* Luke got me out finally, but I had *nacht*mares for months. . . ."

He trailed off and she slid her fingers across his, then spoke briskly, knowing somehow that it would pull him back from the past. "Well, those bats above us are in a state of hibernation, though it's odd they would roost here. The colony usually seeks a cave. We can't really get them to move until spring, so we'll have to leave them and explain to Lilly."

He exhaled. "All right. Let me *geh* down and hold you as you climb. Your skirts could be dangerous as you move backward."

"Caleb?"

"*Jah*?"

"I—I won't tell anyone about your fear. I'm *gut* at keeping secrets." For some reason, it felt important that he know something about her character. *Of course, he could become my mail-order groom one day soon.* The thought made her shiver, alive and pulsing with warmth. Then she had to force herself to concentrate on her descent.

* * *

"You only finished two on the list?" Birchbark's voice rang out in the space of the snug cabin. Then he sneezed so hard that Fred started baying.

Caleb resisted the urge to throttle his host. Instead, he concentrated on the other man's pantry. "How did you fill these shelves so fast? Is there a root cellar? Stop sneezing! Are you sick?"

"Simmer down, *buwe*. The pantry likely wasn't as empty as you thought."

Caleb stared at the fresh jelly jars, quarts of tomatoes, and yellow beans and shook his head. "I know what I saw."

"*Ach!*" Birchbark yanked the green curtain closed. "Ferget the pantry. Tell me what ya learned on yer two handyman jobs."

"What I learned? You mean between delivering a baby and discovering a snug colony of bats? What else is there?"

Birchbark continued inexorably. "I didn't ask ya what ya did; I asked ya what ya learned."

What I learned . . . That Abigail is soft, empathetic, and kind . . . yet she has surprising strength when it's needed, like Nan Troyer when she gave birth to her dochder. . . . That Lilly Smucker is afraid of having a spuk haus *despite Abigail's explanation about the bats. . . .* He blinked, realizing Birchbark watched him with keen eyes.

"I learned that *Gott* made women strong, fear is real, and you've got a *narrisch* sense of what a handyman does."

"*Gut.*" Birchbark sneezed then belched. "Now we're gittin' somewheres. . . ."

Chapter Eight

In the snow shine of the new morning, Mercy glanced back at the runner sled behind her that bore her basketed collection of special soaps and sachets. She was proud that she had her homemade goods in several stores in the *Englisch* town of Farwell and grateful that she did a brisk trade. She also took in sewing and was always in demand to make long dresses that the *Englisch* girls wore to dances.

Today, she had two fitting appointments for the so-called *Englisch* Snow Ball held on Christmas Eve, and she had to restock her goat milk soaps with newly made holiday scents like bayberry and pine. Perhaps she'd make enough money to buy Joshua something nice for the day after Christmas—which was the time the Mountain *Amisch* usually exchanged gifts.

She walked through the snow and allowed memories to flood her mind. Joshua's *fater* had had a keen white smile, honey-brown eyes, and nicely disheveled hair as he'd held her hips while they ice skated together on Stehley's Pond. She'd been nineteen years *auld* and the world had seemed easy and *wunderbaar*. Then her mother had died and, in a matter of weeks, Mercy had to take on the care of her younger sister, Abigail, and then discovered she was pregnant. The *Englischer* left as soon as things became difficult, and Mercy had never laid eyes on him again.

She sighed aloud. At least the two miles to Farwell had passed quickly as she was lost in memory. She now took to the snowplowed road, making her way to the first store that carried her wares. She entered and became aware that Abigail and Phillip were in the place, laughing over something, their heads bent close together.

Mercy suddenly had a strange feeling pass through her—a bitterness, she decided, that after only a few days, Phillip Miller dared to be so intimate with Abigail in public. Mercy hefted her wicker basket of carefully wrapped and labeled soaps higher on her arm and proceeded to march over to where the two stood.

"Don't you have any shame, Herr Miller?" she hissed. "My sister is not some—some—" Mercy floundered, and she felt herself flush at Phillip's grin.

"Not some woman who would send for a mail-order groom?" he teased in low tones.

Mercy looked at her baby sister and was surprised that she seemed so comfortable with the man's joke—her sister, who was normally so calm and even considered stern.

"Abigail?" Mercy questioned. "What are you doing here?"

"Courting. And I know it's early, but Phillip thought a morning sleigh ride would be *gut*. We stopped in to look things over. You know that Christmas is coming soon."

"Of course, I know."

"Well, is there anything here that you might want?" Abigail asked.

Mercy looked into Phillip's dark eyes and felt her world tilt. "I—" She broke off as a strange and completely outrageous thought pulsed through her mind. *Jah, I want Phillip Miller. Wrap him up to geh. . . .*

Phillip noticed an odd expression on Mercy's face but dismissed it, thinking she was probably calculating how best to get him to leave Blackberry Falls for good. But he felt already comfortable here and had to admit that he found Abigail to be a charming person to talk with— *almost like a friend*, he thought. Then he drew his reflections up short. *Friend? I'm here to find love, jah, but also to marry Abigail as a helpmate for the farming life.*

He realized that Abigail was speaking and came back to the conversation at hand.

"Would you mind, Phillip?"

He nodded readily, having no idea what she was talking about.

"*Gut.*" She smiled. "*Danki.*"

He watched her turn and start to leave the store with her sister and finally found his voice. "Will I be seeing you later?"

"Most certainly." She gave him an airy wave and followed Mercy out the door. Suddenly he felt a gentle touch on his arm and looked down to see a petite, elderly *Englisch* lady smiling up at him.

"She said she was going to help Mercy get some sewing done here in town," the woman confided.

"Was it that obvious I wasn't paying attention?" he asked.

"Only a little."

He bent and kissed her wrinkled cheek. "Thank you."

"I'm sorry to take you away from your courting," Mercy said, as they crunched through the snow.

Abigail heard the unapologetic note in her sister's voice and hid a smile. "*Nee* you're not."

Mercy huffed. "Well, I'm glad for your help anyway. The less time you spend with that—that dark-haired ruffian, the better."

"But that leaves me all the more time to spend with the blond-haired ruffian."

Her own words conjured up the image of Caleb's big body. Those moments in Lilly Smucker's *spuk*ed attic showed he had a willingness to be vulnerable, and Abigail remembered the touch of his lean fingers with a heated feeling in her belly that did much to dispel the chill of the day. She found she had to drag her thoughts back to the moment at hand.

"Anyway, I'm pleased that I got word Tracy Prescott had to change her fitting time," Mercy commented as they sidled past the postman on his rounds through the streets of Farwell.

"Well, I'm glad to give you an extra hand, though I'd much rather work with clay than fine fabrics."

"I know. But it doesn't hurt to do things differently every once in a while."

"Really?" Abigail teased. "This from my *aulder* sister who hates change of any sort?"

She saw Mercy's frown and was about to apologize when Mercy stopped at a stone path between two high hedges. An old white-columned three-story *haus* rose impressively in front of them.

They walked the path to the massive, stained-glass door and Mercy pressed a bell that could be heard echoing inside. The fine glass reverberated with approaching footsteps, and an *Englisch* housekeeper opened the door and greeted them with a smile.

"Here for Tracy's dressmaking? She's in the first room."

Abigail was delighted to discover that "the first room" was actually a lady's sitting room of sorts. A beautiful needlework pattern of pansies stood half-finished on a vertical hoop and a dainty piano decorated the corner. Light filtered in from the giant stained-glass window depicting blue waters, and Tracy stood poised on a dressmaker's stool, wearing the makings of a midnight blue satin gown.

"Oh, Miss Mercy, I'm so glad you've come. And this must be your sister, Abigail?"

Abigail smiled up at the pretty *Englisch* girl. She had long hair, which had been dragged up into a careless ponytail, and a smattering of light freckles across her youthful face. Abigail judged her to be no more than seventeen or so.

"*Jah*, I'm Abigail. It's nice to meet you."

Abigail quietly bent to reach into a sewing basket that sat on the floor and pulled out a tomato-red pincushion. Then she awaited Mercy's instructions as her sister bustled about the dress.

"I'm so sorry you had to come on such short notice, but my mother insists that I go with her to the Winter in the Garden evening—you know, ice sculptures and a silent auction to benefit that little school on Second Street for kids with special needs. . . ."

"Mmm-hmm," Mercy muttered. Abigail knew her sister was focusing on her work, not really hearing what Tracy was saying.

"Pins!" Mercy snapped her fingers and Abigail moved to obey. *It's really fun to watch Mercy when she's so absorbed,* Abigail thought as she placed the small pins along the seam of the ball gown.

Abigail worked with purpose and soon she was sewing the seam by hand. Tracy had put on a pretty flowered robe and was playing a jaunty tune on the piano that sent Abigail's foot tapping.

She wondered what it would be like to dance, to be moved around a ballroom floor with effortless grace in a gown of midnight blue, while Caleb held her close and . . .

Abigail drew her thoughts up sharply and she lost the beat of the music. *Why do I imagine Caleb when it very well might be Phillip I marry?* She vowed then and there to make a concentrated effort to court with Phillip and not to see Caleb for a few days. She was mentally strengthening her resolve when a petite blond-haired *Englisch* woman flew into the room with all the dainty zest of a swallow.

"Oh, my dears, I'm so glad to see your pretty faces. Tracy, stop playing for a moment, will you, darling? Oh, my, you're Mercy's sister, of course!" The woman rushed to embrace Abigail. Then she thrust a cream and gold envelope into Mercy's hand.

"You mustn't mind me. I'm Tracy's mother, Janice. I'm

head of the Winter in the Garden evening that's coming up in two very short weeks. I was hoping—no, praying—that you girls might plead with your bishop to allow the *Amisch* up at Blackberry Falls to partner with us *Englischers* here in Farwell to raise money for those children with needs beyond their parents' means. . . . I know I should have thought of it sooner, but things tend to fly out of my head. Now, I know we work together to support our volunteer firefighters and for the occasional mud sales, but this would be such a wonderful opportunity."

Abigail's head swam with the woman's chatter, but she personally loved the idea of helping this vivacious creature and especially the needy children.

"What would we have to do on our side?" Abigail asked.

"Well . . ." Mrs. Prescott drew breath. "Perhaps you all have some wares you might offer to sell—oh, jellies or Christmas crafts, or Mercy's soaps, or your pottery, dear. Mercy told us you're a potter—what a simple yet grand position to hold. . . . We're also doing a silent auction and perhaps you might put in one of your beautiful quilts to bid on? Now, I'll leave you to Tracy's dress . . . I simply have to get things done today. . . . Tracy, serve the girls brunch when you're through. . . . Mrs. Broom will have it all prepared."

Abigail watched the older woman spin around the dressing dais to the piano and kiss her daughter, then flit out of the room with a cheerful farewell. It was as if a whirlwind passed through the room, Abigail thought kindly, and wondered for a moment what Aenti Fern, the healer, would think of Mrs. Prescott. *They'd probably get on well. I hope Bishop Kore will permit our community to help. . . . Perhaps even Caleb might offer his handyman services to bid on in the silent auction.* . . . Then she drew rein on her wayward thoughts and reminded herself that she was determined to see more of Phillip, and surely he had as much to offer as the other mail-order groom . . .

Mercy waited while Bishop Kore examined the invitation Mrs. Prescott had sent. Her thoughts drifted as she gazed out the window at the snowy afternoon. She and Abigail had joined Tracy for a delicious brunch of dainty sandwiches and a beautiful cinnamon Bundt cake as well as fruit, cheese, and sparkling cider. It had been strange to eat in the wide dining room with its stained-glass ceiling and exotic plants, but stranger still to try to focus on the conversation while her mind kept running back to touch the spot where she'd discovered an affection for Phillip Miller. . . . *What is wrong with me and what kind of sister am I to have thoughts about my sister's man?*

"Great jumpin' frogs and melba toast, of course we'll help!" Bishop Kore's distinctive voice crashed into her reflections and she nearly jumped herself.

"That's *gut*, Bishop. I know it will be a worthy cause. I won't *geh* myself, of course, but I'll send along my winter soaps and—"

"Whoa, my *maedel*! What did you say? Not going? And why in toy ducks and bicycle raffles would you not *geh*?"

Mercy swallowed hard and looked at the pegged wooden floor. She could not admit that she felt an attraction for Phillip and wanted to avoid him at all costs. "I—um—will need to stay home and make supper for Joshua."

"By rabbit tracks and chipmunk feet, I expect Joshua

will be there himself—there's always work for a *buwe* at such a doodaddle!"

"*Jah*, but—"

"*Nee!* You will attend, Mercy!" He smiled at her then. "Besides, it wouldn't be the same without you, and I know that Abigail will appreciate your being there."

Jah, *she'll appreciate my presence but only until she discovers that I've had sweet thoughts about that impossible mail-order groom of hers. . . .*

Chapter Nine

Caleb had set out from Birchbark's cabin in the midafternoon, having been primed with the nebulous information that "Anke Mast" was the next person who needed a handyman. *Not pregnant . . . not pregnant . . .* The refrain echoed in his mind as he plowed waist-deep through the glistening snow. Then his thoughts slipped to the minutes in Frau Smucker's attic—his raw terror at the sight of the bats, and the gentle, soothing compassion of Abigail's touch. He felt his fingers sting inside his gloves when he remembered touching her, seeing her brown eyes lift to his in the haloed light of the lantern.

A distant baying caught his attention, and he shook himself from his reverie. He stopped and turned in time to see his dog, Fred, leaping happily amongst the snow piles, barreling right toward him. He caught the wriggly body against his chest and had to smile. He'd left Fred sleeping peacefully before Birchbark's hearth, but the dog must have awoken and badgered the *auld* man to *geh* out.

Now, Caleb patiently accepted the slobbery licks on his cheeks and almost jumped when he heard a man clear his throat from behind him. He turned with Fred still in his arms and encountered a massive *Amischer* with silver blond hair and a light beard.

"Hello." Caleb nodded.

The *Amischer* cocked his head to one side. "Ya look familiar . . . have we met?"

"*Nee*, not that I know—but I'm new around here. One of the mail-order grooms you've probably heard about . . . Caleb King."

The *Amisch* man broke into a wide smile and swept his hat off, then put it on again. "Yer *bruder*'s one Matthew King, *jah*?"

"*Jah*, he is."

"I'm Abner Mast, and your *bruder* is a *gut* friend of mine. Now put yer hound down so I might shake yer hand like a man."

Caleb let Fred down gently, then had his hand wrung by the other *mon*.

"Aha! Well, I came out ta meet the handyman and found ya instead. A *gut* thing . . ."

"I think you've found us both actually. Birchbark has sent me to be . . . handy . . . for someone named Anke Mast. Is she related to you?"

"Related? *Ach*, she's my bride of just a few days now!"

"Well, congratulations then!" Caleb smiled and shook hands once more; then he stood back. "Shouldn't you be on your honeymoon?"

Amischers usually made the rounds of friends and family to celebrate their weddings, especially in the winter.

Abner laughed. "So we are, but we married in a very quiet way, as my Anke wanted. And we're, uh, honeymooning at home, as it wuz."

"Well, what can I do for you?" Caleb eyed Abner's work-worn hands and wondered how he might help the newlyweds.

"*Ach*, it's not me who be wantin' ta have ya. It's Anke. So, bring yer dog and *kumme* along."

Caleb followed Abner Mast through the deep snow with Fred wriggling happily along behind. They passed the general store and the big Stolfus cabin, then came to an icy stream running parallel to a much smaller cabin. The front porch was dressed in pine garlands, and a wreath of holly with bright red berries hung on the door.

Abner tugged on the latch and invited Caleb inside.

"Anke? The handyman's here. He's brought a hound." Abner nudged Caleb. "She loves a *gut* dog."

"*Ach, gut!* Just in time for a fresh sugar cookie with teaberry icing. Abigail's getting 'em out of the cookstove now."

Caleb half froze and swallowed. *Abigail? Abigail, the mail-order groom seeker, is here?* He cleared his throat and concentrated on slipping off his wet boots. He found himself standing awkwardly in the snug little cabin, and he wondered if this was part of courting her—being willing to feel strange in his own body. Then she looked at him and he knew a peculiar warmth in his chest.

"Do you want a cookie?" she asked merrily. Her words didn't seem to match her eyes, and he shook his head slowly. *Why do I feel that she is truly sober inside despite the smile on her lips?*

"*Ach*, now—we'll wait until they're iced," Abner said as he wrapped one of his big arms around his new wife. "Now, Anke, let's give the *buwe* a drink and then he'll do yer bidding. What do ya say?"

Caleb glanced away when Abner boldly kissed his wife. *What is it to love? To cherish a woman as a vessel of* Gott *'s making?* The words of Abigail's ad swam behind his eyes as he covertly took in her fine figure.

He was startled from his thoughts when Anke handed him a frosty mug. "It's eggnog—my own mixing."

"*Danki.* I'm sure it's delicious." He took a long pull of the drink, then licked his upper lip. The frothy brew was refreshing and tasted only faintly of alcohol. He smiled in appreciation and sat at the table where Abner indicated. He was directly across from Abigail; trays of large, glistening sugar cookies sat between them. He could feel the heat from the pans, and it made him aware of the flush on her pretty cheeks. He took another drink of the eggnog and felt content.

He watched Abigail stir the bright pink teaberry icing and thought of the sweet taste of the berries themselves. "I love teaberries," he remarked to the room at large.

"*Ach, gut!*" Anke exclaimed. "Ya can take some cookies home ta Birchbark for ya both. But right now, I wonder if I might speak ta ya a wee bit in private?"

"Surely." Caleb put down his mug and got to his feet, his long legs knocking the underside of the table. He avoided Abigail's gaze and followed Anke through to the living room. The *aulder* woman looked up at him with gentle eyes.

"Birchbark said ya would have the heart fer this as a proper handyman. . . ."

Here we geh, Caleb thought grimly though he kept a smile on his face. He was prepared for everything from feeding a *boppli* rhino to the potential delivery of twin giraffes, so he was pleasantly surprised when Anke told him how he might help her.

"Ya see, it's a present for Abner, for the Christmastime. I bought it with my own money and had George Stauffer hide it in our big shed."

Caleb nodded. "I'll do my best, Frau Mast."

"*Ach, danki*. But ya must keep it a secret, though Abigail knows, of course."

He cleared his throat, still warmed inside by the eggnog. "She's a talented artist. Perhaps she might help me a bit with the design."

"*Ach*, that would be *wunderbaar*! I'll tell her later." Anke pressed his hand, and Caleb drew her in for a brief hug.

When she went back toward the kitchen, Caleb followed her. Delicious, eggnoggy thoughts swirled in his head, thoughts that had little to do with the now-iced cookies. As he watched Abigail scrape a fingertip of icing from the bowl and put it to her lips, he stopped dead. *Yep, definitely more sugar here than teaberry-iced cookies. . . .*

Abigail stepped out into the gloaming. The trip to town with Phillip that morning had been pleasant and working with Mercy peaceful. Then an afternoon of cookie baking with Anke had left her happy. She traced the word over in her mind—*Happy? Me? Surely I've had joy in the purposeful work of my pottery, but something about Caleb standing there in his blue shirt and dark pants, a large cookie in his hand, has made me feeling the stirrings of some new freedom. . . . More freedom than I've known since Zinnia's death. . . .*

Impulsively, she turned from Abner and Anke's cabin, having insisted that she'd prefer to *geh* home alone. She moved through the snow until she could see the faint hint of lantern light shining through a crack in Abner's back shed. She glanced once behind her, feeling as though someone watched her. Then she strengthened her resolve and told herself it was only her imagination that there were eyes behind her. She thought of the Bible verse about *Derr Herr* providing peace to those who fixed their minds on Him and pressed on toward the shed. She paused for a moment before reaching for the cold latch, then slid the door open, feeling her heart skip a beat.

Caleb stood in a loose, paint-stained, once-white shirt, his suspenders lowered to hang against his long, black-clad legs. She felt as if she had captured him in some state of intimacy, and she almost backed away.

"Abigail?"

His voice was a bit rough and she noticed another half-empty glass of eggnog atop an old barrel.

"*Sei se gut, kumme* inside," he said. "Though it's not much warmer in here . . . I have to keep the back door open for ventilation."

She did as he asked, noticing for the first time that he held a paintbrush.

"*Ach*, Caleb, you're working on the sled for Anke! But isn't it late? Surely you could have started tomorrow?"

He nodded. "True. But back home I worked a lot at *nacht*. It's peaceful. Besides, I was waiting for a certain cookie baker to retire for the evening." He gave her a slow smile that caused her heart to flutter.

"I see."

"You didn't think I'd let you walk home alone?"

Abigail considered. "I'm fine being alone."

He put the paintbrush down and came toward her. "I know that. I can tell. . . . But why then did you write the ad? Why did you want a mail-order groom in the first place?"

She looked up into his sea-blue eyes and her thoughts slammed against each other.

She thought of the strange feeling that she was being watched from behind and wondered briefly if the past had eyes. She thought of the pull of the water and her regret over going swimming that day so long ago. . . . Then she remembered that she stood warm and safe in Abner's shed with a steady-eyed man before her. Asking her . . .

"I suppose I saw the success of Tabitha and Matthew's match, so I wrote the ad," she blurted.

He took a step nearer her and she caught the rich pine scent of his skin.

"And I wanted . . ." She paused, searching her heart and mind. *What had she wanted?*

Caleb had moved to stand before her. She swallowed and found her eyes level with his bare throat. He reached a lean finger to stroke the curve of her cheek and she knew that color rushed beneath her skin to meet his touch. "You wanted," he whispered. "What do you . . . want . . . sweet Abigail?"

She wet her lips, not knowing how to reply. *What do I want? Freedom? Peace? Love?* His gentle touch was destroying the cloak of secrecy she usually kept wrapped around her. She barely understood the response of her body to his rough voice. He bent as if to kiss her and she looked down, uncertain as to what to do. Then Fred caught the scent of some small creature stirring in the shed and let out a loud baying, shattering the silence and breaking the spell that had held her mesmerized only moments before.

Caleb linked his arm through Abigail's as they walked toward her home and tried to remember that he was probably half-drunk from Anke's seemingly innocent eggnog. He certainly felt a little warm, and there was a tightness in his belly at Abigail's nearness. He took a deep breath of the cold *nacht* air to center his head.

"Would you like me to help you work on the sled in the evenings?" Abigail's voice was tentative.

"*Jah*, that would be great. I think I can get the base coat on and then allow you to do the decorative work. The velvet in the seat needs to be sewn, and the reins need to be replaced."

"*Ach*, and don't forget the sleigh bells," she added.

He smiled and stopped still in a beam of moonlight, letting Fred run on ahead. Then he turned and looked down at Abigail.

"Is there something wrong?"

"*Nee*," he whispered. "But I like that you remembered the bells—that merry part of life."

He watched a slight frown touch her lips. "Well, 'merry' doesn't normally describe me, I'm afraid."

"Why not?" He reached his right hand to gently cup her cheek.

He watched while she seemed to debate within herself as to what answer she might give and regretted that he had troubled her with his question. He lowered his hand and mentally wrenched himself away from her. "Never mind, Abigail. We'd best get you home; it's cold out tonight."

He would have moved on if she hadn't laid a black-mittened hand on his sleeve. "*Nee*, wait. You told me about the bats. That was a trust. I'd like to trust you the same way."

"You don't have to—you can tell me in your own time or not at all. I don't expect you to—"

"*Sei se gut*, Caleb. I think I wasn't entirely truthful with you in my ad."

He smiled, staring down at her. "Soooo, you're already married? Or have two other mail-order grooms waiting in the wings?"

He stopped his gentle teasing when she shook her head. "*Nee*, but I am perhaps a lot more serious than you might think. I—I've made some bad decisions in my life."

"Who hasn't?" he asked somewhat roughly, thinking of his *fater*. "We all have dark waters within us, but it is *Derr Herr* who illuminates us and brings us new life."

"I know that." She paused. "At least, some of the time."

He nodded. "Well, don't think that I'm saying I know it all the time either. It's hard to hold on to real Truth." He became aware of the minutes passing and reluctantly took in her windblown cheeks. He slipped his arm around her, pulling her close. "Let me see you home, Abigail. You're going to freeze out here."

He felt her yield against him and he set a brisk pace, following Fred's tracks in the snowy trail of moonlight.

Chapter Ten

The news spread about Bishop Kore's desire that the *Amisch* of Blackberry Falls participate in Farwell's Winter in the Garden benefit, and both young and *auld Amisch* hurried to find treasures that might be donated for the silent auction or any other of the festive booths listed in the invitation Mercy had circulated. And, as if doing penance for her personal thoughts about Phillip, Mercy lost herself in a fever of work, leading right up to the *nacht* of the benefit.

She made a double batch of goat's milk soap, mixing in festive scents like peppermint, pine, and bayberry. She also dug out a beautiful bright yellow crocheted baby's blanket and stayed up late at *nacht* to finish the stitches she had abandoned long ago due to a lack of time. She had forgotten how comforting it was to rock and stitch by bright lantern light. She even found herself humming snatches of songs from her girlhood, and the bitterness she'd felt during the last years seemed to fall around her feet, like a tattered gown.

She was in such a frame of mind one afternoon when there was a brisk knock at her front door. She opened it, expecting to find Ann Bly with some fresh holly and ivy, but instead, it was Phillip. She blinked as she stared up into his handsome face and immediately her guard went up—she was once more the abandoned and foolish young pregnant woman who had no one to blame but herself.

"*Jah*. What do you want?" she snapped.

"Not much really," he said. "I'd like to give Abigail a surprise at the benefit in Farwell and needed your advice."

Mercy's throat burned; she knew at once both happiness for her sister and a heavy jealousy for herself. *This is ridiculous. . . . He's nearly Abigail's betrothed.* Gott *forgive me.*

"So, what do you think?"

Mercy stared up at him. "Uh . . . what?"

He rolled his eyes. "You haven't heard a word I've said."

"I did so. *Kumme* in out of the cold."

"*Danki.*" He took off his hat, revealing his dark tousled hair.

She turned away from him and carefully smoothed the folds of the yellow blanket she had placed on the kitchen table.

"That's pretty," he said from over her shoulder. She watched as his lean fingers stroked the yarn, inches from her own hand. She felt surrounded by him and closed her eyes for a moment.

"My *mamm* crocheted back home," he said.

She tried to make her voice stern. *Abigail's mon . . . this is Abigail's mon. . . .* "Where is home? Surely you had to travel far to come to Blackberry Falls?"

She sensed him move away and opened her eyes. He

sat down at the table. She wanted to frown but couldn't manage the gesture.

He gave her a sunny smile, and she slid into the chair across from him. "Home was Lockport, PA."

"And—and was that close to Renova? I mean, you saw Abigail's ad. . . ."

"Forty minutes by horse between the two places. I caught sight of the ad by chance in a little diner—but then, perhaps it wasn't chance. I feel *Gott* worked to bring me here."

Mercy nodded automatically. "*Jah*, surely. . . ." *For Abigail . . . Abigail's mail-order groom.*

"So, what do you think of the fresh flowers idea?"

She looked up at him, having a sudden image of him offering her flowers. She pursed her lips and shook her head. *Nee,* her mind whispered. "*Nee,*" she said abruptly.

She saw surprise on his handsome face and then concern. "*Ach*, is there something against such things in Blackberry Falls that I don't know about?"

She exhaled slowly. *This is for Abigail.* "I'm sorry," she said finally. "Fresh flowers for Christmas would be nice." *There. It's true,* she thought. "Now, please *geh* on. I've got a lot to do for the fundraiser."

"Well, *danki*, Mercy. I appreciate your advice." He rose from the table, then stopped, staring down at her. "Say, uh, would you and Joshua like a sleigh ride to the festival?"

"Tad's staying overnight." As she made the excuse, she felt her heart pound in her ears.

"No matter. Then we can keep him out of trouble and you can help me choose Abigail's flowers."

She nodded, and he put his hat on and left with a quiet

click of the cabin door. "Of course, he only offered so I could help pick out Abigail's gift," she muttered aloud, but then she permitted herself, with wistful fingers, to trace the path of his hand in the folds of the yellow blanket.

Caleb whistled softly as he worked on the Christmas sled for Anke Mast. He'd stripped off his own coat and shirt and had donned an *auld* work shirt of Abner's as he painted. But his mind drifted to the minutes Abigail had been in the shed with him a few *nachts* past and he found himself wishing she was with him now. He thought his wish had been granted at the sound of the wooden door being slid open, and he felt his breath catch. But, instead of Abigail, it was Phillip, the other mail-order groom.

Caleb stifled a groan. He had work to do and didn't want to be waylaid by the competition; nor did he want the secret of the sled to get out.

"What can I do for you?" Caleb asked, noting the expectancy in the other man's stance.

"We've never met formally. That's why I stopped here. I'm Phillip."

"And I'm Caleb." He reluctantly shook the other man's outstretched hand, then went back to his painting, hoping Phillip would leave because of the paint fumes. But then the niggling of his conscience forced words from his mouth. "So, you have been writing to Abigail?"

"Yep. I answered her ad and feel that I can provide most of what she wants, although I don't mean to sound prideful."

Caleb sighed to himself. He instinctively knew that

Phillip wasn't baiting him and that, in other circumstances, he'd probably accept the other man as a friend.

"You're doing fine work on the sled here."

"*Jah, danki*. But not a word about it. It's a surprise from Anke to her new husband."

"I know. Abigail told me this morning when I was at her cabin. She's planning on coming over later to help with the decoration."

Caleb nodded, immediately envisioning Abigail locked in Phillip's arms in a sultry embrace. He wondered if she allowed the other mail-order groom any kissing and immediately regretted the notion. He was about to say something out of frustration when Phillip spoke in a casual tone.

"*Jah*. Abigail and I spend a lot of time looking at seed catalogs."

"Seed catalogs?" Caleb repeated blankly.

"Sure. I'm a farmer by trade and it feels *gut* to study some of the plant varieties together. I especially like the heirloom tomatoes."

"Okaaay." Caleb felt the tension in his body ease.

If they're studying tomatoes, they can't have all that much time to do other things. . . .

"*Jah*, I expect she'll make an excellent farmer's wife. . . . But her sister, *ach*, that woman has it in for me and for you, by the way."

Caleb smiled, despite Phillip's assumption that Abigail would be his. "That's okay. I've known people like Mercy. They're wounded inside, and it is difficult for them to accept change in life."

"I guess I'm a big change in her life then."

"*Jah*, maybe you—" Caleb broke off as the shed door slid open once more.

Abigail peeked her pretty, bonneted head around the door. "Sorry. I can come back later. I don't want to interrupt the two of you."

Caleb watched her beautiful eyes widen as she processed the sight of both mail-order grooms together.

"Is everything all right?" she questioned.

Caleb moved to put the paintbrush down and step closer to her, intending on providing reassurance, but he ran smack-dab into Phillip and backed off. Caleb watched Phillip lay a big hand on her shoulder and pat her almost absently. *Seed catalogs . . . and vague touches. . . . Abigail looks comfortable but not especially excited. . . .* Caleb's thoughts ricocheted around his brain, and then he realized he'd stepped too close to the sled and black paint now stained the fabric of the old work shirt he wore.

"Everything's fine," Caleb said softly. He picked the paintbrush up again and worked with swift, even strokes. He wanted to concentrate on something other than the strange situation he was in. Maybe he was foolish to even think that he had a chance with Abigail. . . . He looked up as he heard the shed door open. Phillip gave a brief wave and slid it closed.

"Where did he *geh*?" Caleb asked as Abigail regarded him with a steady gaze.

"He said he had an errand in Farwell before the benefit. . . . I thought I'd work on the designs for the sled . . . that is, if I'm not in the way?"

Caleb swiped at his cheek and nodded with a smile. "I don't think you could ever be in my way."

She stepped closer and smiled up at him.

"What?" he asked.

"You've got paint on your cheek," she said softly, and he blinked, feeling foolish as he grabbed a rag.

"Here. Let me," she said.

He stood with hands at his sides, awkward as a colt, while she worked at his cheek. He could tell that she was nervous because a pulse thrummed visibly in her throat.

"There!" She stood on her tiptoes, surveying her handiwork, then surprised him with a quick buss on his clean cheek.

He drew her close and slanted his head, kissing her with gentle strength. He was amazed, then thrilled, when she slid her slender arms about his neck and returned the soft caress of his mouth. . . .

Abigail was falling, lost in a sweet blur somewhere between burgeoning passion and the faint thought that she shouldn't find such intense pleasure in the touch of his lips.

When she finally broke away, she stared up into his blue eyes, noticing the faint shadow of his beard and the realization that the burn on her cheeks was caused by his intimate touch. She must have appeared somewhat shocked because he took a step away. "I'm sorry," he muttered. "You've got paint all over your cloak."

She looked down at herself and vaguely registered the black stains, darker than even the wool fabric.

Caleb easily undid the pins at her throat and tossed her cloak onto a nearby hay bale. He slung his own heavy coat around her shoulders and bundled her in its warmth.

"Caleb, what are you going to wear? You'll freeze!"

He smiled down at her. "I owe you a new cloak. But if that is the price for such a kiss, it is small and surely not equal to the bounty I found with you."

"I've never had a kiss from a man," she admitted. "Only from my *fater*."

She glanced up at him and saw that his cheeks became ruddy and flushed at her confession. She stood stock-still when he reached his right hand to run his thumb across her bottom lip. "Virgin lips?" he asked softly.

She nodded, practically holding her breath. *Virgin . . . virgin . . . while he must surely . . .*

He smiled down at her. "I never thought I had much talent for kissing."

"And have you had much practice?" Abigail asked, surprising herself, but for some reason it seemed important to know.

He shook his head and his blue eyes brightened. "*Nee*—honestly. During *rumspringa* I kissed two *Englisch* sisters but neither one seemed especially moved. *Nee*—not much experience at all." He ran a finger down her hot cheek. "But I'd like to . . . practice."

Suddenly, Abigail thought of Phillip. *Perhaps it was wrong to wantonly kiss Caleb when she hadn't so much as moved past the turnip seed page with Phillip—yet, aren't I'm courting Caleb as well?* She swallowed hard and stepped away. "*Ach*, I'd better start on the trim where the sled has dried up front."

He gave her a solemn nod. "*Jah*, surely, and I've got to finish up here. I'm going to do a few ice sculptures for the benefit tonight."

"*Ach*, that sounds lovely!"

He shrugged with a smile. "*Gut* job for a handyman."

She watched him seem to struggle with something and almost asked him what troubled him, but then he spoke.

"Would you like a sleigh ride to the benefit tonight? I think Birchbark's got some kind of sled I could clean up."

She felt her heart sink. "*Ach, nee.* I've made other plans to get there. I'm sorry."

"No need to fret. I understand."

Abigail nodded, looking away. *I hope he does understand because I must* geh *to the cemetery tonight. . . .*

Chapter Eleven

Phillip couldn't help but notice the warming scents of Christmas that drifted to him as he held Mercy's basket of soaps while she resisted his helping hand and scrambled into the sleigh. Joshua and Tad sat at the ready in the back, each one grinning with suppressed excitement. Phillip passed the basket back to Joshua and glanced sideways at Mercy.

Her red hair was peeking in soft tendrils from the side of her bonnet and she hugged herself tightly, her arms around her middle as if she were freezing . . . or perhaps defensive. He reached down and pulled up the pile of quilts Grossmuder Mildred had insisted he take. He settled the soft weight across Mercy with tentative hands, then lifted a pail of steaming hot baked potatoes to her.

"Grossmuder Mildred said to snuggle these against you somewhere to keep extra warm."

She was about to reach inside when he stopped her and used his own heavily gloved hand. "Where are your mittens?" he asked as he dropped a hot potato in her quilted lap.

"I forgot them."

He flung several potatoes into the back at the *buwes* who laughed in return. Then he took off his gloves and passed them to Mercy.

"Wear these." For some reason, the thought of her being cold bothered him.

He picked up the reins, then clicked to the horse that Bishop Kore had loaned him, and they were off in a spray of snow.

Mercy felt the warmth of the potato permeate her middle and she relaxed a bit from her initial stiff posture. The intimate touch of Phillip's large gloves nearly made her cry. *I have been so lonely,* she admitted to herself as she clenched her hands inside the gloves. *When was the last time someone has touched me? Fourteen years ago . . . so long . . . but Phillip belongs to Abigail, to her life, not mine. Though living with him as a* bruder-*in-law will be impossible. . . . Perhaps I should move away. . . .*

"Relax," he called over the whooshing sound of the runners on the snow.

Mercy nodded. "I'm fine." *Not fine . . . not fine.*

"Can we go faster?" Tad hollered from the back.

Phillip laughed and looked at her. A flash of white teeth, and she realized that he was waiting for her approval to let the horse fly.

"I'm not an *auld* lady," Mercy snapped. "*Geh* as fast as you want!"

"Yes, ma'am!"

He managed the reins with ease and soon they were sliding so fast over the snow that Mercy could feel her heart jump in her throat, but she felt safe too—and she wished the ride would never end. . . .

Once he'd returned to the cabin, Caleb had to resist the urge to grit his teeth when Birchbark began another roaring stream of sneezing.

"I ain't sick," the *auld* man rasped when he'd finished.

"And I'm a wood sprite," Caleb returned drily. "I'm going for the healer. You might have pneumonia."

"I do not! And, so help me, if I git ahold of you, *buwe*. . . ." Birchbark made a show of flinging the quilts back, but soon collapsed against the feather pillows.

Caleb tucked the quilt beneath Birchbark's beard and moved a glass full of water within reach on the bedside table. "What else can I get for you?"

Birchbark sighed and opened bleary eyes. "You goin' down to Farwell ta do them ice sculptures?"

"*Jah*, but I don't have to leave right away. Do you need something?" He watched the *auld* man seem to struggle within himself, then finally shake his head.

"*Nee*, it can wait, I guess. . . ."

"Look, Birchbark, I'm glad to help you. Truly."

"All right. If ye'd *geh* to the pantry over there, I got some baby formula that needs to be delivered ta Farwell. Four cans thereabouts. Mary Stevens ain't got *nee* milk and that young'un needs to be fed. Jeb Stevens is thinkin' 'bout stealin' the formula—he's been outta work fer two months now and things are pretty tight."

Caleb listened to the strange explanation, then went to the pantry and found the four yellow cans.

"Put 'em in my pack and carry that 'cross the mountain."

Caleb decided it would only frustrate the sick *mon* if he disagreed, so he loaded the cans into the massive backpack and drew on his coat. He shrugged on the backpack and faced the bed. "All right, I'm *gut*. Though I doubt Tommy will fancy having to carry both me and this giant pack of yours."

"He'll be fine but will be wantin' an extra measure of oats when you tie him up at Farwell. Mind that ya see he gits it."

Caleb nodded, not wanting to ask if Birchbark could talk to an animal long-distance, as it were. He grabbed his black hat, bid Birchbark *gut*bye, and set out through the door into the wintry gloaming.

Abigail resolutely pulled off her black mittens and knelt in the snow, careless of the cold enveloping her. She'd brought a lantern even though it was barely dark, but she could have walked the *Amisch* cemetery blindfolded if it had been necessary. It was a week and a few days before Christmas, and Abigail always visited the cemetery alone on the anniversary of Zinnia's death.

Abigail sighed as she laid the tiny vessel of forced tulip bulbs in the place she scraped clear of snow. She closed her eyes and was suddenly no longer cold as she remembered the hot, August sun and the shimmer of the deep water downstream from Blackberry Falls. Abigail had been fourteen, tall and lanky and dressed in an *Englisch* bathing suit of yellow, red, and green. Zinnia had been there, her red hair a perfect foil for the sheen of the water. Zinnia was short and stocky, strong from all her hard work on her *fater*'s farm. And then there was Heather; coy and dark-haired with green eyes that could shine warmly or glitter with malice. Abigail had never really understood why she considered the other girls to be her friends. *Especially after they* . . . A sudden sound from the forest brought her quickly to her feet. She scanned the tree line and once more felt as though she were being watched.

She drew a deep breath, dismissing the idea that the *nacht* had eyes, and turned back to the grave. There was much to do besides thinking of the past. . . . Even now she should be in Farwell. She had some pottery pieces for the Winter in the Garden benefit and wondered with a pleasant shiver of warmth whether Caleb might be there. She frowned to herself. *Phillip.* . . . *I promised myself I'd spend more time with Phillip.* . . . But it was Caleb's blue eyes that haunted each footstep until she got back into the small sleigh and clicked to Amber, her faithful mare, to begin the journey to Farwell.

Caleb reluctantly mounted the steps and gave a quick knock on the Stevenses' simple door. He'd had no trouble finding the place, but now that he was here, he felt utterly ridiculous delivering infant formula to a woman who had no milk. He shuddered, recalling the baby delivery. . . . *Maybe I can just leave the stuff right here by the door.* . . . He began to shrug off the large pack when the door was flung open from the inside.

Caleb stared into the work-lined face of a man who looked both angry and desperate. "Uh . . . Jeb?"

"Yeah . . . whadda ya want?"

"Well, I heard . . . that is . . . Birchbark told me . . ."

Caleb felt his face flame and eased a finger under the collar of his coat.

"Birchbark? How d'you know him?" The man squinted suspiciously.

"I'm . . . uh . . . rooming with him for a while. He said . . . you were thinking about maybe doing something desperate tonight. . . ." Caleb watched the emotions shift across the other man's face.

"Yeah . . . well." Jeb bent his head. "You know what they say about desperate people doing desperate things. My Mary's . . . well, I expect Birchbark's told ya."

Caleb nodded. "He sent formula. I've got it right . . ." He shrugged at the pack, feeling for some reason that the load had grown heavier.

"Here! Come in, won't ya?"

Caleb staggered through the door. "*Jah, danki.*" He entered the simple home and nodded to the young woman who held a small baby, swaddled and wearing a blue cap. The little one was fussing loudly.

Caleb yanked off the pack and eased it to the floor. "Uh, Birchbark sent some formula." He knelt and hastily undid the pack, then sat back in surprise. "What the . . . ?"

The pack was laden with formula, diapers, and home-made applesauce. And then all manner of other *boppli* goods spilled out onto the floor. Caleb blinked, then ran a hand across his eyes. He knew there had been nothing in the pack but four cans of formula.

Jeb clapped him on the shoulder, bringing him back to the moment.

"That Birchbark—I see he's workin' ahead of time this year! What do you say, Mary?"

Caleb glanced over at the young mother, whose sudden smile lit her from within.

"Thank you," she mouthed over the *boppli*'s wails.

"You're welcome," he hollered over the din, then noticed that Jeb was neatly stacking the baby things on the scarred wooden table in the center of the room.

"I can tell ya that Birchbark's never let anyone else carry his pack, not so's I noticed. He must trust ya."

Caleb nodded, feeling as if he was forgetting something. Then he withdrew his pocketbook from his pants and took out some cash. Giving the money to Jeb seemed to make the situation feel less strange. He gathered up the pack, resisting the urge to look inside, threw his pocketbook in, and headed back into the coming *nacht*.

Then he remembered Tommy's oats and he muttered to himself, leading the horse toward the sound of orchestra music that emanated from the center of town.

Chapter Twelve

Abigail looked around the town square of Farwell with delight. Beautiful, festive music came from the gazebo where several smiling townspeople, dressed in formal black suits and bright red scarves, were playing their stringed instruments. Folks milled about, pausing now and then to talk to each other, and all sent warm smiles her way even as they gave brief glances toward her long cloak and bonnet. She hadn't been able to quite get the black paint off her *gut* cloak, but she was a little glad about that as she recalled the amazing first kiss she had received from Caleb. It would be easy to get lost in dreams, she thought, looking around. It had started to snow very lightly and the pine trees in the square glistened with colored lights and bright decorations. She wondered where Caleb might be ice sculpting, then started in surprise as she heard Mercy call her name.

Abigail looked up and saw Mercy and Phillip coming toward her. Mercy looked troubled while Phillip's bright smile flashed white against the gentle snow. He carried a small white cardboard box that was adorned with a dark green bow.

"Mercy, are you all right?" Abigail asked as they stopped. "You're wearing gloves that are much too big for you. Are you cold? I have an extra blanket in the sleigh and I—"

"I'm fine," Mercy said as she stripped off the gloves. She slapped them against Phillip's arm, and he caught them just before they fell. "I need to *geh* check on my soap stock. I hope you both have a *wunderbaar* time."

Abigail watched as Mercy turned and headed back down the street. She clearly wanted nothing to do with Phillip, though he too seemed puzzled by her sister's behavior. Abigail decided to find Mercy later in the evening and discover what was bothering her.

For now, Abigail remembered her resolve to spend more time with Phillip and moved with him as he gently pulled her down on a snow-dusted bench near the sidewalk. He held out the white box with its sumptuous bow and she took it with pleasure. It was nice to get a present, she thought.

She lifted the lid with its velvet ties, then smiled down into the careful nesting of gold-flecked tissue paper that surrounded the gift. Carefully, she pulled back the thin paper and lifted the flowers from their cradle. "*Ach*, Phillip! They're beautiful." She held the wrist corsage of velvet red roses, baby's breath, and tiny ferns near her face and inhaled the heavenly scent. "*Danki*, Phillip."

"You're welcome. Mercy helped me pick them out. You can wear them on your wrist and sort of . . . hide them beneath your cloak. I know we are plain folk, but it shouldn't hurt for one *nacht*. I thought—I thought when I got them about us maybe planting rosebushes on our farm one day."

Abigail froze inside at his shy but steady look. *What am I playing at?* she wondered. *Phillip already has us married and living on a farm. . . . What about my pottery? And rosebushes . . . And a mail-order groom on my terms?*

She looked at the roses, absently running one finger over the delicate petals. "*Ach*, Phillip, I—"

"Here. Let me help you get them on your wrist." He leaned closer to her and she blinked back sudden tears. *He is so trusting but I—I would rather have a corsage of weeds if only they were from Caleb. . . .*

Mercy jostled her way into one of the town's crowded specialty gift shops, her eyes automatically drawn to the festive display where her soaps were nestled on a tartan scarf. She walked over to the counter, feeling her heart race. *How could I return his kindness to me by slapping him with his own gloves?* She put her fingers to her lips as an errant giggle nearly choked her with surprise, but she sobered quickly. Picking out the roses for Abigail had been terrible—*Forgive me,* Gott, *but I wanted them for myself. . . .*

Even on the brief sleigh ride into town, she had to admit to herself that she had a nagging fantasy of what it might be like to sit beside Phillip as his *frau*. . . . She nearly jumped when Joshua called to her.

"*Mamm*, Tad and I each wanted to do some sledding on the big hill behind the church. Is that okay?"

"*Jah*," she answered absently, missing the mischief in Tad's eyes. The two *buwes* ran out of the store and she added more soaps from her basket to the display. Then, satisfied, she turned, only to run full tilt into Phillip's broad chest.

Her arms felt hot where he steadied her, and she had no idea what to say, which was a rare thing. "Wh—where's Abigail?" She knew she sounded angry, but it was better than wallowing in misery that she couldn't have her sister's suitor. "Did she like the roses?" *There. I'm doing the honorable thing by asking after the flowers. . . .*

"She liked them." Phillip nodded, but there was something in his voice that made her pause. She looked up into his handsome face and could see the shimmer of doubt in his fine eyes.

"What's wrong?" she asked, the words out of her mouth before she could help herself.

He shook his head, then guided her backward to avoid an *Englisch* woman who obviously wanted to see Mercy's soaps but had a screaming toddler in tow. Mercy watched Phillip turn sideways, then stoop to face the furious little boy. Phillip began to whistle, and immediately, the child quieted and Mercy blinked in disbelief.

"Oh, thank you," the mother whispered, two soaps in her hand. "He's a handful sometimes and I wanted to get some Christmas shopping done."

Phillip rose to his feet, patting the child on the head. "You're more than welcome."

The pair walked off and Mercy looked up at Phillip. "I wish you had been here when Joshua was little." She swallowed then coughed at the implications of what she'd said. Despite her discomfiture, Phillip merely expressed understanding.

"I bet it was hard to be a single *mamm*."

"*Jah*," she agreed after a long moment. She didn't like

to talk about the early days of Joshua's life, and no one but Abigail questioned her about that time.

"I'm sorry if I've made you uncomfortable, Mercy. Please forgive me."

Mercy nodded and sought to quickly change the subject. "Uh, you were telling me about the flowers and Abigail. . . ."

"*Ach, jah.*" He moved to idly run a lean finger across the edge of a bayberry soap. "I—I think I must spend more time with her. I don't know that she really wants to become a farmer's wife."

Something inside Mercy rose up in hope. *I would be a farmer's wife . . . his helpmeet and beloved* frau *. . .* But she soon crashed into the reality of Phillip bidding her goodbye without even a backward glance.

Phillip wandered along the sidewalks without noticing the festivity around him. He felt defeated somehow, as if he truly stood no chance of winning Abigail's hand and heart. But there could be far worse things, he considered. Like Mercy raising a *sohn* alone. *Oh, the community would have helped but there would have been gossip as well.* He frowned then heard the low pulse of organ music. He stopped in the street, realizing he'd drifted away from the bustle of the shops to a back street where an old-fashioned redbrick church stood. It had high stained-glass windows that flickered with light from within. He felt drawn to the wide stone steps and eased open the heavy door. He stepped inside and saw a large group of worshippers in the long wooden pews. They were standing and singing

"Silent Night" or, as he knew it, "*Stille Nacht.*" He loved the *auld* carol and found himself singing along as he stepped into one of the back pews beneath the choir loft. It felt *gut* to be united with others in something, and as he sang the verses, he felt his spirits rise. He knew a peace that was only interrupted by the strange sight of a small colored ball bouncing like a missile down the center aisle.

The organist continued unaware, and two more Super Balls ricocheted off the pews, one hitting an older woman in the back and another bouncing off the bald head of a man halfway up the aisle. Both turned around with indignant expressions and Phillip had to suppress a smile. The balls were coming from the empty choir loft behind him, and he had a *gut* idea of who the bouncers were. Then a black ball landed somewhere near the organist, who broke off her playing with a discordant screech. "Mouse!" she screamed. "There's a mouse!"

The church was in an uproar in seconds, with everyone looking for the mouse. Two more balls followed, adding to the furor, and Phillip slipped quietly from his pew and headed outside into the light snow. He didn't have to wait long before he caught sight of two shadowy figures stealing out of the church and past the lighted garland decorations on a nearby tree.

"That was great!"

Phillip recognized Tad's strident voice and didn't wait for a reply from the other culprit. He stepped out of the shadows, struggling to keep the laughter from his words. "It was a great prank, *buwes*. But what would your mothers have to say?"

* * *

White Christmas lights lined the cobblestone path, and Abigail knew that she was the lone spectator in the hedge maze, at least for the moment. She couldn't help but covertly admire the strength in Caleb's arms and back as she stood behind the tall shrubbery. He'd removed his coat and hat and had rolled up the sleeves of his dark blue shirt. She watched with quiet intent as the shape of an evergreen was coaxed from the block of ice by Caleb's confident strikes of the hammer and chisel.

He paused to study his work, then turned and looked directly at her through the snow-dusted branches. "I thought it might be you, Abigail." His voice sounded husky.

She swallowed and slipped around the tall hedge to face him. "And why did you think that?"

He smiled and laid aside his tools, then walked toward her. She felt for a moment a curious and tantalizing thrill in her breast, almost as if some big snow cat held her in thrall. She resisted the urge to lean back against the hedge for support, then caught the glorious scent of him as he neared—snow and pine and the tantalizing note of bayberry. He smelled like Christmas.

"I could feel you," he whispered as he ran a lean finger down her cheek. "Does that make any sense?"

She wanted to say *nee*, but some impulse bubbled up inside her and she decided that a bit of truth might be warranted. "*Jah*," she said quietly. "I—I think I can feel your nearness too at times." She swallowed hard when he took a step closer, almost as though he was compelled by her admission.

She was very aware of the warmth of his big body despite the nip in the air, and she shivered a bit with pleasure as his clever fingers undid the ties of her bonnet and eased it back. Then he bent his head and whispered in her ear.

"Mmmm . . . you smell like roses. I haven't stopped thinking about you all afternoon." He smiled down at her as he confessed his feelings, and she raised her mittened hands to his chest and heard his sharp intake of breath. He drew nearer, slanting his head, and her mouth burned as she waited for his kiss.

But, instead, she felt a sudden laugh in his chest as he rocked his long legs forward then bent his back to catch the scent of the flowers secured on her wrist. "Now, my pretty, I know your secret. Mmmm . . . roses in winter. Where did you find them?"

Abigail badly wanted him to ignore the flowers and proceed with the kissing, but she couldn't help but be truthful. "They were an early Christmas gift—from Phillip."

He gave her a wry smile. "Smart man, my rival. But he increases my pleasure so I can't complain."

Abigail swallowed. "Was it—is it a pleasure to kiss me?"

He groaned. "*Jah*, sweet pleasure that I would taste again."

She waited with delicious expectation, but then she felt him wrench himself from her, and she stared in confusion at his broad back as he lifted his tools and began to strike at the ice again.

"Caleb? What is it?"

He half laughed, then stopped working and glanced at her over his shoulder. "I know what I want, Abigail. And we are alone in such a place that one kiss may lead to another and another. . . . I need to treat you with dignity and respect."

"Why, I believe you're shy, Caleb King." The bold

words were out of her mouth before she could think, but when he made no reply, she took an impulsive step forward. She drew a deep breath. "Perhaps, it is you who needs courting. . . ."

She would have continued when feminine laughter echoed from nearby. Abigail made haste to tug the strings of her dark bonnet close about her chin and slipped once more behind the high hedge. The smart tap of high heels echoed on the cobbled walkway and three *Englisch* women in dark boots and pretty coats soon came into view.

Abigail bit her lip, wondering if she might slip away, but then she froze in place as the young women stopped near where Caleb was working.

"*Gut* evening, ladies." He paused in his sculpting to smile easily at them, and Abigail felt a sudden prick of jealousy. She was amazed at herself. Why shouldn't he interact with the guests? But then one of the women cooed softly as she ran a pointed fingertip down the evergreen ice sculpture, then trailed the same finger across the muscles in Caleb's left arm.

"You're Amish, right?" she asked, sidling closer to him.

"*Jah* . . . or . . . yeah, I guess you'd say."

Abigail watched as he nodded to the other two girls, who were smiling rather seductively. What did they expect? Abigail thought indignantly. That he'd lay aside his tools and kiss each of them? The thought made her flush. Wasn't that exactly what she wanted from him?

"Are you married, honey?" The brunette, with hair like a waterfall, asked the question softly.

Abigail couldn't stand to wait for his reply. She pulled the edges of her second-best cloak tight around her and tiptoed away from the hedge to lose herself deeper in the maze.

Caleb had finished the star and tree and had stepped back into the shadows of the maze as more people came to admire the ice sculptures. He knew Abigail had gone, probably soon after the women had stopped and expressed their interest in him and all things *Amisch*. The truth was, he'd felt overwhelmed by the forwardness of the *Englisch* girls, and it had surprised him. He realized that he far preferred Abigail's quiet reserve and the gentle pink of her parted lips lifting to his mouth.

His own thoughts aroused him and he automatically navigated the maze, always keeping his right hand on the snowy branches. He was able to quickly exit the high hedges and found himself on a well-lit street that was filled with families and happy chatter. He recognized that he was very near the school for the unique *kinner* when an *auld* woman asked with a charming smile if he'd like to purchase a raffle ticket for a lovely pottery serving plate.

"It's to benefit the school," she said. "As is everything tonight! The tickets are a dollar each."

Caleb knew instinctively that it was a plate of Abigail's design, and he wanted it on the spot. *It'll give me something to remember her by if she chooses Phillip as her mail-order groo*m. . . . He pushed the anxious thought aside and reached into his pocket for his wallet, then had a sudden memory of tossing it into Birchbark's pack when he'd left the *Englisch haus* earlier that *nacht*. The pack was with Tommy, who was tied up at a convenient shed.

"I'll be right back, ma'am. Please save me twenty-five tickets."

He turned and walked as quickly as he could through the friendly throng, hoping he'd run into Abigail. But he made it to the faint light of the shed without seeing anyone he knew and found Tommy still contentedly chewing his feed bag of oats. Caleb patted the horse fondly, then reached for the oversized pack, lowering it to the ground to find his wallet. But when he opened the top flap and reached inside, he pulled out a heavy, gaily wrapped package, with red ribbons that caught in the *nacht* breeze.

Caleb sank to his knees in the snow, holding the package and wondering if he was truly losing his mind. He let his fingers play with the ribbons, then slowly turned over the gift tag. The thin card was easy to read.

FOR THE CHRYSALIS SCHOOL

He sighed aloud and absently patted Tommy, who was nudging him. Then he reached into the sack once more and found his wallet. He had half a mind to stay where he was and not to deliver the package to the school, but, in his heart, he knew he could never do such a thing.

"Well, one thing's for sure," he muttered grimly to Tommy as he got to his feet. "Birchbark and I are going to have a long talk about this pack."

Chapter Thirteen

Caleb walked back to the day school as quickly as he could. He didn't want to miss the raffle for Abigail's work, and he was glad when the same *aulder* woman came smilingly toward him with a handful of tickets. "I saved you twenty-five exactly," she said, and Caleb gladly handed over the money. "Thank you, Mr. uh . . . ?"

"King. I'm Caleb King."

"And I'm Miss Barbara, the school's principal."

"Well, then, I think this gift should *geh* to you." He slid the present from beneath his right arm and handed it over gratefully. He was all too glad to pass the gift on; he didn't want to think about where it had come from or what was inside—pack or no.

"Would you like to come inside the school?" Miss Barbara asked. "The raffle is about to begin."

"*Jah*, surely."

He followed the principal inside the door and admired the vibrant paintings of butterflies that graced the interior walls. Folks began to press forward, and Caleb stepped aside, pausing across from the small room that must be the school library. He didn't see Abigail, and he wondered if she was with Phillip. He pushed the frustrating thought aside and listened as they began to call ticket numbers. But then he felt an impatient tug at his arm. A sprite of an *Englisch* girl was staring up at him through thick, purple cat's-eye glasses.

"Don't you want to see the library?" she whispered, pulling at him. He smiled at her insistence.

"I'm sorry," a woman nearby said softly. "She's pretty demanding at times."

Caleb looked down into the lady's tired eyes. "She's fine," he said. "You're Mom?"

She nodded, and Caleb felt another insistent tug at his hand. "Do you want to see?"

"All right," he said at Mom's nod. He allowed himself to be pulled into the room, which was hardly bigger than two closets, yet was packed to overflowing with books of all kinds.

"I'm Miranda," his guide announced, indicating that he should plop down on the blue bean bag next to hers.

"I'm Caleb." He sat down awkwardly, surprised when she pried a thin black-spined book from the shelf nearest her.

"I wrote this," she said proudly, handing it to him.

He looked at the detailed, colored cover which depicted Miranda with a long fall of yellow hair and a stick-necked body surrounded by dogs of every shape and color. "*Miranda's Dogs,*" Caleb read carefully. "Do you have dogs at home?"

Miranda shook her head. "No. We don't have any yard. Do you have dogs?"

"Well, I have Fred. He's my dog and Tommy's my horse."

"Oh." She nodded, taking the book back. "I'll read it to you."

"'Miranda does not have dogs. Miranda loves dogs. Miranda has autism. She wonders if dogs have autism. When Miranda grows up, she will have dogs. The End.'"

She gazed over at him, clearly awaiting his response, but for a moment, he could make no sound. The child had touched his heart with a few simple words that held worlds of meaning. He suddenly hoped that whatever was in the gift from the pack, it was something priceless.

"Well, what did you think?" Miranda asked.

"It was *wunderbaar*—that's something wonderful."

She nodded. "That's what my mommy says about me. Okay. See ya." She hopped up and ran out the door, leaving him to unwind his long legs with a bit less ease. When he glanced up, he saw Abigail staring at him.

Abigail watched as he got to his feet and collected his hat. "You're kind," she said simply.

She watched him flush a ruddy color, and his gaze skittered away from hers. "They need a new library," he pointed out, clearly wanting to change the subject.

"Maybe they'll get one after tonight," she said quietly. "The principal just opened a gift of three gold nuggets. I can only imagine what they're worth."

Caleb coughed faintly. "Three—gold nuggets? Do you know where—"

"Number seventy-seven!"

The school's principal had gotten hold of a microphone and Abigail watched as Caleb shuffled through the tickets he'd pulled from his pocket. "I've got it," he muttered after a moment. "I'd better *geh* claim my prize. I hope it's your pottery, Abigail."

She let him brush past, then stepped out into the small crowd to watch him as he reached the prize table. The principal seemed to be in a flurry of excitement once he got there, and she leaned across the table to press the microphone to her bosom and whisper something that caused Caleb to flush and nod, then step away. But she called him back once more and handed him the serving plate while the onlookers clapped.

Abigail was curious as to the exchange between the principal and her mail-order groom. *Her*, she thought suddenly. Was he hers? She pushed the idea aside as Caleb made his way back to the place she was standing, and she felt a strange thrill of pleasure wash down her back.

He was so very handsome, but he was more than that, she knew. Kind, caring, considerate—she didn't care if he read or wrote poetry as her ad had specified. The way he moved was poetry and his kindness to the child in the library touched Abigail's heart in a way she would never forget. Jah*, he is more than fine. . . .* But then she felt the brush of rose petals against her wrist and bit her lip. It seemed almost treacherous to dismiss Phillip when she remembered his kindness and hopes for the future, and she resolved once more to give the other mail-order

groom his proper chance at becoming her husband—
though the thought brought sadness to her heart. . . .

Phillip threw the small, confiscated ball up into the
falling snow, where it shone in the brightness of the
streetlamp. He had walked the *buwes* some distance from
the church and now paused as he considered their crimes.

He caught the ball, then stared at the two. Tad looked
thoroughly unrepentant, but Joshua was clearly miser-
able. "Well," Phillip began, "as I said, it was a *gut* prank
and life should have some room for pranks but not at the
expense of others. You nearly terrified the organist, and I
bet the congregation is still looking for the invisible
rodent."

"Are you going to tell my *mamm*?" Joshua asked with
resignation.

"*Nee*. I'm not. She—she's got enough worries, I sus-
pect. But I will make sure that you both do some work
with me on the upcoming seed exchange."

"Seed exchange?" Tad's eyes glimmered as if he was
considering what havoc might be created with a packet
of seeds.

"*Jah*," Phillip continued. "And even if you never farm
the land, you will gain some knowledge—which is something no one can ever take from you." He bounced the
ball lightly off the top of Tad's head, then turned to lead
them back to the festivities.

Mercy had wandered from the main street of shops and
found herself feeling deeply alone as the crowd of people

laughed gaily around her. She sought the relative solace of a small diner when she realized she'd eaten nothing since early that morning.

The space held only a few customers and Mercy picked up the menu, intending only to get tea. But the cheerful *Englisch* waitress who came to her table made the special sound good.

"I'll take your drink order, honey. But the cook makes a mean hot roast beef sandwich with mashed potatoes on the side."

Mercy considered and decided that it had been a long time since anyone but Abigail had cooked something for her. "I'll take tea and the special."

"Comin' right up."

Mercy gave a covert glance around the diner. She realized that everyone seemed to have someone to sit with, and loneliness engulfed her once more. She had read once about eating alone and the difficulty it presented. She looked down at her work-worn hands, then almost started when a bell clanged and the diner door opened, allowing blowing snow to enter.

She swallowed hard when she saw that it was Phillip and the *buwes* and almost wished that she could crawl under the seat. But it only took a few seconds before Phillip saw her and the *buwes* crowded into the booth, one on each side of the table. Mercy longed to *geh* and fix her hat and damp *kapp* but then she sternly repressed the idea. *I needn't make myself look better for him—he's Abigail's man. . . .*

"Mercy, hello." Phillip hung his black hat on a coat rack attached to the table and smiled at her as he sat down.

"Where have you been?" She wanted to sound soft and feminine, she realized, but her tone bit just the same.

"*Ach*, seeing things, bouncing ideas around. If I have your permission, Joshua and Tad are going to help me with some of the heirloom seeds for the seed exchange in January."

Mercy lifted her chin and looked into Phillip's dark eyes. "I know I can speak for Tad's *fater* . . . the *buwes* can participate, but only if they won't be a bother."

"No bother at all."

"Well . . . all right."

"And you might help, too," Phillip invited with a surprised look on his handsome face—almost as though he couldn't believe what he'd said.

But Mercy didn't want a handout of quality time. "*Nee*," she responded stiffly. "I'll stay at home. That's where I belong. . . ."

Abigail noticed that Caleb seemed more than a little relieved when they left the school and stepped out into the *nacht* air. Musical notes drifted and faded around them as Caleb led her back into the maze, which glistened with white lights.

"Where do you suppose those gold nuggets came from?" she asked, wondering what was on his mind.

"I don't know." He shook his head slowly. "They could have been in someone's family a long time."

She agreed, then stopped and took an impulsive step toward him, forgetting her resolve to spend more time with Phillip. "I wonder," she whispered, "if I might court you a bit?" She bit her bottom lip, trying to guess what he'd say, then felt a surge of power as she did when something beautiful had cooled inside the kiln at the pottery. He nodded slightly and she stripped off a single mitten to hold her bare palm open to the falling snow. She didn't really know what she was doing but she felt sensuous and wanted to communicate that feeling to him.

Carefully, she lifted her palm to his right cheek. She pressed the dusting of snow against his sculpted cheekbone and felt him shiver, whether with cold or anticipation, she didn't know. But then she stood on tiptoe and put her mouth against his wet cheek and tenderly began to kiss, then, lick, at the wet snow. She felt a groan reverberate in his chest and she smiled, continuing until all hint of moisture was gone. Then she swallowed and looked into his ocean-blue eyes.

His pupils were large and dark, and he slanted his head and brought his mouth down on hers, quick and hard. She thrilled to his touch and couldn't help but notice the way his big body rocked against her, tantalizing her with desire she had never felt before. She was about to tangle her arms about his neck when a cackle of female laughter made her freeze. She felt the tension in Caleb's body as he slowly turned her around and held her in front of him, his arms providing a comforting circle.

She recognized the other *Amisch* woman—It was Heather Lambert, the frenemy from Abigail's adolescence in Blackberry Falls. Abigail rarely encountered Heather these days—only at church meeting, or the occasional community picnic. But now, Abigail felt trapped and somehow guilty of the pleasure she'd found in Caleb's arms. Heather's smirk was easy to see in the light from the

Christmas bulbs, and Abigail longed suddenly to be back in the refuge of her pottery. Her feelings must have communicated themselves to Caleb as he began to rock her gently from side to side.

"Heather," Abigail said coolly. "What is it that you want?" *Because you surely don't want to be pleasant— your face shows nothing but venom. You only want to taunt and to threaten.* Abigail clung to the words inside her head. *I'm not guilty . . . not guilty . . .*

"I was simply passing and couldn't believe it was you, Abigail!" Heather purred. "But then, I heard you were courting two men. Where's the other? I wonder if they know just how clever you can be behind that sweet mask of yours?"

"I don't know you, but you clearly have nothing of merit to say here. So, you'd best *geh* on," Caleb rumbled low.

Abigail felt her eyes prick with tears to hear his defense of her—even though he didn't know the circumstances . . . the truth . . .

"Of course, I'll *geh*," Heather simpered. "And leave you both . . . alone. But one thing you might ask of your courting partner, by and by, is what she was doing in the Blackberry Falls *Amisch* cemetery tonight."

"You were there," Abigail snapped before she could think.

"*Nee*—I simply know your dedication to a mutual friend." Heather's laughter carried on the *nacht* air as she tightened her bonnet strings and walked away.

Long moments passed before Abigail slowly turned around to face him, ready for a frustrating line of questioning. But he said nothing—instead simply pulled her close. She felt the tenderness of his touch and was about to apologize for the ugliness of the past few minutes when he bent and nuzzled her neck. He took her mittenless hand in his and whispered softly in her ear. "Sweet Abigail, *sei se gut*. . . . Court me again."

And she did.

Chapter Fourteen

"Three gold nuggets. Three! And enough *boppli* supplies to choke a horse." Caleb paused as Birchbark began to cough.

Caleb sighed and poured a teaspoon of the honey-and-lemon mixture the healer had left that morning, then spooned it into the *auld* man's mouth.

"Listen," Caleb continued when the coughing stopped abruptly, "I don't believe in Santa Claus—I'm too *auld*. You've got me thinking I'm *narrisch*."

"Well, mebbe ya are."

"*Nee* . . . I'm not crazy. You are! Or this whole place is. . . ."

"Mebbe yer crazy in love."

Caleb drew a deep breath as images of Abigail kissing him pulsed behind his eyes. He turned around from Birchbark's bed and faced the window in the cabin. *Crazy in love? I don't even truly know what love is. It's got to be more than snow kissing, even though that makes my blood heat. . . .*

"See, that got ya thinkin'," Birchbark said with a hoot of laughter.

Caleb closed his eyes. "Tell me about the gold, *sei se gut*."

"What's ta know?"

"Somehow you put that gold in that pack, and I can't explain it." Caleb opened his eyes and half turned to stare at the wily *aulder* man.

Birchbark must have sensed Caleb's growing frustration because he suddenly became serious. "All right. All right. Simmer down and I'll tell ya a tale of Blackberry Falls."

Caleb dropped into a chair. "Fine. I'm listening."

"Blackberry Falls was sacred to the Susquehannock tribe. So much so that they brought their dead to be buried in mounds of earth with all of their valuables, too. But when the tribe was gone and much time had passed, the burial mounds began to be dug up by explorers and treasure hunters. Only a few of the Susquehannocks still rest in peace in the forests around Blackberry Falls." Birchbark thumped himself on the chest. "And I know where they are, but I pledged never ta talk except to an honest man near the end of my days."

Caleb sighed. "So, the gold was from a burial mound? How did it get into the pack?"

"I told ya about the gold. Now that's enough jabberin' fer one day. I needs me sleep. *Ach*, and don't ferget that John Stolfus is on yer handyman's list ta tend to." Caleb was about to protest, then watched helplessly as Birchbark turned on his side and snuggled deeper into the quilts.

* * *

Abigail came blinking awake as a knock sounded on the front door of her cabin. She had been dreaming—warm, luscious dreams of kissing Caleb in the snow the *nacht* before. . . . But now, the knock sounded again and she hastily grabbed a robe and hurried to open the door.

Phillip stood outside wearing a lopsided smile. He held a small, pink piglet under one arm. "*Gut* morning."

Abigail could barely hear his words due to the outraged squealing of the baby pig. "Where did you find him?" she shouted, motioning the unlikely pair inside. She went to a yellow cabinet in the kitchen and pulled out a container of various bottles, then snatched up a thick glass container that she used for milk. Filling the bottle, she turned, and, without preamble, stuck it into the tiny, squealing mouth.

The silence was deafening. And Phillip laughed a bit as the piglet suckled. "I'm sorry to wake you, Abigail. Someone left this little one in a basket on Grossmuder Mildred's porch. It's a wonder he didn't freeze to death. Grossmuder Mildred agreed—uh—thought I should bring it here—you are so kind, Abigail."

"*Ach, danki*," Abigail muttered, pulling the edges of her robe more tightly about her. She could only imagine the picture she presented to Phillip. Her hair hung free, reaching beyond her hips; her robe was not made for the chill of the winter, and she had *nee* prayer *kapp* on her head. All in all, she felt rather exposed, though she wondered vaguely how she might feel if it was Caleb who stood before her. She shivered a bit when she considered her bold courting of Caleb the *nacht* before.

"You're cold," Phillip observed, looking for some place to lay the now-contented piglet.

"I'm fine," Abigail said as she indicated a wicker basket in the small sitting place. "We can put him here for now."

Phillip gently laid the drowsy piglet on the quilt that was folded in the basket. "This is the way it is on a farm," he said softly. "You have to be prepared for anything and everything."

Abigail nodded. "Life is like that too." She wanted to pull away from his talk of life on a farm—still, she knew that she was perhaps, again, not giving him a fair chance at becoming her mail-order groom. "Uh . . . *danki* again for the flowers you gave me. I put them in the icebox to stay fresh."

"*Jah*, I wanted you to enjoy them."

"Well, I did." She pushed aside the thought that she'd enjoyed the roses all the more because their heady scent had added to the intensity of kissing Caleb.

There was a brief silence as the piglet nestled down deeper in the quilt folds; then Phillip cleared his throat. "*Ach*, Abigail, you're so beautiful, but I guess I shouldn't be looking at you this way."

Abigail wet her lips and realized that she should probably be ashamed for answering the door dressed as she was. "Well, I best *geh* and . . . get ready for the day. . . ."

She was just about to step past him when it came to her that she had feelings of desire for Caleb fueled by damp kisses, but she'd tried no intimacy with Phillip. *How can I be sure . . . unless?* She stood still and rose on her tiptoes to brush her mouth against his. Nothing but a vague feeling pleasure was all she felt, and she told herself she must try again. . . .

* * *

Phillip tried hard not to gasp in surprise when Abigail squeezed the muscles of his arms and started to kiss him. It wasn't that he didn't feel pleasure, but he was startled by her boldness. And, even as he touched her thin shoulders, it occurred to him that he wished she was a little plumper so his fingers might touch deep softness. Abigail had moved to kiss him a second time when he heard a soft knock and then felt cold air swirl about his legs. He almost broke the kiss, but Abigail thankfully pulled away first. He didn't really want anyone to see Abigail being so forward. But then he looked up.

Mercy stood just inside the door. There was a stricken look on her face, and the curves of her cheeks had taken on a reddish hue.

He wanted to say something to her because he could tell that she was upset. Perhaps she was ashamed of Abigail's behavior. "Mercy . . . we . . . I . . ."

"Of course, we and I. . . . You're courting, aren't you? What is the surprise?"

Her sharp tone woke the piglet, and its frantic squeals once more filled the air. Abigail picked up the pig and Phillip saw her frown at her sister. "Mercy, it was only a kiss."

"And you in your dressing gown with your hair down!"

Phillip interrupted as gently as he could above the squeals. "I woke Abigail with this homeless piglet and she . . . we . . ."

"I said there is no surprise, Phillip."

"*Gut* morning to you both." She turned slowly and shut the door behind her.

Phillip avoided Abigail's eyes and, for some strange reason, felt as sad as the piglet himself.

Mercy blinked back stinging tears as she plowed through the snow, unsure of where she was headed. Somehow, the prospect of Phillip courting with Abigail had never seemed completely real until she'd seen them kissing.

She was so absorbed in her thoughts that she ran full speed into Caleb, who steadied her briefly.

"I'm fine," she snapped, hastily rubbing at her cheeks, then jerking away from him.

"Hmmm . . . okay. Do you think Abigail is up already? I was going to pay her a visit."

Mercy seemed to rally and gave him a lopsided smile. "Uh . . . *nee*. Sound asleep. I just came from there. There was nothing to see."

"All right," he said. "Then I have to stop by the Stolfus *haus*. I suppose I'll do that now."

Mercy didn't want to take any chances that Caleb might *geh* back to Abigail's while Phillip was still there. In some perverse way, she wanted Phillip to be happy, even if it meant her own unhappiness.

"I'll walk with you awhile, if I may?" she said in a bright tone.

"Surely. Can I, uh, help you through the snow?" He offered her a strong arm and she took it with tentative fingers.

"So, you are a handyman? I've heard it through the community grapevine of course."

"*Jah*, my *fater* wanted me to be a farmer . . . but it just didn't take."

Mercy sighed. "We can't please everyone, and that's a hard lesson learned for some folks."

"But you've learned it, eh?"

She frowned, thinking that she didn't please Phillip but decided that was only a selfish thought. *Derr Herr* wanted His *kinner* to love each other as well as themselves. "*Jah*," she answered finally. "I've learned it."

She became aware of the sounds of young voices in the air and saw that there was some fierce sledding going on. She was glad to see Joshua headed down the hill on a runner sled. She decided that the honey cornbread she carried in her basket for Abigail would instead make a nice midmorning snack for Joshua.

Mercy glanced up at Caleb and spoke politely. "You'll have to excuse me. I see my *sohn* and have a treat for him."

Caleb tipped his hat and smiled. "Thank you for allowing me to help you. And, I must say, you're nothing like Phillip says you are. Have a *gut* day."

Mercy watched Caleb walk off, and for the second time that morning felt as though she'd been struck a personal blow. "First the kiss and now this?" she muttered aloud. *What must Phillip think of me? Probably it's all true. . . .*

Caleb mounted the steps of the huge cabin and struck the iron knocker against the wood. The great door was quickly answered, and a young, fresh-faced *Amisch maedel* invited him inside.

"*Ach*, I'm sure glad ye've *kumme*. How did you know about Herr Stolfus?"

Caleb swung the door closed behind him and looked at her. "What do I know about Herr Stolfus?"

"Why, that he's stuck!"

"Stuck?" Images ran rampant through Caleb's head. Was the *mon* stuck in the couch, outside, beneath a water buffalo. . . .

"Under the sink, he is. And a mite angry. . . ."

Caleb swept off his hat and handed it to her. "Of course, he's angry, but at least he's not pregnant."

"Wh—at?"

"Never mind. Can you take me to the sink—Miss uh—?"

"Rebecca. Rebecca Bly. If ye'll *kumme* this way?"

She led him into a cavernous living room and through a swinging door to a large kitchen. Caleb briefly noted that the woodwork was incredible, but then all of his focus was on the pair of legs protruding from the bottom of a sink. Even in Pennsylvania Dutch, the angry voice that went with the pair of legs uttered more original swear words than Caleb had ever heard. He glanced at Rebecca, who looked distinctly uncomfortable.

"*Geh* on into the next room," Caleb said kindly. "I'll call if I need something."

He waited until the girl left, then went to the sink and dropped to his knees. Up close, the loud swearing made Caleb's ears pop, and he wondered why John Stolfus was on the list that Birchbark had given him—all Herr Stolfus needed was a quick pull.

"Herr Stolfus? I'm going to get you out!"

The swearing stopped abruptly but the voice still raged. "Get me out? Ye'll never do it in a thousand years."

Caleb laughed silently. "I've delivered a baby and now I'm delivering you from a sink."

"What! What'd you say? I ain't no babe that you must pull out! I still got strength left in me bones."

Caleb felt his mirth fade away. There was something poignant in the other man's words; a cry that he was still worthwhile, and Caleb suddenly understood his temper.

"All right. All right. I am going to get you out, but I need you to help. I need you."

"Nah . . . nobody needs me now."

Caleb eased his head and shoulders as far in as he could so that he could see the *auld* man's face. "You're John, right? I'm Caleb."

"Huh! Another mail-order groom. Your *bruder* married my daughter. She took over running the mill for me recently."

"I've heard," Caleb muttered, not liking the man's pallor. "Are you hurt in any way, sir?"

"Probably busted a rib crawlin' under here. I should have gotten Abner or Matthew to help. Stubborn *auld* fool—that's what I am."

"*Derr Herr* says to call no man a fool, not even yourself," Caleb muttered. "You know what? I'm going to need a piece of wood to put under your back so I can get you out a bit easier."

"Well, the workshop is beyond the living room. *Geh* help yourself."

Caleb got out and followed John's directions. He entered the clean workshop, and it only took him a minute to find an appropriately sized piece of wood to be a backboard. He was leaving the workshop when an incredible wooden dollhouse caught his eye. The piece must have involved hours of work—on the gingerbread decoration alone. But he quickly moved on and headed back into the kitchen.

John was quiet now and Caleb looked up as the kitchen door opened. His *aulder bruder* Matthew stood there, staring at John's legs for a moment. "Caleb? What's wrong here?"

"John's all right. Maybe a cracked rib. . . . Can you help me get him out? I figure we can use this wood as a backboard of sorts."

"All right. John," Matthew called. "I know what strength you've got in those legs. You help push your way through while we get this wood into position. We're just going to have you roll on your side for a second."

Somehow, through the combined efforts of all three men, two hours later, John sat propped up in his own bed while Aenti Fern, the healer, tended to him. She gave him a drink of some powerful tea, and when his eyes began to close, she shooed Caleb and Matthew away. Just then, Tabitha came to the door, seeking her *fater*.

"She'll sit with him all *nacht*. I know her determination," Matthew commented as they made their way down the broad, carved staircase. "Say, why not *kumme* to my *haus* for some venison steaks, little *bruder*?"

"Sounds good to me," Caleb agreed. "In any case, I've been wanting to talk to you."

"Something wrong?"

Caleb shook his head with a rueful smile. "*Nee . . . ach*, maybe something's right. . . ."

"You want to talk about women, don't you?"

"Guess so," Caleb answered.

Matthew laughed. "I'm not sure I'll be much help."

"Well, then, I'll take what I can get, big *bruder*. . . ."

Chapter Fifteen

Abigail stared down at the piglet she held in her arms while feeding him another bottle. She hadn't really been able to concentrate on her pottery, and it wasn't only because of the antics of the baby pig.

Her mind flashed back to that morning when she'd purposefully kissed Phillip and had truly felt . . . not much of anything. He must have found her quite brazen, because he'd disentangled himself from her the minute Mercy had left the cabin.

"Uh, Abigail," he'd mumbled. "Mercy saw . . ."

"And that's fine, I think." Abigail had felt her temper snap because she was beginning to realize that only when she courted Caleb did she feel such heated intensity.

She'd soon shown Phillip out then dithered the day away, taking care of the piglet. She would have to find the creature a home, and she knew where she needed to *geh*. She laid the satiated pig back in his wicker basket and wrapped him snug in the quilt.

She decided she would make the most of the fading daylight and head up to Birchbark's cabin. She hoped that

Caleb might be there but realized that he could easily be off on a repair somewhere. Still, she added another quilt and two bottles to the wicker basket, then lifted it gently from the floor. She slipped outside into the cold and lashed the basket to a runner sled. Then she hitched up Amber and they set off with the sled in tow.

She had gone only a few hundred feet when a cloaked figure stepped out of the woods and stood in the path of the horse, holding a lantern high.

Amber startled and it took all of Abigail's strength to keep her from rearing backward.

"Who's there?" she called in irritation. "You could have been killed!"

The person threw their hood back and Abigail saw Heather's face in the shadowed light. For a moment, she felt the old tension rise in her throat but then she rallied. "What is it, Heather?" she asked, attempting to keep her tone level.

"*Ach*, if you had killed me, just think of the stories that would *geh* round. . . ."

For a moment, Abigail froze. Then the piglet began to squeal.

"If you would step aside!" Abigail commanded.

"I will. But only after I give you a warning or perhaps, a consideration. Maybe the reason you sent for those mail-order grooms is because the men of Blackberry Falls have long memories, and you know no one here would have you. What will happen if one or both of your mail-order men happen to learn the truth?"

Abigail briskly slapped the reins, ignoring the other

girl, and Amber moved forward, forcing Heather back into the snowy forest. . . .

Caleb rubbed the back of his neck as he left his *bruder*'s cabin. As Matthew had predicted, Tabitha would not leave her *fater*'s side, so Caleb had the rare chance to have supper alone with his *aulder bruder*.

Caleb had waited inside the beautiful cabin while his *bruder* cooked the steaks, baked potatoes, and heated up a jar of yellow wax beans, sweet with summer's taste.

"So, you want to talk about women?" Matthew asked with a raised dark eyebrow, and Caleb agreed.

"What do you want to know?"

Caleb sighed. "I want to know about one woman, Abigail."

"She is Tabitha's best friend, but she is always reserved around me. I'm afraid I can't tell you much."

Caleb chewed his potato thoughtfully as he considered her lack of reservation in kissing him. He ended up shifting uncomfortably on his chair and forced himself to focus on the food instead.

"Well, how is the courting going? I've heard that Phillip is at the pottery a fair amount."

Caleb shrugged. "I suppose it has to be a fair courting."

"There's fair, and there's fair. Don't you worry that she's kissing him too?"

"What do you mean—'too'? Who says I'm kissing her?"

Matthew grinned at him. "I recognize the dazed look."

Caleb felt his cheeks burn as he cleared his throat. "Well, maybe she's kissing me. . . ."

Matthew laughed out loud. "Then that's the best of all. I love it when Tabitha—uh—kisses me."

They had gone on to a mutual discussion of the fine art of kissing, until Caleb reluctantly got up to go.

Now, he was halfway up to Birchbark's cabin when a fierce drop in temperature warned him that a blizzard was coming up fast. But he wasn't prepared for the rage of the storm as it came roaring down Blackberry Falls, filling the air with icy shards and a whiteout of snow. Caleb struggled to maintain his direction and prayed that Abigail was somewhere safe. . . .

Abigail listened to the fury of the storm and took another sip of the hot cocoa that Birchbark had made her. She moved quietly on the bentwood rocker, trying to calm her nerves and praying that Caleb was safe at the Stolfus *haus.*

"Stop frettin', Abigail. The *buwe's* fine." Birchbark tapped the tiny piglet snuggled over his broad shoulder, then grunted his approval. "Out like a light." Birchbark laid the sleeping pig in the wicker basket near the hearth, then pulled on a ratty sweater. "It sure is blowin'," he muttered as he tossed another log on the fire. Abigail watched him sit briefly to pull on an extra pair of socks that she was sure he'd gotten from the *Englisch*—they had bright green frogs with coral pink tongues on them, and she tried hard not to stare.

A heavy thud sounded against the door and Birchbark

crossed the room in two strides, opening it and allowing the whirl of the storm to whip round the room. It was Caleb. Abigail got to her feet and reached his side as Birchbark hauled him in, then slammed the door.

Caleb's breaths were muffled by his black scarf but still sounded harsh in the relative quiet of the room.

"His eyelids are bleeding," Abigail exclaimed.

"Ice shards. They're driven into his clothes, too." Birchbark wasted no time peeling Caleb's icy outdoor clothes off, then dumped him without ceremony onto the big feather bed. "He'll live, Fred."

Abigail heard Birchbark speak to the anxious dog and thought that she could have used a few reassuring words herself.

"All right, Abigail. Jest keep them quilts piled on him, and he'll warm up. I've got ta *geh* ta work!"

"To work?" Abigail stared at Birchbark, thinking he was truly *narrisch*.

"Awww, let him *geh*!" Caleb groaned from the bed. "He'll be fine."

Birchbark gave a hearty laugh while Abigail stared at him. He stepped into huge boots which hid the green frogs from view, then added a long coat made of furs. Finally he hefted his large pack across his shoulders and nodded at Abigail. "I'll keep the piggy as me own. Call him Nutflake . . . ha!" He pulled on his fur mittens and stalked to the door, opening it to give a glimpse of the mad, driving snow. Then he stepped into the fray and slammed the door behind him.

"I've always heard that Birchbark was *narrisch*, but I

never believed it until now," Abigail said as she began tugging Caleb's boots off. "He's going to freeze to death."

"*Nee*, he won't, and *jah*, he's crazy. But he'll be back—trust me." He folded his arms behind his head and his blue eyes flashed up at her as she layered another quilt on top of him. "You do realize that we're most likely trapped alone here until the snow and ice let up?"

She couldn't stop the flush of color that warmed her cheeks. "To tell the truth, I've already thought of that."

He smiled up at her—a warm, sensuous smile that seemed to strike sparks off her heart and mind. "Would you like to share your thoughts?" he asked.

"*Jah*." She sat down on the edge of the bed. "I think we should tell each other stories. . . ."

Mercy muttered to herself as she dried dishes in her warm little cabin. She wasn't worried overmuch about Joshua and Tad in the storm since they were sheltered at the school*haus* with Ann Bly, their experienced teacher. They were practicing for the annual Christmas program, which the whole community always enjoyed. Ann would never let them out in the storm even if she had to burn the desks as firewood.

Still, she prayed for her *sohn* in her mutterings and finally allowed herself to sit down in the small rocking chair near the hearth. She rocked for a few moments, realizing that she felt lonely, which made no sense. She was often alone when Joshua was out—but something about the whistling of the storm outside made her feel forlorn and lost. She knew the source of such thoughts . . . it was the idea that Phillip had spoken to Caleb and whoever else about her, behind her back. . . . *I've had enough of people talking about me, more than enough since before Joshua's birth and in all the years after. . . . People in Blackberry Falls have long memories. . . . Still, not all were unkind and maybe the lack of acceptance I feel is more about me than it is about them. . . .*

It was on the heels of this revelatory thought that a muffled pounding sounded at the door. Mercy resisted the urge to take the gun from the doily drawer in her *gross-muder*'s worktable. Instead she straightened her spine and went to unlatch the door. Phillip fell heavily against her, covered in snow and ice but dripping blood from his forehead.

It took all her strength to half drag him inside. "What happened?" she demanded as she grabbed a doily from the nearby drawer and watched it turn crimson too fast.

"Hit by a tree limb, I think," Phillip groaned.

She didn't reply but helped him to the *auld* couch. "Lie down," she ordered.

"Yes, ma'am." He half laughed.

Mercy frowned. His big body hung over the bottom and side of the couch, but she told herself that there was no way she'd take him into her bed. Even the thought of the word *bed* caused her to feel a hot flush in her cheeks.

I'm a fool, she told herself as she hurried to grab towels and a medical kit that she kept for Joshua's occasional bumps and cuts.

She bent over Phillip and realized that the blow to his forehead was not as bad as she'd first thought. "The head just bleeds a lot," she muttered to herself, as she cleaned the wound and wrapped a bandage around his head. She didn't forget that she was still angry with him for talking about her, but her focus now was on being gentle and kind.

"You might have a concussion," she said softly, surveying the knot that protruded from his head to the edge of the bandage.

"I do feel like I could *geh* to sleep."

"Absolutely not!" She was surprised at the fear she felt. She'd read somewhere once that a concussed person should not *geh* to sleep anytime soon after the injury.

"I'll keep you up," she vowed.

"That sounds great," he muttered in mock horror.

But Mercy didn't smile as she covered him with a quilt, then slid her rocker close to the couch. . . .

Phillip gazed at Mercy and realized that she looked blurry. Lantern light cascaded around her and he thought her hair shone beautifully but remembered in time that she didn't like to talk about her hair. "You have a halo," he commented instead. "And I lost my glasses in the storm."

She groaned aloud. "You'll never find them. And you'll have to *geh* to Farwell to get another pair."

"I'll *geh* tomorrow."

"Tomorrow is Sunday," she reminded him. "We have church service."

"Right . . . I forgot." He sighed, feeling as though his eyelashes weighed a ton. *If I can just* geh *to sleep for a few—*

"*Nee* sleeping!" She jerked him by his shirt collar, and he opened his eyes wide at the pain in his head.

"All right . . . all right. I know you'd prefer me dead, but do you have to torture me too?"

He watched her outline recede.

"I would never want to see you dead," she said stiffly.

"Because of Abigail?" he asked, not really expecting a reply.

But then Mercy's answer shot across his consciousness and set his head to pounding worse than any shaking might.

"*Nee*," she whispered. "Because of me."

Chapter Sixteen

Caleb stared at Abigail in surprise and confusion. "Tell each other stories?" he asked. "What kind of stories?"

"Courting stories," she answered promptly.

"Are . . . are there such things in Blackberry Falls?"

Abigail laughed. "I think there should be. Maybe I've just made them up."

"*Ach*, now I remember—your ad. It asked for poetry and a *gut* reading voice; is that right?"

"*Jah*, I did write that, but now it seems a bit silly. I should have written about the value of *gut* kissing instead."

He saw her blush but had to ask the question that teased at his mind.

"Have you experienced *gut* kissing?"

"*Jah*, perhaps you know it, too."

"I do, sweet *maedel*, but I wonder—" He broke off, feeling silly himself now.

"What is it?"

"Nothing," he said.

"*Nee*, speak, *sei se gut*."

"I wonder if Phillip has kissed you?"

"Is—is that your business?"

He heard the tinge of anger in her pretty voice and regretted his words.

"*Nee*, it's not mine to know. Forgive me," he said stiffly.

"I'll answer your question," she said into the silence. "Phillip has not kissed me, but I have kissed him."

"Oh . . ." Caleb recalled begging her to kiss him, to court him, in the maze at Farwell. And he remembered all too well how he had responded to her kissing. Now he wondered if Phillip had done the same.

Abigail sighed aloud. "I suppose I ought to tell you the truth. . . ."

He waited, his breath tight.

"I kissed Phillip because of you. Because of how much I enjoy kissing you . . . I wanted to see if it felt the same with the other mail-order groom."

Caleb didn't really want to hear the answer but asked anyway. "And did it?"

"*Nee*," she said flatly.

He resisted the urge to smile.

Mercy bit her lip and found her heart pounding. She couldn't believe that she had essentially admitted to Phillip that she cared for him.

She glanced over to where he lay and saw that he no longer looked drowsy but was watching her with keen intent.

"What did you say?"

Mercy shook her head. *Perhaps he didn't hear me correctly.* She rose from her chair and headed to the small kitchen area. "I've got scalloped potatoes and ham casserole ready. Would you like a plate?"

She waited, hoping he'd let the previous conversation drop, and to both her disappointment and relief, he did.

"That sounds delicious. *Danki!* I was supposed to go back to Grossmuder Mildred's for chicken and biscuits but—I got hit in the head. Obviously."

Mercy scooped a healthy portion of the casserole onto a blue plate and added a serving of the bright green beans she'd put up the past summer. *Who would have thought that when I canned these beans I would be feeding a man I barely know. Yet he is a* gut *man—kind . . . and Abigail's . . .*

She swallowed hard as she put the plate on a tray and added a cup of tea. She carefully brought the food and drink to the couch. She gestured with her chin and Phillip grabbed the side table and eased it close to him before lying back with a sigh of what sounded like pleasure.

"*Danki*, Mercy. I would bless the food if it pleases you?" He gave her a myopic stare and she nodded hard.

"Dear *Fater* in Heaven, I thank You for the bounty of this meal and for the gentle hands that have worked on its preparation. I pray that Joshua and Tad are enjoying themselves at the school and that the storm will ease up. In the Name of *Derr Herr*. Amen."

She nodded in agreement, then offered him a cloth napkin. *It's going to be all right,* her mind whispered. *He didn't hear . . . he didn't hear. . . .*

She watched him take an enthusiastic bite of the casserole. "Mmmm," he praised. "It's delicious!"

"*Danki.*" She turned and headed back to the cookstove, but his rich voice stopped her.

"Hey, Mercy?"

"*Jah?*" She turned back to face him, thinking she had left something off his tray.

"What did you mean when you said that you care for me?"

Abigail gave Caleb what she knew to be a rather prim look that was at odds with her admission of how much she enjoyed kissing him. She knew instinctively that she had pleased him, and she longed to test the warmth of his mouth once more. *I am brazen . . . and he looks like he would be more than pleased if I were to bend down and . . .*

"Stop that," he said roughly.

She blinked. "Stop what?"

"You—you're looking at my mouth."

She felt warmth course through her veins and was hypnotized by his words. And his mouth . . .

She swallowed hard and looked away from him for a moment. Then she felt his hand against her cheek, brushing, touching, making her close her eyes with pleasure.

"*Ach*, Abigail, I think—"

She opened her eyes and bounced off the bed, moving to the relative safety of the rocker by the fire.

"Now," she said firmly, "we will tell courting stories—so that we may *kumme* to know each other better."

His blue eyes flashed with a hint of mischief, but he nodded just the same. "All right. But first, since we are doing this in the name of courting, I say we *geh* also with a much *aulder* courting tradition."

Abigail gave him a suspicious look. "What *aulder* tradition?"

"Bundling! You know . . . you lie next to me atop the quilts and I lie beneath them. You have to admit that being physically close might also foster better courting stories." He smiled at her and she wasn't sure what to say.

It was true that bundling was still practiced by some couples as a means of knowing each other better. Usually a bundling board was placed down the center of the bed, but in a pinch, under-over quilt bundling was permitted.

"Abigail, please. Perhaps the heat of your body near mine will warm me. I'm still cold."

When he said he was cold, her heart went out to him and she rose from the rocker to tentatively lie down atop the mound of quilts while Caleb moved over to make room for her.

"See," he whispered. "I feel warmer already. Now, *sei se gut*, begin your courting story."

Abigail thought for a moment. "I am used to being alone."

"So, you don't need company? That doesn't bode well for your mail-order groom, does it?"

She turned her head to look into his eyes, cherishing the rich fall of his blond hair and the fine arch of his brows. "I wouldn't mind some people's company."

"Ah . . ."

"I should like to tell you the worst about me," Abigail whispered.

"How bad could the worst be?" His tone was light, but his bright blue eyes had grown serious and kind. He worked a hand out from beneath the quilts and used a lean finger to solemnly tap the tip of her nose. "Please tell me, my sweet."

Abigail drew a deep breath. "When I was seventeen, I had just started work on my own in the pottery. I went to church meeting, of course, and the occasional social gathering, but as I said—I preferred to be alone. Yet, even by myself, when customers came by or Tabitha visited a bit, I caught word of what was going on in the community." She paused, then looked away from his steady gaze. "I came to know that Zinnia Stolfus, a girl my age, had breast cancer. I knew her, of course, from school . . . but I did nothing to help her or the community in ministering to her. I never called on her or made her food. I would see her from a distance—her hair gone. Her parents took her to Farwell and beyond, trying to find help. The community had fundraisers for her but I never participated or gave even a dollar to help her. I—rarely even prayed for her. She died within a year. . . . I didn't *geh* to the funeral. I told Bishop Kore that I was sick . . . and . . . that is all. You may tell me what you think of me now."

She felt him lean up on one elbow and gently turn her chin so that she was staring up at him, his face close to hers and the fall of his hair caressing her cheek. "I think, Abigail, that you have told me a courting story, true— but I know enough about you to understand that there was some reason for what you did. I don't believe that you have a cruel bone in your body. So, tell me the rest, Abigail. . . ."

She shook her head, feeling tears run down either side of her face. Caleb bent and slowly traced the path of her tears with his mouth, down then up again. "Please, Abigail. Tell me. Trust me."

She drew a sobbing breath. "I—can't."

He drew her close, quilts and all. "*Jah*. You are so strong. You can."

Abigail choked out the words, trying to concentrate on forming the sounds in her head as a distraction, but in the end, she simply told him. . . .

Phillip watched as Mercy stalked over to him and pressed a small hand against his bandaged head. "Feverish, you must be," she declared. "Thinking up some nonsense about me caring for you! You are my sister's future husband—get that through your daft head!"

He looked at her thoughtfully. "Perhaps I will become your *bruder*-in-law but perhaps not."

"One suits as well as the other, if you ask me. Though I'll not see Abigail's heart broken on any account."

"I know that." He kept his voice soothing. He didn't want her to be upset—not because her mood bothered him, but rather to spare her all pain. He wondered at this protectiveness on his part when all that he had done with Abigail was peruse seed catalogs.

"It's *gut* you know that—it will save a lot of discord in the future," Mercy fumed.

Phillip smiled at her. "Do you expect—uh—discord?"

"Eat your food," Mercy bit out. "It'll grow cold."

Dutifully, he picked up his fork and dug into the rich potatoes. He wanted to say something more to Mercy, but she had turned from him and was pumping water into the sink to wash the dishes.

He thought about getting up to help her, then realized that a nice nap might be in *gut* order after such a delicious meal. He closed his eyes and felt himself drifting slowly to sleep. . . .

Caleb eased his body from the bed as Abigail slept on, exhausted by her story. He saw through the window that the storm had abated much as Abigail's tears had done. He was angry for her, angry at the past, perhaps even angry with *Gott*. . . . He silently tested his thoughts against the *Gott* Who had made him and remembered the story of Jacob who wrestled an angel of *Derr Herr* for a full night. In the morning, Jacob's hip was hurt, but *Gott* gave him a new name—Israel.

Caleb moved to stare out the frosty window at the huge snowdrifts and knew in his spirit that *Gott* didn't mind when you wrestled with Him. . . . He thought back to Abigail's story and could see it happening in his mind . . . Abigail at fourteen, dressed in an *Englischer* bathing suit of yellow, red, and green though she couldn't swim—the sunlight on the water—three girls wading waist-deep, seemingly innocent—and then Abigail being attacked by the other two. Thrust beneath the surface, her mouth open, choking on the cool water, and then when she almost got to the top, being pushed under again. . . . She finally managed to free herself and stagger away from her tormentors, who laughed as her as she gasped to catch her breath.

It was enough of a horror story to make him shudder. Abigail might have been killed. Drowned. She had never spoken to either girl again despite the closeness of the

Blackberry Falls community . . . and when Zinnia got cancer . . .

"Caleb?"

He turned quickly at Abigail's soft call. She had sat up on the bed and her hair had fallen from her *kapp*. She looked confused as she glanced around the room, and Caleb hurried to sit on the edge of the bed beside her.

"Abigail, you were really sleeping deeply."

He watched her regain her focus. "I remember. I told you—"

"*Jah*," he said, then reached out to finger comb the long tendrils of her hair. "You spoke the truth. That confession will free you now."

"I can never be free of what I did or didn't do. I cannot change the past. Even Heather is a grim reminder of what happened."

"Forget Heather," he said quietly. "When I think that you might have drowned because of those two . . ."

Abigail let her shoulders fall forward. "I realized—in telling you, that I should have extended kindness to Zinnia. Forgiven her . . . and now I can't."

Caleb pulled her gently against his chest. "Perhaps you might have responded differently, but you were hurt, still hurt. Maybe even wondering where *Gott* was when you were under that water. . . ."

Abigail began to sob softly and he rocked her slowly, from side to side. "*Jah*," she choked. "Where was *Gott*? I don't understand. . . ."

"*Gott* was with you the whole time," Caleb said, reaching to stroke her back and the fall of her hair.

"If *Gott* was with me, then why did He allow me to be under that water?"

"*Gott*'s ways are not our ways, and you didn't drown. And you can learn from Zinnia's death and perhaps extend forgiveness to Heather or at least try. . . ."

"*Jah*," she whispered, then lifted her head as his lips found her damp mouth and she was lost in the gentleness of his caress.

Phillip became aware of being shaken so hard, he felt as if his head would fall off. He opened his eyes and found Mercy kneeling beside the couch, shouting his name and pulling at his shoulders.

"I—I'm awake, Mercy. . . ." he managed, and she must have heard because she collapsed against his chest in apparent relief.

"*Ach*, Praise *Derr Herr*," she mumbled. Then she seemed to rally and lifted her head, looking into his eyes. "I—You fell asleep."

He nodded and impulsively leaned forward to tuck a strand of her hair behind her ear.

She froze like a baby rabbit. He could tell she was holding her breath as he trailed his hand down to touch her tender, frantic pulse point. Phillip caught his own breath, compelled to act but not completely sure of what he was doing. Then something flashed in Mercy's eyes and she got up from her knees.

He looked up at her, realizing that tears sparkled in her eyes.

"You're addled," she said in an unsteady tone. "And I will never again be someone's castoff! Never!"

He tried to speak but she turned and hurried away to the main bedroom of the little cabin, then slammed the door.

Chapter Seventeen

Blackberry Falls buzzed with energy following the snowstorm as cabins were dug out by all who were able to do so. Abigail felt as though a burden had been lifted from her shoulders after talking with Caleb. She also felt a childlike delight in realizing that Christmas would soon be upon them.

She was happy when Tabitha came for a visit, leaving Caleb and Matthew to *geh* out on Birchbark's sled for some business or another. Abigail made tea and joyfully opened the small gift that Tabitha had carved for her. Tabitha was an expert carver, and Abigail had a mantel of small creatures created by her friend's hand.

Abigail unwrapped the green tissue paper and carefully lifted the sea creature up in her hands. "It's a manatee and its *boppli*! Why, they're beautiful."

Tabitha nodded. "I thought that poplar would best capture the arch in the back and the fluid tail. I wanted to give you something different this year."

"*Ach*, I love it. I can't wait to put it on the mantel to join its *wunderbaar* family of wooden forest creatures. This is the first time you've carved a *mamm* and babe!"

Abigail set the manatee on the mantel and then stirred a sugar cube into the mint tea.

"Well, *jah* . . . I wanted to convey some news to you with the pair."

Abigail looked up. "You're pregnant!"

Tabitha laughed. "*Jah!* No one knows but Matthew!"

"It's *wunderbaar* news." Abigail reached across the table to hold her friend's hand.

"*Jah!* Praise *Gott*," Tabitha said with a gentle smile. "Now tell me—how's Caleb?"

"Don't you mean how are both mail-order grooms?" Abigail laughed.

"Why do I feel like that's not a true laugh?"

"*Ach*, it's not. I—I haven't seen much of Phillip . . . not even the *nacht* of the winter fundraiser when he gave me roses to wear on my wrist. I feel like I'm cheating him, Tabitha. Like I never spend any time with him but I'm always seeing Caleb. We're somehow drawn together."

"Perhaps you are meant to be. He sent no letter in response to your ad but came on faith. That matters. How was the *nacht* in Birchbark's cabin?"

Abigail lowered her gaze from her friend's eyes. She had never even told Tabitha what she had revealed to Caleb. "It was . . . different from what you might expect."

"You mean no kissing? No sitting before the fire together? No romantic words?"

"Well . . ." Abigail laughed more naturally then. "Maybe a few kisses . . ."

"This is a *narrisch* plan!" Caleb hollered up to where Birchbark sat on the high seat of the long flatbed sled.

Matthew merely shook his head at his younger *bruder* and smiled. Each man was stationed on either side of a mound of evergreen garlands and Christmas trees of all sizes.

Caleb jumped on the pile of greenery as it began to tip when Birchbark hit a dip. Somehow, Birchbark managed to talk the horses up though they were belly-deep in the snow.

"There now!" Birchbark yelled back to them. "Quit yer bellyachin', Caleb King! Ya should have tied the greens down better!"

Caleb groaned and let his face fall forward into the delicate pile. It smelled like Christmas and bright life and a thousand other things that he loved—but he wondered if the sensation of being alive was all the more sharp and palpable because of his growing relationship with Abigail. A relationship that *Gott* seemed to favor, at least for now. He pushed aside the fact that she might choose Phillip as her mail-order groom but then was jolted away from such thoughts as Matthew jumped up beside him and nearly landed on his back.

"We're going to lose this whole load if Birchbark doesn't slow the sled down," Caleb groaned.

"I heard that!" Birchbark yelled.

"Good!" Caleb yelled back.

He thought back to earlier that morning when Birchbark had grunted out the Christmas tree project as they ate Caleb's bacon scramble and fried potatoes.

"We'll use the flatbed sleigh I got rigged up and we'll get enough Christmas trees and garlands to make Blackberry Falls sing!"

Caleb had resisted the urge to sigh aloud. He'd learned

enough about Birchbark to understand that you never knew entirely what the *auld* coot was up to. He also knew that if he came out saying that the whole idea was *narrisch*, Birchbark would be all the more determined to make him *geh*.

"Folks are barely dug out, *buwe*." Birchbark pointed with his fork. "And it's a service ta them that are *auld* or shut-ins."

At the time, it had seemed like a reasonable explanation to Caleb, and he had enjoyed cutting trees and branches with Matthew. But now, as Birchbark piloted the sled to a shaky stop, he wondered how the whole plan was going to work out.

"What are you two doin' lyin' down up there?"

"He grows on you," Matthew said with a grin while Caleb shook his head.

Birchbark had gotten down and now went to pound at the cabin door. A tall, broad-shouldered *Amisch* man came out to greet them.

"This here's Samson Lambert, *buwe*. A good shot and a fair aim! Samson, pick your tree."

Caleb could see that the big man limped heavily as he stepped out onto the porch steps.

"I'll have the white pine down toward the bottom there!"

"Caleb, Matthew, pull that tree out!" Birchbark yelled.

Caleb now felt that he hadn't had the right attitude about the job so he grabbed the bottom tree with a zest and the feeling that others really did need help at times. Birchbark's generosity made him feel that Blackberry Falls was a healthy community, though he understood that a lot could lie beneath the surface . . . even the kind of terrible events that Abigail had described to him. . . .

Matthew helped him get the tree down and then they retied the mound of greenery to the long sleigh bed. Birchbark was talking to the very large Samson when Caleb and his *bruder* stopped at the bottom of the front steps with the tree.

"*Ach*, just right for the family," Samson said with satisfaction.

Caleb knew that many *Amisch* communities did not have large Christmas trees—his family certainly hadn't . . . but Samson clearly embraced the idea.

"*Kumme* in!" Samson called. "We'll have a hot cider together!"

So, they wrestled the tree into the cabin and sat down at the large table while their host poured hot cider into glass mugs for them. No one else was around, and Samson clearly wanted company.

"Do you have *kinner*?" Caleb asked as he sipped the cinnamon-laced drink.

"*Jah!*" Samson smiled. "Two *buwes* and my oldest, Heather."

Heather . . . The name danced behind Caleb's eyes. . . . Surely it couldn't be the Heather who had . . . He broke off the idea midthought as the girl he recognized from the fundraiser came through the front door.

"*Fater*, what are you up to now? Surely we don't need a tree!" Then she caught sight of the guests and Caleb thought it was like watching a veil drop in place as she smiled with sudden charm.

"*Ach*, the mail-order groom. I saw you not long ago. When was—"

"I was kissing my potential wife. You interrupted us, I believe." Caleb looked around with a sunny smile as Birchbark kicked him hard under the table.

Caleb resisted the urge to yelp as Heather frowned. "I don't know what you're talking about." She sniffed.

"*Ach*, well, perhaps it was my imagination that you were there."

"Perhaps," she agreed. "Well, you'll excuse me, gentlemen. I must get to cooking *Fater*'s lunch."

Caleb and the other men soon left with a more subdued Samson waving from the doorway. When Samson had gone back inside, Birchbark glared at Caleb. "A fine example of charity you be, *buwe*."

Caleb frowned. "I'll admit my fault and try to improve my attitude."

"Hmmm!" Birchbark huffed. "See that ya do, Caleb King. See that ya do. . . ."

Mercy had not laid eyes on Phillip since the *nacht* of the big snow. When she had composed herself, she had *kumme* out into the living room, only to find that Phillip had gone. She fretted about his head injury, pushing aside the tender moments that she had experienced with him. She had prayed that he had made it to Grossmuder Mildred's cabin in the blowing snow. It was Joshua, coming home the next morning from the school, who had told her that he'd seen Phillip, digging out Grossmuder Mildred's cabin.

Mercy was grateful that Phillip had strength enough to be outside, but she wasn't sure how she would feel when she saw him again. She finally decided that perhaps he would not remember the tenderness he'd displayed to her; probably his behavior had been caused by his head wound, in any case.

But now she was outside tending the goats, and she found that the hard work did much to drive Phillip from her mind—until he came whistling up to her cabin.

"*Gut* day, Mercy. I thought I'd stop by and thank you for taking care of me the other *nacht*."

Mercy nodded. "It was nothing that deserves thanks."

"Ahhh, still have a poker up your back, I see."

She frowned at his teasing and was about to suggest that he take his leave when Birchbark pulled up with bells jingling on a huge flatbed sled. Mercy watched as Phillip greeted the *aulder* man and his two sidekicks. "Which tree will it be, Mercy?" he asked.

She tightened her lips, thinking that she had not had a large tree in many years, but then she felt something relax inside of her at Phillip's flash of a smile.

Why shouldn't I celebrate? she thought and stepped out of the goat pen. "I'll take the little blue spruce," she called. "And some garland, *sei se gut*."

Phillip joined Matthew and Caleb as they wrestled the spruce from the mound. Then Mercy watched while Phillip grabbed an armful of pretty garland and Birchbark bid her *gut* day as the ramshackle sled took off once more.

Phillip smiled at her as he held the blue spruce by its trunk and dragged it down the snowy hill to her cabin door.

"Is Joshua home?" he asked.

"*Jah*, he's just finished his chores. Do you need his help?"

"Well, if you don't think it's too forward, I thought I'd

help you both with the decorations—unless you're too busy right now?"

"But don't you want, er, need to *geh* see Abigail?" Mercy stammered.

"Not right now. Later, perhaps. So, what do you say about decorating?"

Mercy didn't want to pass up the opportunity. She said yes.

Phillip was pleased when Mercy agreed to a morning of decorating. He couldn't quite recall the *nacht* of his head injury and wondered if he had behaved appropriately with her. *Not that I would have stepped out of line,* he mused. Still, there was something that niggled at his consciousness, but he decided everything was well or Mercy wouldn't have let him inside.

As it was, she invited him in graciously, then called Joshua to help with the tree. They wrestled the five-foot blue spruce into the small cabin while Mercy brought an *auld* can to be filled with stones and water to keep the tree fresh.

The Mountain *Amisch* of Blackberry Falls did not overdo decorations, but Phillip was pleased to see that Mercy had baked and strung on dainty ribbon several rows of small gingerbread creatures. She had also strung popcorn and cranberries as well as various types of sweets in tiny knots.

"I'm so glad that you were prepared for a tree!" Phillip smiled and gestured to the simple ornaments.

He watched Mercy flush a becoming shade of pink and was surprised that he felt what amounted to an electric shock run down his spine. He almost shook his head, then decided his head wound might be more serious than he thought. He looked away from her, concentrating on the tree as he and Joshua got it set up straight.

"Well, actually, these decorations were for Abigail, but I suppose we can—"

"Use them nicely here," Phillip finished for her and watched as she gave him a slow nod.

What is wrong with me? he asked himself. Then, as if to prove he was *narrisch*, his gaze strayed to Mercy's full bosom and he almost poked himself in the eye with a tree branch. *Definitely crazy . . . I need to spend more time with Abigail. . . .*

But he enjoyed hanging up the garlands and decorating the tree with the small family. Afterward, Joshua challenged him to a game of checkers, and against his better judgment, he sat down to play. He was aware that Mercy was baking something that smelled delicious in the small kitchen but willed himself to concentrate on the game pieces and not to stare at Mercy's soft back. . . .

Chapter Eighteen

Caleb was struck by the thought that he had never paid a visit to the healer, Aenti Fern, who was at the bottom of the "handyman" list that Birchbark had given him. So, it was no surprise when Birchbark eased on the brake in front of the path to her cabin, then stopped the flatbed sleigh.

"*Geh* on up, *buwe*. And pick any tree for Aenti Fern— she'll make it as she sees fit anyway. I'll be waitin' here."

Caleb jumped down from the flatbed and grabbed a mid-sized white pine, leaving Birchbark and Matthew sitting up front. He dragged it up the snowy incline, somehow feeling that it was he who needed healing done for him, though he wasn't exactly sure why. He knocked on the worn wood of the rounded front door, waiting with the tree behind him.

He heard footsteps come near from within the cabin and the door opened slowly. He had to duck to enter. He pulled the tree in, then turned in the muted interior light to greet the healer. But, to his surprise, there seemed to be no one there, and he had a momentary eerie feeling— similar to what he'd felt with the bats.

He forced himself to continue inside and to shut the door behind him. Something passed by his cheek—the feel of gossamer threads. He whirled around, nearly tripping into the tree. Then he straightened and recalled Birchbark's words about Aenti Fern. *Ya'll need my help with Aenti Fern.* . . . Caleb considered going out and getting Birchbark to lend him a hand, but he decided that *Derr Herr* was more than enough to help him. . . . A thread of lyrics whispered through his mind—"Even in the dark you can still see the light . . ."

He walked farther inside and bumped his hip against a tabletop. He reached out instinctively, and his fingers touched rounded glass. A lamp. He dropped the tree and turned up the flame.

He started when his gaze swept what seemed to be an empty room. "Aenti Fern? I've brought a Christmas tree for you. Birchbark sent me. Uh, I'm Caleb King."

Something rose from the far corner of the cabin and he nearly dropped the lamp.

"Doesn't that *mon* know not to send you when I be working? *Kumme* and sit a while with me while I decorate the tree."

"But Birchbark—"

"He'll wait! Sit, *buwe*."

Caleb eased himself down onto a child-sized chair that he now noticed and lifted his arms to the tabletop.

"Now, let me find my ornaments. I know I shouldn't use them as they're not plain, but the bishop doesn't mind because they are so full of history." She rooted in a large dresser drawer and pulled out her hand with a high laugh.

Caleb got to his feet again, prepared to help her erect the tree, but she waved him back down.

"*Nee, buwe*. I've got it."

He blinked and saw that the pine was standing beautifully upright near the open front hutch.

"Now, Caleb King, you'll hand me the ornaments. Be careful, mind you."

Caleb reached into the large box she'd set on the table in front of him. He picked up a clear glass ornament that somehow seemed to be lit from the inside. He peered into it and saw a baby lamb illuminated by a bright star. He turned the glass carefully. "It's *Derr Herr*."

"*Jah*, He is First and will always be first. Now hand me the ball carefully."

Caleb did as he was told, easing his finger inside the ribbon loop, then passing it to Aenti Fern.

She hung it at the top of the tree, then turned to him once more. "Another one, *buwe*."

Caleb lifted a second ornament and peered inside the halo of light. He watched intently as he saw a blond-haired *kind* take to a sled on a mountain of snow. The *buwe* laughed, then seemed to notice the frozen pond beside him.

Caleb exhaled sharply. "I know that *buwe*—it's me. I remember that Matthew fell through the ice and I pulled him out. He had bad pneumonia that Christmas. Where did you get this?"

"Hmmm, let me think. . . . You had the feeling that you were in need of healing when you came in here, *jah*?"

Caleb passed her the ornament. "*Jah*, I did, but I never expected this."

"When your *bruder* had pneumonia on Christmas, what did you do with your Christmas orange and peppermint?"

Caleb hung his head. "I gave him mine, too."

"*Ach*, and did any but *Gott* see your kindness? *Nee*, I think not! Lift yer head, Caleb King—there is nothing to be ashamed of in love and kindness."

He looked up into her strange gray eyes and nodded mutely.

"Choose another, *buwe*. I haven't got all day."

Just as he was about to draw another ball from the box, a loud pounding on the door sounded, along with a big belch.

"It's Birchbark." Caleb got back up and moved to open the door.

Birchbark stepped inside, tall and round in his dark furs. "*Ach*, Mistress Fern, I thought it might be best if I helped the *buwe* with the next ornament."

"Suit yerself, but there'll be *nee* bellowing. I'm behind, as it is."

"*Jah*," Birchbark agreed; then he placed a firm hand on Caleb's shoulder. "Draw on, *buwe*."

Caleb did as he was told. He looked inside the ball and felt a sinking in his stomach. "This belongs on *nee* Christmas tree."

"*Nee?*" Aenti Fern asked. "You must know that sorrow builds us as much as happiness."

Caleb felt tears fill his eyes and shook his head. "I don't want to see this."

"What is it that ya see, *buwe?*" Birchbark rumbled softly.

Caleb felt choked but managed to get the words out.

"My *mamm* died on Christmas. This is me, crying in my bed. My *fater* is hitting me, trying to make me be quiet. But it didn't matter—I had to cry for her."

"Surely ya did," Birchbark said. "Now, Aenti Fern, if you please, one last ornament before we *geh*."

Caleb drew a ball that was illuminated but had nothing except snow inside it. "I don't see anything."

"It's the future, Caleb King. What makes your Christmas is up to you," Aenti Fern whispered. "For there are penny Christmases and wealthy trees, dripping in gold, but perhaps *nee* Christmas like the one you make and offer ta *Gott*."

Birchbark made a sound of agreement deep in his throat and Caleb got up. It didn't seem appropriate, but he stepped around the table and bent to kiss Aenti Fern's cheek. "*Danki*, but I did nothing to help you as a handyman."

"You'd be surprised." Aenti Fern nodded. "*Kumme* and see me anytime."

Birchbark drew him inexorably to the door and then outside.

"She's hard to understand," Caleb muttered.

Birchbark laughed. "Ya have *nee* idea."

Caleb finished the day with Birchbark and his tree mission to find that the whole flatbed sled was nearly empty. He gave Matthew a brief hug as his *bruder* got off at the cabin he and Tabitha shared.

"Now, don't be tryin' that hug stuff with me, *buwe*!" Birchbark muttered loudly as he got the sled going again.

"Don't hold your breath!" Caleb quipped.

"Hmmm . . . all right, here's where ya get off."

Caleb glanced at the wide path that led out to the pottery.

"*Kumme* on, *buwe*. *Geh* fer a little *nacht* courtin' an' take that last little fir tree with ya."

Caleb didn't need more prodding. He caught up the last tree, then jumped down from the sled and waved *gut*bye to Birchbark. He started down the snowy path to the pottery. He hoped that Abigail was home and was delighted when he saw the pottery lit warmly against the coming *nacht*. He hurried his steps and got to the cabin door, only to realize that Abigail was probably out back.

"Hello!" he called, not wanting to startle her.

"Hello!" he heard her echo, and he went to the back door of the pottery with a smile on his face. He propped the tree against the side of the cabin, then stepped inside the pleasant warmth and walked to her where she sat at the potter's wheel, her hands wet with clay.

"*Ach,* Caleb . . . I'm sorry but I must finish this plate. It is a Christmas gift from Abner to Anke, but he doesn't want anyone but you and I to know about it."

"Don't hurry," he said cheerfully. "I'll find some way to entertain myself."

He took off his coat and hat, then walked behind her. He could see the zigzag part in her hair where it met her *kapp*. He was fascinated by her hair, imagining what it might be like to have her as his *frau* and to enjoy the privilege of seeing her hair loose and flowing down her back.

He cleared his throat and she looked up at him, revealing the pale, delicate line of her throat and neck. He couldn't help himself. . . . He bent and kissed her upside-down beautiful mouth, swiping at her lips with his tongue, then hearing a sound as if from far away—his own voice groaning in pleasure.

He pulled away for a brief moment, then eased the stool she sat on out from the pottery wheel. He came around and knelt between her gray-stained hands, facing her, with the work she was doing at his back. *For a moment*, he thought. *A moment's kiss* . . . Then he leaned into her and whispered softly, "Court me, Abigail . . . *Sei se gut* . . ."

Something creative and free burst forth in Abigail's mind at Caleb's request. She watched his lashes lower against the flush of his cheeks and then lift again as he looked into her eyes. His blue eyes reminded her of seas she had only viewed in pictures, and his pupils were dark and dilated as if he burned with fever. But still she hesitated. Her damp hands would surely ruin his white shirt, but perhaps if he took it off . . .

Her gaze must have communicated the thought to his mind like an electric current because he eagerly slipped down his suspenders and found the closures at his throat, moving slowly downward. She watched his lean fingers work, her heart pounding in her throat. Then she helped him push the fabric from his broad shoulders.

He shivered, but she knew that it was more from excitement than cold, and she felt a kindling response in her belly. "Touch me," he whispered in a husky tone, and she responded instinctively, her gray-hued fingers running down his smooth chest, then brushing upward again. She felt more than heard the groan in his chest when she finally drew him closer that she might kiss his mouth. She kissed him the way she'd felt him kiss her, letting her burning lips play against the shape of his, then tentatively running her tongue along his mouth until she felt him yield and their kisses mingled, breath to breath—each kiss more passionate than the one before.

She ran her hands over his shoulders and down his arms, almost as though she were marking him for her own, branding him with gray streaks, knowing it would take a while to wash the markings off. She pictured him standing at a washbasin, her fingerprints all over his chest and shoulders, and the time it would take him to wash away her touch. . . .

"The Lord calls to us with love, a love that forgives, remembers, and cost much in the death of *Gott*'s *Sohn*."

Bishop Kore's voice rang out to the rafters of the Mast barn. The bishop's communication had changed, as it always did, from odd speech to a striking power and wisdom that reflected the power of *Derr Herr*. But still, her mind drifted. From where she sat with the older women, she could easily make out Phillip's tall frame and dark hair. She wondered if it might be acceptable to offer him a Christmas gift and what that might be.

Then her conscience objected. Why should I offer him anything? Wouldn't that take away from any gift that Abigail might give? She tussled with the problem until she suddenly realized that people were getting to their feet and she hastily joined them. Since it was so cold, the community would eat in shifts inside the Mast home. The women would serve the men first; then the men would return the service. It was generally a time of relaxation, talk, and laughter, but Mercy felt tense and torn over her feelings for Phillip.

Abigail caught up with Mercy as they made their way outside the barn. Mercy put her arm around Abigail's waist and her younger sister returned the hug.

"*Ach*, I love Christmastime!" Abigail said gaily.

"*Jah*," Mercy returned.

"Mercy! Are you here in this moment? Where are your thoughts today?"

Mercy forced herself to smile. "*Ach*, just a lot of things to do in the next week."

"I'll help you," Abigail said stoutly.

"I know. *Danki*."

They'd entered the packed Mast *haus* and took off their long cloaks and woolen bonnets and soon became part of the organized chaos of serving.

Mercy felt distinctly uncomfortable as she brought around the creamed and buttered sweet corn to where Phillip was seated—surprisingly next to Caleb.

Mercy waited a few seconds until Phillip half turned from the bench and took the bowl from her hands. Mercy shivered as he smiled his thanks and let his lean fingers brush the underside of her breast. *Surely, he didn't mean it*, she thought, but her breast tingled just the same. She made haste to *geh* back to the kitchen and to find something else to serve.

Mercy nearly jumped when she felt a light touch on her arm. It was Abigail.

"Mercy, we're out of walnuts for the chicken salad.

Grace Fisher said the store was unlocked as usual, so I'm
going to run over and get some more."

"All right. Be careful of the ice—it's glazed over the
snow in places."

Mercy watched her sister weave through the crowd
for a moment, then turned to accept a bowl of steamed
carrots. Reining in her emotions, she deliberately avoided
Phillip's table.

Abigail hurried over to the Fisher store, careful to hold
the railing of the white front stairs. The general store was
also known as Cubby's, though Abigail thought it was an
odd name since Sam Fisher was nothing like a cute cub.
Abigail knew that the man was less than kind to everyone
and even worse to his wife and children. When she tried
the latch on the store front, it was locked. She found it
odd because usually everybody kept their doors unlatched
during the day and even sometimes at *nacht*. But she
climbed back down the stairs, deciding to try the door to
the house, which was connected to the store.

The back steps had been salted so she crept her
way up and tried the latch. This time the door opened
silently and she made her way into the *haus*, wiping her
feet on the woven mat as she did so. She walked through
the living room, feeling uneasy for some reason, and
had almost reached the green curtain that led to the
store when some sound made her stop. She thought it
was odd because she'd seen the Fishers during church
meeting. Perhaps someone passing through had stopped
in to take food.

She pulled the cloth curtain back slowly and could not contain the surprised gasp that came from her lips when she recognized Sam Fisher and Heather clasped in a sultry embrace, their clothes in disarray. Abigail tried to step back, instinctively knowing that Sam was furious while Heather merely smirked at her.

"*Nee*," Sam bit out, his dark eyes menacing as he tore himself from Heather. He caught Abigail's wrist in a painful grasp, then yanked her close to him. "Ya'll say nuthin' of this. Nuthin', or else I'll beat you within an inch of yer life, girl. Understand?"

Abigail nodded but Sam still didn't let her *geh*. Instead he reached up to grab her cheeks, squeezing the fine bones until Abigail cried out. Sam laughed. "*Gut*. And don't bother tellin' them mail-order fellas of yours either—not if ya wanna see them breathin'. Now *geh* on with ya."

Abigail staggered backward into the curtain, then turned and ran to the back door. She was sobbing softly and barely felt her tears as they froze in the icy air. She rounded the *haus* and store and nearly missed the snowy path. She slipped twice and then fell hard, her weight coming down on the same wrist Sam had brutalized. She was scrambling to get up when she felt strong hands grasp her around the waist.

"*Nee!*" she cried out, until she heard his voice. . . .

Caleb pulled Abigail close and felt her deep shudders of cold and pain.

"It's all right, sweet. How badly did you hurt yourself?" He swept her up in his arms and she clung to him like a limpet. He stalked across to the Mast *haus*, and not wanting to draw attention to her, went in the side door of the large cabin where a hallway contained a row of cloaks and coats and an old leather sofa. The hum of conversation could be heard through the wall as Caleb laid her down carefully. He knelt beside her.

"I'll get Aenti Fern to help us. Just wait here, sweetheart."

"*Nee*—" Her eyes pleaded with him. "Please don't leave me. Please."

"All right." He nodded as he gently opened her cloak. Her wrists were bleeding from where she'd scraped them on the ice, and she had bruises on her face as well as abrasions on the palms of her hands.

He tore open the cotton of her sleeves then pulled his shirt out of his waistband and quickly tore strips from the bottom to bandage her cuts. He was very gentle, but still she cried out, and his heart ached for her.

He gathered her close, rocking her against his shoulder.

"Do you want me to make our excuses and take you home?"

"*Jah*," she whispered.

He unwound her arms from about his neck and tucked his shirt back in. "I'll be right back, Abigail."

He got up, feeling troubled. *Abigail always seemed so confident, so strong. Could something have frightened her out in the icy snow?* He quietly opened the door to the next room and made his way to where Mercy was spooning out carrots to the last of the men having their dinners. He whispered briefly to Mercy, then headed back to the large, empty room where Abigail lay on the couch.

Her eyes looked terrified and he made low, soothing

sounds as he picked her up once more. As before, she clung to him and, once outside, he hurriedly lifted her up behind him on Tommy. He wanted to get her home as soon as possible.

Abigail unclenched her eyes as Caleb finished cleaning her arms and rewrapping her wrist. She looked up at him and felt tears trickle down the sides of her face. He kissed her, following the trail of her tears. She was in her bed; he'd turned his back while she slipped out of her damp clothes and fumbled into a flannel *nacht*gown.

"Ready?" he asked.

She jumped under the mound of quilts and shivered. "*Jah.*"

He turned back to her, pulled a ladder-back rocker closer to the bed, and sat down. "You take a rest, sweetheart. I'll sit here and stand guard."

"What do you mean?"

She was surprised at the fear in her voice, and he leaned forward and caught her hand in his. "Nothing. It was only a figure of speech. I'm sorry. Will you tell me why you are so frightened?"

"I—I'm not—only shaken from the fall." She hoped she sounded convincing. The truth was she had only been so frightened one other time in her life, and Heather had been part of that too. She realized that Caleb had been speaking to her and brought her attention back to the present.

"I said, try to sleep, sweetheart. I will stay with you. Tomorrow we will *geh* and see Aenti Fern."

"I—I'm fine, really. I don't need the healer. I'd much rather finish the sleigh for Anke."

She watched him study her intently and she strove to meet his gaze. Finally, he nodded and looked away. "All right. The sled it is. But now, rest. I will *geh* and fetch you something to eat. You never got your turn to eat lunch. I'm a dab hand at cooking as long as you've got the basics in your kitchen."

"I do," she assured him.

He got up from the chair and leaned over her, bracing his arms on either side. Then he bent to kiss her, once and gentle.

"*Danki*," she whispered.

"I love you."

She looked up into his blue eyes and saw nothing but truth. It filled her with a joy that drove away the fear of the past hours and echoed what lay in her own heart.

"I love you," she breathed.

Chapter Nineteen

Caleb looked around Abigail's neat kitchen, moving almost automatically. *I love you . . . I love you. . . . The words came so easily for me, and I expected nothing in return . . . but she said she loves me. . . .* He felt joy in his heart that made the tips of his fingers tingle. But he forced himself to concentrate on making a simple vegetable soup and some quick biscuits. He remembered that Birchbark had told him not to reveal his talent for cooking to any woman, and he smiled as he loaded the wooden tray he found on the small counter. But when he entered Abigail's bedroom, he discovered that she'd fallen fast asleep, not even rousing when he put the tray on her dresser top.

He was about to sit in the rocking chair once more but then decided that he'd prepare a surprise for Abigail, to cheer her when she awoke. He went back to the small kitchen and found the ingredients for gingerbread and a jar of cookie cutters. Soon he'd rolled out the rich dough with a light dusting of flour. When he'd exhausted the shapes of the cookie cutters, he took a knife and cut some shapes of his own—Christmas trees, deer, and a clever lover's knot framed in a heart. Then he carefully used the knife tip to put a small hole in the top of each piece. He placed the shapes on the small cookie sheet and put the first batch into the cookstove. He was washing the bowls when Mercy came into the *haus* without knocking. Her *sohn* and Phillip followed.

Caleb shushed everyone, then spoke low. "Abigail's sleeping, but I have vegetable soup and biscuits for supper."

"You made it?" Mercy asked doubtfully.

Caleb watched as Phillip teased Mercy. "Not all men are farmers."

"And what's wrong with farmers?" she asked, then blushed berry red.

It was a strange thing for Caleb to see that Phillip and Mercy had forged some sort of connection—a togetherness that was more than potential *bruder*- and sister-in-law. *She loves him,* he thought, *but what does Phillip feel?* Caleb was determined to find out.

He was ladling out soup to Joshua when Abigail walked into the dining room. Her hair was a tousled mess but she looked beautiful. Caleb filled a crockery bowl of soup for her and put it on the table.

"Are you all right?" he asked softly as she sat down to the soup. "I should tend your arms again."

"I'm hungry," she said simply, and he left her to taste the hearty broth.

Mercy began to empty the basket she had brought in with her, loading the table with tempting dishes. "I thought you might want something, Abigail. I've got the ham, scalloped potatoes, some candied carrots, and a piece of pineapple upside-down cake . . . I know it's your favorite."

She watched as Abigail nodded, then hovered over her bowl of soup. There was something wrong with her younger sister, and it went deeper than the wounds on her arms. She had never seen Abigail so shaken in spirit as she appeared at the moment. Mercy plopped down on the bench across the table from where Abigail ate.

"What's wrong?" Mercy asked over the rumble of male voices in the kitchen. "You've got bruises on your face."

"I know," Abigail muttered. "Just a bad fall."

"You should have allowed Aenti Fern to tend you."

"Why are you here with Phillip?"

Mercy swallowed hard and bit her bottom lip. "I . . . he . . . we came home from the Sunday dinner together. I had been walking with Joshua, and Phillip—"

"You like him, Mercy. Right?" Abigail pointed with her spoon. "Don't deny it."

Mercy sighed, longing to hide her face in her apron. "*Jah*, Abigail. I'm so very sorry. Anyway, I'm sure that he doesn't favor me in the least."

"Uh-huh . . . I think I'll try the ham. It smells delicious."

Mercy hastened to undo the cover from the plate and waited until Abigail had served herself. "Please, Abigail, *sei se gut* . . . I never meant to fall—"

"I love Caleb."

Mercy straightened on the bench. "What? It's not even Valentine's Day. You still have time to choose."

"Who are you arguing for, Mercy?" Abigail smiled.

"Why, I don't even know what to say. . . ."

"Don't say anything. Let us be sure of Phillip for you, and then I propose a double wedding—on Valentine's Day."

Mercy couldn't believe what she was hearing, but it sparked a joy in her that she had not felt since Joshua's birth. It made her feel clean and whole as she allowed her sister's plan to dance through her mind. *A double wedding—on Valentine's Day . . .*

Phillip noticed that Joshua was very quiet, holding his crock and wolfing down the soup with appetite. The *buwe* sat quietly in his place at the table, and Phillip remembered what it was like to be fourteen and feel that he didn't know his place or purpose in the world. Phillip went casually to where Joshua sat and asked him to get his coat so they could step outside.

Joshua seemed surprised but complied all the same. Phillip stood with him as they both half turned to look at the moon hanging in the frosty air. Phillip cleared his throat. "I remember being your age—half *buwe*, half man. It was hard, being fourteen—especially with a friend like your Tad."

Phillip knew he'd gained the *buwe*'s attention.

"You had a friend like Tad?" Joshua's voice was incredulous.

"Yep . . . and truth be told, I had no *fater*. And that seemed the worst."

"*Jah*." Joshua nodded. "I don't want to hurt my *mamm,* but having no *daed* is hard every now and then."

"I think your *mamm* is a strong person, and she would

be glad to talk with you. Chances are that it's been hard for her too, not having a husband."

Joshua swallowed and fisted his hands inside his coat pockets. "I think that she's happy though since you've *kumme*."

Phillip felt his face heat with a flush at the *buwe*'s words. *Has Mercy been happy since I've* kumme *to court Abigail? And what do I owe Abigail now that I have so much feeling for her sister?*

He turned to put a hand on Joshua's shoulder. "I care for your *mamm* and for you. We must see what *Gott* wills for us all."

The *buwe* nodded. "I—I hope He wills— Well, I'm glad He brought you here."

"I feel the same. Now, let's *geh* back inside before your *mamm* misses us."

Phillip led the way back to the warmly lit windows of the pottery and began to pray under his breath that *Gott* would somehow bring His glory to this new relationship with Mercy and Joshua even though he still felt bound to Abigail.

Chapter Twenty

Caleb listened to Birchbark's gratifying burps as he finished his omelet. "*Gut* cookin', *buwe*!"

"*Danki*," Caleb replied as he began to gather the dishes.

"Well, tomorrow's Christmas Eve, and I've got a list fer ya."

Caleb gave him a wry smile. "A list? Do you want me to check it twice?"

"Watch yer mouth. *Nee*, I do the checkin', but I do want ya to take the pack with ya."

"*Ach*, *nee*. I'm not pulling rabbits out of that thing and having no way to explain where they came from."

"Since when have ya pulled out rabbits, I'd like ta know?" Birchbark gave him a toothy smile. "*Nee*, this is jest a few simple things ta do. Ya can even take Abigail along, if she'll have ya."

Birchbark's last comment rankled and Caleb frowned. "What do you mean, if she'll have me?"

"Ha!" Birchbark laughed. "Got ya, *buwe*! Even Fred is laughin'."

Caleb cast a dark look at his dog and shook his head. "All right, Birchbark. Give me the list."

Abigail loved to make hard candy for the Christmas program at school. And after her frightening encounter with Sam Fisher and Heather, she wanted to do something complicated to take her mind off her fear from the previous day. She had just poured a batch of steaming red liquid candy onto a cookie sheet when a knock at her door made her jump.

She told herself that it was ridiculous to be afraid in her own home so she straightened her spine and lifted her chin. "*Kumme* in," she called.

She felt both relieved and excited when Caleb entered. Her cheeks warmed when she thought about his tender care of her wrists and then his declaration of love. She was proud she had told him the truth right back—*I love you.*

"*Gut* morning, my pretty." Caleb came forward and slid his cold hands around the warmth of her sides. She put her bowl and spoon on the counter and turned in his arms. She shivered in delight, loving the pine and snow scent of him. Then she stretched on her tiptoes and kissed him without reservation.

"Mmmm," he whispered, his lashes lowered. "You taste like sugar and cinnamon—sweet, like Christmas."

She laughed a bit at his compliment, then glanced over her shoulder. "I've poured some shatter candy. It should be about ready. Would you like to have the hammer?"

"Shatter candy! I haven't had it in years. *Jah*, I'd like to try."

Abigail smiled, then turned and lifted the small silver hammer from its hanging place on a nearby beam. She was about to turn back to him when she felt his big hands splay the width of her waist as he bent and began to suck softly, here and there, on the back of her neck. "Maybe this is the better sweet." He emphasized his point with more kisses until she felt as if she were melting at his touch.

"Do you—do you want the hammer? The candy's bound to be set."

He laughed. "*Jah*, I'll shatter the candy, but I promise to return to your tender neck for another kind of sweet."

"Anytime, Herr King."

Abigail watched as he struck the flattened candy on the cookie sheet. It had always been a delight to watch the hard candy splinter into shards, creating bundles of sweets with no two alike. She had pink mosquito netting at hand and began to cut it to serve as the wrapping for the candies.

"*Ach*, I'm looking forward to the school program this afternoon," Abigail said, knowing she sounded happy.

"And may I sit with you?" he asked, trailing his lean fingers down her arm.

"I'd like that," she murmured. "I'd also like it if Phillip sat with Mercy."

He put the small silver hammer on the counter and turned her in his arms. "So, you too have noticed that there is . . . something between them?"

Abigail nodded. "I guess this leaves me with only one mail-order groom." She felt herself flush at the implications of what she'd said, but Caleb seemed not to know any such reticence. Instead, his bright blue eyes gleamed like secret treasure, and she watched in amazement as he slowly slid his hands from her waist, to her thighs, and downward until he was on one knee before her. . . .

Caleb felt humbled by the love that *Gott* had permitted him in finding Abigail through her mail-order groom ad. He pressed his head against her skirts, then looked up into her beautiful face. "Abigail, marry me *sei se gut*."

He had no ring to give, nor was one needed. The *Amisch* of Blackberry Falls wore no jewelry, not even a wedding band.

"*Ach*, Caleb! *Jah, jah, jah*. Three times over I will marry you, but I think that we should keep it secret until Valentine's Day." She bent and kissed the firm line of his lips. "I want to make sure that Mercy is not hurt in any way."

He caught her about the legs, hugging her to his broad shoulder. Then he got to his feet, lifting her with him, and she laughed helplessly as he turned about. "I agree about Mercy—and Phillip. And, to celebrate us, I think we should"—he dropped her on her bed—"have a pillow fight."

He grabbed a pillow while she was still righting herself and gently swung at the side of her head.

"Unfair!" She giggled.

He watched her snatch another pillow as she knelt upright on the bed and whack him hard. Two goose feathers flew into the air as testament to her swing, and he found himself laughing out loud. After a few more hits, he collapsed beside her on the bed and both gasped for air.

Finally, he turned on his side and looked at her; bosom

heaving, *kapp* askew, her pretty face framed by loose tendrils of hair—she was, in all, a delight to his heart.

"Would you care to *kumme* with me on some errands that Birchbark has tasked me with? I'd love your company."

She turned her head to look at him. "I wish I could, but I still have to net the candy and help prepare for the scholars' presentation."

"Well"—he moved to kiss her—"we still have a few minutes here to catch our breath."

He smiled against her mouth, thinking that if they weren't careful, the candy and errands would be soon forgotten.

As far as Mercy was concerned, the day was not going in the right direction—not by a long shot. She'd been up before dawn making raisin buns and then had gone on to sugar doughnuts, but in turning one batch, she had burnt her hand and it smarted badly. Then she'd caught her breath as someone knocked on the door. She wrapped her hand in a damp tea cloth and went to answer the door, wondering who it could be. Joshua had sleepily staggered out to tend to the goats, so she doubted it was her *sohn*.

She opened the door and felt her heartbeat rush to life in her throat when she saw that it was Phillip. He looked still sleepy as his dark lashes lowered to take in her hand in its makeshift bandage.

"What happened?" He reached to tenderly pull away the cloth.

Mercy's instinct was to slap his lean fingers away, but

his touch soon reminded her how much she cared for him and she gentled under his hands.

"Mercy, this is a bad burn. *Kumme* with me."

"I'm in the middle of frying doughnuts. I don't have time to see Aenti Fern!" She could smell the grease burning on the morning air.

"Wait here," he commanded, brushing past her briefly. She followed him, of course, then watched as he calmly dealt with the frying fat and the three burning treats still left in the pan. She was amazed at his expertise.

"I thought you were a farmer," she murmured as he turned and bumped into her.

He laughed and swung her up in his strong arms. "A farmer, *jah*, but I must know how to run the farm*haus* too, Mercy. Don't you agree?"

Mercy wrapped her arms around his neck. "Put me down! I'm too heavy."

"I'll not putting you down until we've seen to that hand of yours."

There was nothing she could say as he stalked through the cabin to the front door and kicked it open. She noticed that he wasn't even breathing hard, and she had the vague thought that perhaps she wasn't as heavy as she believed.

Then he dropped to his knees in the snow. Mercy found her bottom snuggled against his thighs but he barely seemed to notice. He took her injured hand and plunged it deep into the snow. The relief from the burn was almost immediate.

"You could have just gotten a pail of snow and done the same," Mercy pointed out. She felt flustered by his warm embrace and couldn't recall being so close to a man since Joshua's father. She was startled from her thoughts by Phillip's lifting her once more, but this time, he spoke softly in her ear.

"I could have gotten a pail—true. But then I wouldn't have had the opportunity to hold you, Mercy. And I think that you need to be held—everybody does once in a while."

Mercy's first reaction was to tell Phillip to go away to some place where dainty little women knew how to keep a man from leaving. Instead, she felt herself blink back tears at the truth in his words.

Phillip knew that he had touched on some hidden truth in her heart, and he slowed his steps a bit as he walked back inside. *She feels so* gut *in my arms, but what about Abigail?* He reached the door and soberly set Mercy down inside. The thought that he might be betraying Abigail with his feelings for her sister disturbed him, and he quickly said *gut*bye to Mercy and left.

He knew that she'd looked hurt but what else could he do? He was so involved in his thoughts that he ran pell-mell into Caleb, who was wearing a large pack on his back. Caleb struggled visibly to stay upright and would have collapsed had Phillip not reached out and caught him.

"Why the pack?"

"You don't want to know." Caleb shook his head. "Where are you off to?"

"To Abigail's, I guess."

"*Ach* . . . I just came from there. She had to finish some candies for the school program this afternoon."

Phillip noticed that Caleb looked thoughtful.

"I don't suppose you'd want to help me out with, um, a few deliveries today?" Caleb asked.

Phillip realized that he had nothing else vital to do and agreed.

The two men set off to a place called *Auld* Lady Coover's *haus*, and Phillip had no idea what to expect.

"There seem to be a lot of independent women around Blackberry Falls," Caleb commented.

"You mean like Mer—um, Grossmuder Mildred?"

"Yeah . . . Grossmuder Mildred."

There was something in Caleb's voice that made Phillip uneasy. Could the other mail-order groom have an idea about his growing affection for Mercy? He decided that "less said, sooner forgotten," and commented on the over-growth almost blocking the path that led to Frau Coover's place.

Indeed, the snow-laden branches and tangled rose-bushes did nothing to welcome them forward. But they pressed on, Caleb mumbling as his pack got stuck now and then. They finally emerged into a clearing surrounding a curious cabin, where a giant beast of a dog bounced toward them. "WOOOOFFFF!" the dog roared in such a deep tone that the jays fled from the nearby trees.

Phillip sighed. "I'll bet he's friendly."

"I'll bet we could saddle him." Caleb's words were lost as the black beast pushed him over and began to sniff inside the pack.

Phillip started to laugh.

Chapter Twenty-One

Abigail carried her sweets in a wicker basket, planning on getting to the school in time to help with any last-minute preparations. The schoolteacher, Ann Bly, worked at various jobs around the community, including being a seamstress. But today, her creative inspiration would fill the little school full of the spirit of Christmas.

Lost in her thoughts, Abigail took a wrong turn and knew she'd have to circle around the back of Fisher's store to get to the school *haus*. She clenched her basket tighter and had just cleared the store when she heard Heather's voice carry on the wind from behind her.

"Abigail . . . wait for a moment."

"I can't," she called over her shoulder. "I need to get to the school."

But even though Abigail hurried her steps to get away, Heather was soon abreast of her. "Really, Abigail, are you such a *boppli* that you think you've stumbled onto the first sin of Blackberry Falls?"

Abigail tightened her jaw. "I do not judge you. Your own thoughts betray you."

"Sam is going to marry me."

Abigail felt a clutch of fear in her heart. "And what of Grace and her children?"

"We'll have to see now, won't we?"

Abigail stopped dead. "Don't believe a lie, Heather."

"*Ach*, what do you care anyway? You've had to catalog-order your men."

Something about Heather's voice suddenly sounded insecure. Perhaps it was because Abigail had known Heather growing up, but she sensed that Heather was rattled about something.

"Heather, what is it? Did Sam hurt you, too?"

The sudden pallor of the other girl's skin let Abigail know that she had struck close to the mark.

"*Nee*," Heather whispered with venom. "He is going to marry me."

Abigail suddenly realized that it was foolishness to debate with the other girl, and she was glad when Heather flounced on ahead.

Abigail tried to shake off her worrisome thoughts as she approached the bustling school*haus*. She mounted the stone stairs carved into the hill that led to the large, bright cabin where the *kinner* learned. The whole schoolroom was in an uproar with *kinner* hanging garlands of pine, chains of popcorn and cranberries, and generally running to and fro with candy canes in hand. Abigail was almost bowled over as she reached the long buffet table, which fairly groaned beneath an array of food. The whole of Blackberry Falls generally turned out to see the *kinner*'s program, and folks loved to talk and eat afterward.

Abigail saw Tabitha and made her way through the children to reach her friend.

"How's the *boppli*?" Abigail asked as she gave Tabitha a hug of greeting.

"*Wunderbaar!* We told my *fater* yesterday and he cried with joy. Matthew can't stop touching my belly. . . ."

"*Jah*, I bet that's what got you into this predicament in the first place!"

They both laughed, then moved to ask where Ann Bly needed them the most.

Caleb struggled under the huge dog's lapping tongue until a shrill cry came from the direction of the porch.

"Ishmael! Ishmael! *Kumme* here at once!"

The dog obeyed, visibly reluctant until he managed to secure a large soup bone from the pack Caleb was struggling to put back on in the snow. Phillip gave Caleb a hand up and they both made their way across the snow to where a tiny *auld* woman was scolding the black dog, who swept his tail back and forth good-naturedly.

"*Ach*, so it's that time again, eh?" Frau Coover asked, eyeing the pack. "Best ta come inside fer such matters. Don't mind Ishmael. He's a Newfie, a Newfoundland pup that my late husband brought back from his travels. Keeps me company, he does! *Kumme* in. *Kumme* in!"

Caleb struggled to follow Phillip into the cabin. The pack was a pain in the neck, but he knew he had been charged to bring something in it to the *auld* woman.

Inside the cabin, Caleb looked about in fascination. Spools of ribbon, midnight-blue paper with glittery shooting stars, elaborate bows, faerie puppets, and dozens of other oddities decorated the walls.

He shrugged off the pack and propped it against a

knobby cabinet full of tempting candy in clear glass jars—horehound sticks, peppermints, licorice whips, and so on. . . . He longed to reach into a jar. He nearly jumped when Frau Coover seemed to read his mind.

"*Geh* on with ya! Take what ya choose, please!"

Cautiously, Caleb reached a hand to the second shelf and pulled down the jar full of root beer barrels. He took one out and offered the jar to Phillip, who shook his head. Then Caleb replaced the glass and began to suck on one of the sweets. It was strange, he thought, that the candy didn't quite taste like root beer—but rather like something dear and familiar, but just out of reach. He felt as if he were spinning around, though he knew the room was not moving, and he heard laughter coming somewhere both near and far. A woman's face came to mind—Abigail. He wanted to remember her beauty but she disappeared and in her place were the features of his *fater*—cruel and glaring. It was both scary and tiresome to see the man who had given him life but loved him not. . . .

Caleb heard a thump and then the crackling of a fire. He came to his senses and felt himself touching the frame of Birchbark's pack. He looked around the room, and the walls were bare of ornaments—they were simply pine. Phillip sat awkwardly at a tea table while he sipped tea with Frau Coover, and the Newfoundland lay at Caleb's feet—not nearly so big as it had seemed before. He started to speak but Frau Coover waved him silent.

"*Kumme, mei buwe*, have some tea. It's been waiting for you."

"Waiting?" Caleb asked. "How long . . . I mean . . ."

He glanced at the cupboard from which he'd taken the candy and found it full of dishes, neatly arranged.

"It's a special herb tea that I brew myself." Frau Coover smiled with perfect teeth.

"No," Caleb said flatly, but then he remembered his mission. "Uh, I guess I should check the pack for you."

"What fer, *buwe*? I already put things in Birchbark's pack—no need ta take 'em out."

"I don't understand. I've never seen anyone but Birchbark put things in the pack."

Frau Coover laughed and slapped her knees. "*Ach*, the things the young think! Dontcha know that love waits for no man?"

Caleb replied slowly, his thoughts in a haze. "Love . . . ? But the saying is that 'time waits for no man. . . .'"

"Not in Blackberry Falls, it ain't! *Nee*, sir! Dontcha know that *Derr Herr*'s Word speaks of such things?" She smiled. "'Iffin' I speak with the tongue of angels, but have *nee* love . . . I ain't nuthin'.'"

"Uh, right. Right. Phillip, we'd better *geh*. Abigail wouldn't want us to be late for the program."

"I suppose you're right."

Caleb shouldered the awkward pack, resisting the urge to glance inside, and nodded to Frau Coover. "A *gut* day to you, ma'am."

She waved his words away with a smile. "Would you like a few root beer barrels to take on your way?"

"*Nee*," Caleb snapped when Phillip seemed to be ready to accept the candy. "*Nee*, Frau Coover. *Danki*."

Caleb escaped to the clear, crisp winter air and drew in a few deep breaths. "What happened in there?"

Phillip shrugged. "Good tea, I suppose. . . ."

"Yeah," Caleb agreed darkly. "*Gut* tea . . ."

Mercy arrived at the school*haus* flustered and sweating, despite the chill outside. Nothing had turned out right that morning, including Phillip and his talk of being held. She felt all crinkled up inside, even though she knew that Abigail would likely think it was *gut* news that Phillip had been so kind. But Mercy had been having second thoughts. *How could someone as gentle and handsome as Phillip truly desire someone like me? It isn't as though there have been other* Amisch *men over the years who have found me desirable enough to court . . . so why should Phillip?*

She pushed aside the quiet voice that said she had done very little to make anyone believe she wanted another relationship after Joshua's *Englisch fater* had run off. *It was easier for me to cling to my disappointment than it was to break out of the pattern and love someone again.*

She made her way across the crowded classroom floor and hefted her basket onto a clear spot on the winter white of the tablecloth. She was unpacking cinnamon rolls when Abigail came and brushed a kiss of greeting on Mercy's cheek. Oddly, Mercy didn't have the usual feeling of stiffening inside. Instead, she turned and squeezed Abigail's arm.

Mercy saw the surprise in her sister's eyes. "Well, have you caught the Christmas spirit?"

Mercy considered the question and spoke finally. "*Jah*, I think I have!"

Abigail leaned close. "Or have you caught a bigger fish?"

"Shhh," Mercy said above the classroom din. "I haven't caught anything else."

Abigail smiled and Mercy turned back to emptying her basket. The program would start in an hour, and she wondered where Phillip was. She soon found out when he arrived with an arm on Joshua's shoulder.

"What's wrong?" Mercy asked.

"Just some pre-performance nerves here," Phillip answered.

"Why? Be you sick?" Mercy asked her *sohn*.

"*Nee*—though I wish I was."

Mercy frowned. "Why ever would you say something like that?"

Phillip interjected in hushed tones. "Ann Bly told the class that both Lewis Stolfus and Mary Mast are down with flu. They were to have played Mary and Joseph in the program. Ann decided that two from the upper grades should take the job—they could quickly learn the lines."

Mercy couldn't help but smile, then hugged her son. "You'll do well."

Phillip nodded and waved an arm at the other mail-order groom as Caleb entered the classroom. Caleb waved back but then made a beeline for Abigail as she took her seat.

"We'd better go and find some *gut* seats," Mercy said, and Phillip bent low to her ear.

"May I sit with you?"

Mercy flushed but nodded. "*Jah*—Joshua, go and take your place. Folks are arriving."

She watched her disgusted son walk away, then looked up at Phillip. "Are you sure you want to sit with me?"

Phillip gave her a wolfish smile. "Shall I prove it to you here?"

Mercy drew a sharp breath, then lifted her head. She knew there were stares but, for once, they didn't seem judgmental.

Phillip basked in the pleasure of sitting down next to Mercy. Abigail and Caleb sat in front of them, and for some reason, Phillip felt distinctly happy. Then Ann Bly stood to give the customary greetings and went on to thank the bishop for allowing the program.

"And you'll all be surprised by our nativity play this year, though we should pray for the *kinner* who are ill today." Then she motioned to someone at the back, and the double doors were opened with a whoosh of air.

Phillip watched with interest as the nativity play began. In his home church, they did not have a Christmas program, and he thought that it added to the festivities. A parade of animals from local barns were herded down the main aisle and dutifully made it up the stairs to the place where a painted backdrop served as a manger. It was fun to see the *kinner* dressed in robes and head wrappings. He also had a quick glimpse of Tad as a gangly innkeeper and wondered vaguely if the *buwe* had any tricks to play on this occasion.

Then a donkey colt was carefully led in by Joshua, in the role of Joseph, and a pretty young girl who kept her eyes low as they finally left the main floor and awkwardly went up the steps. The donkey colt brayed at being tied so near fresh straw without any chance to eat. Finally,

Ann directed the colt out the back doors, and the room settled down.

Phillip watched Tad and Joshua exchange a quick glance. Ach . . . *what are they up to?*

Joshua held Mary's arm and made the rounds of several colored *hauses*, asking for shelter. But they were denied each time. Then they came to Tad, and Phillip saw the *buwe* peer anxiously toward the back of the crowded room. The doors suddenly opened and closed in quick succession, and Phillip noticed that Tad looked ready to cry.

"That was his *fater* who left," Mercy whispered.

Phillip frowned, then stared up at Tad, praying for him silently.

Joshua came before Tad and steadied Mary. "*Sei se gut*, sir—have you a room for us tonight?"

Phillip saw Tad swallow, and his own throat burned for the boy. "*Nee*, I have nothing."

Tad's voice shook a bit when he called out the expected, "Wait!" but then Phillip saw the *buwe* motion to Joshua. Instead of directing them to the cold stable, he motioned them forward. The crowd buzzed a bit but Tad stood his ground, and soon there was silence.

Tad swallowed hard. "Wait—Joseph and Mary, you can have my room."

He held out a hand to Joshua and the *buwes* shook. The classroom erupted in loud praise of Tad's decision while Ann Bly flitted up and down the aisle like a startled butterfly. The *kinner* on the stage cheered and all of them moved instinctively to circle around Tad and hug him.

Phillip leaned toward Mercy and spoke. "Why did Tad do that and why would his *fater* leave?"

"Tad's *daed* is a bit different in his thinking. Always has been."

Phillip nodded, then spoke. "Will you *kumme* with me, Mercy? I want to *geh* and see Tad and Josh!"

Chapter Twenty-Two

Caleb leaned his bare hip against the ice-cold window-sill. The leaden sky of dawn began to bear rising colors of pink and purple, the Master's touch. And it was Christmas Eve Day. Caleb knew he would never forget the *nacht* before. The program at the school*haus* had been amazing. *I'll give you my room . . . I'll give you my room, Baby Jesus—Savior and* Sohn.

But do I give Him room in my life? Do I allow a dwelling place for Him in my heart? He began to pray softly within himself, asking *Gott* to help him understand how he might better invite the King inside.

"Big thoughts you think, eh, *buwe*?"

Caleb smiled and turned to face Birchbark. "*Jah*, big. And today is Christmas Eve Day!"

Birchbark gave him a half smile. "Bah, humbug."

Caleb laughed out loud. "Now, why do I think you don't mean that?"

"I'll be gone tonight." Birchbark yawned.

"I thought as much. Do you want me to help you with the pack for tonight?"

"The pack—huh! Now, why would I be needin' the pack?"

"It's all right, Birchbark. I understand that you are . . . well . . . Santa Claus, or an angel or something. You don't have to pretend anymore."

"Do you have your head screwed on right?"

"Pretty right," Caleb answered.

Birchbark sighed. "Love waits fer no man."

"*Ach*, here we *geh*!"

"Ya don't understand, *buwe*. But you might one day— mebbe one day. Now *geh* on with yer day. I expect ya ta give Abigail a hello from me."

"I will."

Caleb pulled his shirt on and snapped his suspenders. He grabbed his boots, then slid his coat and hat on quickly. He did want to see Abigail, even though the dawn had barely broken.

"Tommy wants more oats in honor of the day, and Fred says he's goin' with ya."

"Fair enough." Caleb held the door wide and Fred roused himself from Birchbark's bed while a steady blast of cold air and light snow blew inside.

"*Geh* on with ya, Fred. It's freezin' even with my long johners."

Caleb grinned and called a last *gut*bye to Birchbark, then headed down the mountain with his hands in his pockets and a smile on his face.

Abigail was in that languorous place between sleep and waking when she felt the first gentle touch brush her cheek. She wondered if butterflies had come to play in the snow. A second smooth touch gently traced her eyebrows; first one, then the other. She felt herself smile, and the touch moved to her lips. She licked at the fleeting movement and tasted rich vanilla and honey; she arched her neck to get closer to the touch. She caught the scent of pine and began to kiss him back. Her body knew what her mind wanted to savor and she kept her eyes closed.

She imagined he was snow, and frost, and pine and holly—but most of all, he was Christmas Eve! She blinked and stared up into warm blue eyes completely focused upon her.

"Mmmm," she whispered. "It's *wunderbaar* to be kissed awake on Christmas Eve."

"If you'll allow it, I have one request of you on this happy morning."

"What is it?"

"This." He held up one of the pink-wrapped bundles of candy.

She smiled. "Candy?"

"*Jah*." He gave her a lopsided grin. "Would you—kiss me, court me, with this sweetness, though nothing could be as sweet as tasting you."

She sensed that he felt vulnerable asking for the courting and took the pink bag in her hands. "*Ach*, Caleb, may I kiss you with the candy?"

He smiled. "*Jah*, please."

She felt a thrill of anticipation rush through her chest as Caleb lay down beside her. She untied the bag of sweets, selected a pink one, then began to slide it gently across his lips. His lashes fanned out across his ruddy cheeks, and then she lowered her head. . . .

* * *

Caleb felt as if he were dying as she kissed him. Her lips were petal soft and she trailed the honey-sweet candy down the strength of his neck as she let her mouth draw upon him. She loosed the braid of her hair and it fell free, a satiny curtain that lent heightened intimacy to their situation.

"Abigail . . . I think . . . I want—" He groaned when he heard the bell over the pottery door jingle merrily.

She was off the bed in an instant, looking askance at him with her dress in her hands. He rose from the bed immediately and waved at her. "I'll *geh*. You dress."

Caleb's head was still addled from the heady kisses he'd received. He went through the shop to answer the early-morning ringing. He opened the door and was surprised to find Birchbark standing there.

"Somebody took the pack."

Caleb blinked. "What?"

"You heard me."

"Okay." Caleb widened the door. "*Kumme* in. How did it happen?"

"If I knowed how it happened, would I be tellin' ya now?"

Caleb ignored the other man's crankiness; he had a right to be angry.

Abigail entered the pottery shop looking as neat as a new pin. "Birchbark? What's wrong?" Caleb watched her pull out a chair, and the other man took a reluctant seat.

Caleb leaned over to speak softly in her ear. "Someone took his pack."

"Not *the* pack?" Abigail asked.

"*Jah*," Birchbark said. "Somebody who wanted it for evil, not fer *gut*."

"Wait, you know about—the pack?" Caleb asked briefly.

"Of course." She smiled at him, then went to pat Birchbark's grizzled head.

Caleb felt a strong desire to wring the neck of whoever it was who'd taken such a wonderous thing from Birchbark; he didn't like seeing the *auld* man look so downcast.

Caleb opened the door to the daylight, then turned to give Birchbark a resolute stare. "Birchbark, *kumme* with me! Love—love waits for no man."

Caleb smiled at Abigail, then opened the door wider. Birchbark got up from the table and followed Caleb out into the snow. . . .

"I'm telling you, it will be *wunderbaar*—a double wedding on Valentine's Day."

Mercy rolled her eyes at Abigail. "You are a dreamer."

Abigail laughed. "*Jah*, I suppose, but there was nothing dreamy about Phillip sitting by your side during the school program."

Mercy had the grace to flush. "Perhaps he was simply being kind."

"Mercy, it is Christmas Eve—speak the truth!"

Mercy put a plate of snowball cookies on the table and sat down next to her sister. "*Ach*, you're right. I do want that wedding! And I love Phillip, but I refuse to be hurt again as I was those years ago."

Abigail caught Mercy's hand in hers. "The Bible says

that perfect love drives out fear and perfect in Hebrew means whole. Yes, there will be difficult times—as there are in any relationship, but it won't be like it was with the *Englischer*."

Mercy nodded slowly. "You're right, I suppose. But how do I tell Phillip that?"

"We make sure that you bump into him often. Perhaps even let a few of your snowball cookies do the talking."

Mercy laughed. "You're right. I was going to take a plate to Grossmuder Mildred's. I could hope that he's there. . . ."

"Let's do everything we can to get him those cookies!"

Mercy swallowed, then lifted her chin in agreement.

Phillip whistled softly to himself as he dragged the small Christmas tree up the hill to Grossmuder Mildred's. She'd insisted that trees should only be decorated on Christmas Eve and Phillip had agreed. He longed to see Mercy but could not disappoint the kind *auld* lady.

"Here we *geh*!" he cried out, jolliness in his tone as he came through the doorway.

Grossmuder clapped her hands with the joy of a child. "*Ach*, the smell of the pine lets me see it! The *Gut Derr Herr* gives sight to the blind."

Phillip abandoned the tree to *kumme* forward and gently hug her frail form before giving her a buss on the cheek. He straightened, then handed her his fresh hankie when she would have cried at his touch.

"Somebody's comin'. Move outta the way, *buwe*. No sense gettin' shot."

Phillip gently took the gun from her. "Ah, let's not shoot anyone on Christmas Eve."

"Hello! Anyone in there?"

Phillip recognized Mercy's voice and waited, his heart pounding while Grossmuder Mildred invited their guest inside.

Then Phillip hauled the tree aside and smiled down into Mercy's eyes. "Merry Christmas Eve."

Chapter Twenty-Three

As the day wore on, Caleb became convinced that the pack was well and truly gone. He wanted to say something to Birchbark but didn't have the heart to disappoint him further. So, he trudged on, looking in caves and hollows and snow-filled paths for any sign of the *auld* man's missing property.

Finally, Birchbark stopped and hung his head. "It's gone."

Caleb wanted to reassure him but knew it would only be false support. On the heels of that realization came an all-consuming question for Birchbark.

"Uh, Birchbark?"

"What?"

"Does losing the pack mean that well . . . all of the *kinner* around the world aren't going to get their Christmas gifts?"

"'R ya out of yer gourd?"

"*Nee*," Caleb denied sheepishly. "I just thought—"

"Well, there's yer trouble! Always thinkin'—take time to feel, even when it hurts." The older man lifted his head. "We'll *geh* back ta the cabin. You're freezin' and so I be."

Caleb spoke low. "I'm sorry."

"I thank ye."

They started the rigorous climb to the cabin and Birchbark grunted when they passed Sam Fisher coming down the mountain with an armful of firewood. The storekeeper passed them without any expression, though Fred jumped and growled at him.

"Hmmm," Birchbark rumbled when they were out of earshot of the store owner. "Fred says he's up ta no good. And why would a storekeeper be gatherin' firewood far from his store? And on Christmas Eve, ta boot."

"I don't know."

"*Ach*, but perhaps I know. My pack is special. Used fer good or bad dependin' on who holds it. I think Sam Fisher wants it ta swallow all he don't want . . . even his wife and mistress."

"His mistress?" Caleb said blankly. "Who is that?"

"*Ach*, let's *geh* on an' stop yer yammerin'." Birchbark showed renewed determination and Caleb followed gladly.

While she worked, Abigail spent a good part of the day praying that Birchbark's pack might be found. But amid the flurry of shoppers, those either picking up pottery already ordered or looking for a last-minute pottery present, she didn't see Caleb. So she knew that the search must still be on.

She had sat down to have a refreshing cup of licorice tea when the shop bell rang once more. Abigail looked up and saw Grace Fisher enter hurriedly, almost as if she were being pursued.

Abigail saw with shock that a red mark curved around the pallor of Grace's face. Her bottom lip was split, and it was clear that she was trying to hide her injuries beneath her bonnet.

"Grace," Abigail said gently as she rounded the counter to touch the other woman's hand. "What happened? What can I do to help you?"

Grace shook her head. "My two *buwes*—I thought you might have piggy banks for them."

"Of course, but won't you sit down for a minute or two? I can make more tea."

"*Nee, danki.* I am *gut* at soothing myself. If you could hurry, I need to get back to the store. . . . Anke is keeping an eye on things until I return."

"Certainly, I will hurry." Abigail went to the back pottery and pulled two banks off a narrow shelf. Then she rolled them carefully in newspaper and slipped them into a brown bag.

She returned to the front of the pottery to find Grace standing tensely beside the counter. She handed Grace the bag.

"Merry Christmas Eve," Abigail murmured, longing to do something to help the other woman but knowing it would probably cause more harm than *gut*. Still, when Grace pulled a small pocketbook from her cloak, Abigail shook her head. "There's no charge."

"How much is it, please? I—I don't want your pity."

"Of course." Abigail hastily scribbled out a total in her small accounts book. "It's three dollars, *sei se gut.*"

Grace carefully counted out the change then lifted the bag. "*Danki*, Abigail."

Abigail called her thanks but Grace was already out

the door. Abigail sank down on a stool and started to pray, realizing there was much that needed to be given—not only on Christmas but every day.

Caleb stripped off his sodden clothes and hastily dressed to *geh* to Abigail's. Half the day spent in futile search had exhausted him, though he supposed they'd made some sort of progress now that Birchbark seemed certain Sam Fisher was the culprit. Still, Caleb longed for the peace he found in the potter's presence.

"Fred wants ta *geh* with ya," Birchbark muttered as he changed his long johns.

"Will you still be gone over*nacht*?"

Birchbark lifted his chin. "'Course I will."

"Well, then, I'll see you tomorrow." Caleb nodded, then opened the door.

"*Buwe?*" Birchbark said gruffly. "I mean—uh—Caleb?"

"*Jah?*"

"*Danki* fer yer help taday. Much appreciated."

Caleb knew it was hard for the *auld* man to offer such thanks and he smiled as he stepped out into the snow shine.

Mercy watched Phillip devour the snowball cookies while Grossmuder Mildred clapped at the gaiety she could feel in the small cabin.

"I think you outta *geh* home and make some more of these! Phillip, *geh* and help her."

"*Jah*, but to leave you here alone wouldn't be fair,"

Mercy said, even though she wanted Phillip to *kumme* with her.

"*Nee*." The *auld* woman struck the hardwood floor with her ironwood cane. "*Geh!* And enjoy the rest of the day! Some of the men will bring me down to the singing tonight."

"As you wish," Phillip said, bending to kiss her cheek.

Mercy did the same and then they hurried off the top of the hill. Phillip stopped suddenly and turned to look down at her, excitement in his handsome face.

"I have an idea!"

"*Jah?*" she questioned cautiously.

"I'll be right back."

She watched him for a minute, then turned to look at the view of Blackberry Falls below. *Gott* had blessed the land of endless mountains. The tiny village of Blackberry Falls glowed with warm lantern light, soft and bright. Some kind of joy filled her until she realized that it was the first time in a long time that she didn't feel anger toward *Gott*. She knew now that the bitterness that had led to her sharp tongue and cold heart had come from within and she—

"Mercy! Look what I found in the shed."

He carried a long runner sled, and his eyes glowed with pleasure. "What do you say, Mercy?"

She swallowed hard. She'd been terrified of racing sleds ever since a childhood accident. But when she saw how happy he was, she smiled and clambered onto the front of the sled while he sat in a close embrace, his long legs bent around her. He pulled hard on the rope and then they were off! The feel of the wind and cold on her face—*ach*! It was amazing. But they soon hit a rock, hidden by the snow, that caused them to bounce into the air. She squeezed her eyes shut and started to scream, but somehow Phillip managed to right the sled and she laughed out loud as they landed with a sharp spray of ice.

Chapter Twenty-Four

In the late afternoon, Caleb was on his way to Abigail's when Fred barked sharply at him from behind.

"All right. *Kumme* on, *buwe*."

Still, the dog stood stiff, barking furiously. Caleb turned and started to climb up the hill after his pet. He figured the dog had probably treed a raccoon and wanted to show off. But as soon as he reached Fred, the dog turned and ran ahead, barking loudly.

Caleb sighed and wished that Birchbark was there to interpret. Then his thoughts sped up and he wondered if all was well at the cabin. But when they reached it, Fred lured him on, higher up the mountain. They finally reached a spot where Caleb could see an odd path winding through a stand of pine trees and heavy brush. Two cardinals welcomed him, tweeting from different snow-covered bushes, their vibrant color all the more beautiful against the pristine white. Even Fred didn't scare them away, and Caleb started down the path.

He turned a corner and ran in to Mercy's *sohn* and his friend. He didn't really know the two *buwes* but could recognize the grim expressions on both their faces.

"What is it?" Caleb asked.

The *buwe* he knew as Tad spoke in a choked tone. "That—trickster, Sam Fisher, was here this morning. He was mean to my *fater*. Why, I'd like to punch that man. . . ."

"Will you take me to your dad?" Caleb asked.

The *buwes* turned and started back down the path, and Caleb followed. There was a hush about the place, and even Fred had stopped barking.

They came in sight of a small cabin, maintained neatly. But the strange image of an *auld* man, dressed only in long johns and running about the cabin, disturbed Caleb greatly. "You *buwes geh* and find Phillip."

"I hate to leave Daed alone. He's . . . well . . . he's got nerves, they say." Tad's voice was full of despair.

Caleb put a bracing hand on Tad's shoulder. "I will stay with him."

Tad nodded and the two *buwes* turned away while Caleb began to walk slowly toward the wild-haired man. Somehow, Caleb knew instinctively that remaining calm would calm the other man.

"Hello, I'm Caleb. What's your name?"

The other man, looking around himself furtively, hopped from one bare foot to the other. "I be Zechariah and he knowed it."

"Zechariah, why don't we *geh* inside? I be cold," Caleb soothed.

"Can't. Can't leave 'cause he'll be back."

"Who?" Caleb asked.

"That mean one. Scared me with that gun but I didn't break. I knowed where I put it and I keep it well."

"Great job, Zechariah. You kept things safe."

"I show ya," the *auld* man whispered. "You be *gut*—I know. I know things that other people don't."

"I think you're smart," Caleb whispered back.

"Folks don't think that—but now I show ya."

Caleb followed the man deep into a stand of firs, wishing he could coax Zechariah into the cabin.

"Folks—they look down and around but not up. Not where *Gott* be. Look up!"

Caleb obeyed. He looked up at the pines dusted with snow, and then something flashed into view . . . a frame of wood, oddly out of place. He looked again—it was Birchbark's pack!

"Seed it. Didn't ya?" Zechariah asked.

Caleb broke into a broad smile. "How did you get it up there?"

"Rope and pulley. I did it and he couldn't find it! Was that snake, Fisher, what stole it. He wants it ta use fer bad things, but I stole it back. He said he'd kill me if I didn't give it up. Think he'll do that?"

"No," Caleb said tightly. "You can come stay with Birchbark and me. And Tad, too."

"*Jah, jah*, Birchbark's my friend. He knows me."

"*Gut!* Now let's get you dressed and lower that pack down."

The Stolfus *haus* fairly gleamed with candlelight, and silence reigned over the worshippers gathered there. It was a time of reflection and personal prayer. The candles reminded them of the ever-increasing fragility of life but also of the great power of every life that knew *Derr Herr*.

And then the candles were extinguished, and Bishop Kore got up to give his Christmas sermon.

Caleb had noticed that the Fisher family was not present and knew that Zechariah was safe in a back room with Phillip and Tad and Joshua. As he listened to the sermon, Caleb was fascinated by the bishop's two sides, his strange sense of humor and his beautiful elegance as he applied the Word to everyday life.

The bishop stood by a single lit lantern and the groups on the benches settled in for what surely would be a long talk.

Bishop Kore stroked his long gray beard and looked thoughtful. "Well, it's said that we should keep Christmas all the year but I cannot do that. *Nee*, instead I mess up, make mistakes, and fail. I even think that I have failed *Gott* and that there will be no place to hide from Him and His disappointment in me. But this last thing is a lie. *Gott* doesn't see me as a failure, or worthless, or as someone who never measures up enough. You see, there's a difference between enough and abundance. We, as humans, think in terms of enough. We're not *gut* enough, didn't do enough, were not enough. . . . The concept of enough haunts us. But *Gott*, He deals in abundance. He wants us to have abundant life, overflowing, raining down . . . Abundant love . . . and abundant peace. *Derr Herr* says that He gives peace but not as the world gives, because the world doesn't seek peace in a manger with shepherds as attendants. So, look for abundance this Christmas, and may you find it in *Gott*."

Caleb watched the bishop's eyes as they seemed to twinkle in the light and knew that what the *auld* man said, no matter how crazy, was Truth.

* * *

Phillip sat quietly with Zechariah as the old man moved back and forth in a bentwood rocker. Phillip had insisted on sitting with the wiry man, his *sohn* Tad and also Joshua, in a room distant from the other worshippers. The candlelight service had ended in the large hall and there was now the distant murmur of people enjoying party foods for Christmas Eve. Zechariah had not felt comfortable earlier, but now Phillip noticed the *auld* man sniff the air with appreciation.

"Smells like ham, don't it?"

Phillip smiled. "Would you feel comfortable getting some food or should I get it for you?"

"Don't feel right going out there, but I be hungry."

Phillip rose and clapped a hand on Zechariah's thin shoulder, bid the *buwes* to stay, then left the room.

He saw Mercy busily serving hot cocoa while smiling and talking with the guests. Phillip knew that this was a Christmas Eve he would surely remember the rest of his life. Colors seemed brighter and the tea sweeter and the tall tree that dazzled with candles shone with beautiful elegance even though it was unadorned with ornaments or glitter.

Phillip knew that it was enough to have one Christmas like this, and he was grateful in his heart for such an evening. He blinked then smiled as he discovered that Mercy was no more than two feet away.

"Your thoughts are deep tonight," Mercy murmured as she passed him the last cup of cocoa from her tray.

He smiled down at her, noting the beautiful curves of her face. And the shine of her red hair. "Would you share a cup with me?" he asked, offering her a drink of the cocoa.

She took a cautious sip. "It's hot!" She passed the cup back.

"It is indeed." Phillip laughed. "Would you help me gather up some food for the brood in the back?"

Mercy held out her tray. "Let's get some plates."

Phillip followed her willingly.

Mercy felt a warm cascade of heat down her back, knowing Phillip followed close behind her. It was a wonder to her that she felt comfortable, and moreover beautiful, when she knew his eyes were on her. She felt him move by her side down the long tables lined with food—ham, roast beef, venison, mashed potatoes, mashed sweet potatoes, and mashed turnips and then sweets of every kind with side dishes in between. Mercy filled the tray with large portions, knowing how Tad and Joshua loved their treats. She was also pleased to be able to meet Tad's *fater*. She knew that Tad was very protective of his *daed*, and she couldn't blame the *buwe*. Mental illness, including anxiety, was not well understood among the *Amisch*.

Phillip held the door to one of the back rooms open for her and she slipped quietly inside with the steaming tray. Tad's *fater* jumped up from the rocking chair and bowed to her. She smiled at the *auld* man in return and slid the tray onto a nearby reading table.

Tad and his *fater* made a beeline for the food, while Joshua hung back for a bit until Phillip gently motioned him forward.

"Thank you," Mercy whispered, "for being so kind to the *buwes*."

"It's my pleasure. Truly."

She nodded, knowing that he spoke the truth.

Later that evening, Abigail looked intently at Caleb as he took her inside the pottery. His coat radiated cold, but she knew that beneath it and his shirt was the alluring promise of the bare skin of his chest. She went into his arms, lifting her mouth for the taste of his kiss. It was like drinking dandelion wine on a hot summer day. "Mmmm, sir. You are intoxicating."

She watched him flush, and then he lifted the pack he'd set behind him. "I—uh . . . well I spoke to *Derr Herr* about the abundance of Birchbark's pack. You see, I was wishing hard for something—so, here goes!"

She watched him put his hand inside the pack, and then he smiled as he withdrew his arm to reveal a large wrapped gift. He handed it to her. "Merry Christmas." His voice low and warm. It made her want to kiss him forever. But she wondered what his gift was. She looked down and untied the red ribbon, then gently opened the paper to reveal a heavy black cloak. She let the mysterious fabric spread out, then looked up at him. "A woman's cloak!"

He grinned at her. "Indeed, a woman's cloak—one without paint."

"*Ach, danki*, Caleb. I love it!"

"There's one more thing, my sweet." He took the cloak from her and turned it over to reveal a black satiny piece of lining—a pocket, small and intimate, that she could easily access. "What's this?"

"You remember your ad? Something about poetry?"

Her smile grew. "Shall I see what's in the pocket?"

"If you'll allow me?"

She nodded and he reached two lean fingers inside to withdraw a sheet of white paper. Then he cleared his throat.

> *"Ever before me—gossamer wings*
> *Honey hair and secret kisses.*
> *She is more than the sum of her beauty*
> *Wisdom and gaiety—hands that make and mold*
> *She's not afraid of the fire that burns bright*
> *Within her—waiting for my touch."*

He looked up at her and she watched the color *kumme* into his cheeks. She knew it took a lot of courage for a man to speak so.

"Caleb, that was beautiful. . . . Is that truly the way you see me?"

"*Nee* . . . To my eyes, you are even more than all this. I love you, Abigail. Merry Christmas."

She laid her head on his chest, listening to the warm and steady beating of his heart and knew that she was home.

Chapter Twenty-Five

Caleb knew that the Mountain *Amisch* traditionally spent Christmas Day as a time of quiet family reflection and prayer. Still, he was glad that his *bruder* Matthew had invited him to spend the afternoon at his *haus*. Birchbark still hadn't returned and Caleb knew that Abigail was probably spending the day at Mercy's *haus*. So, it made him feel a little less lonely to be with his *bruder*.

He'd brought a cluster of holly and some winterberry as decoration for Tabitha and Matthew's fine wooden table as well as a glass jar of cranberry applesauce from Birchbark's abundant pantry. He knocked on the door, a beautiful example of fine woodworking, and was surprised when Anke opened it.

"*Kumme* in! *Kumme*, Caleb! The others are in the kitchen." Her voice dropped to a whisper. "Abner loves the sleigh. He took me for a ride, and we will *geh* home later the same way."

Caleb smiled down at her, then wondered who was in the kitchen, as a burst of laughter, quickly quieted, filled the air.

Anke led him in, and Caleb was happily surprised to

find not only his *bruder* and Tabitha, but Abner, John Stolfus and Mercy, as well as a person who caused his heart to speed up—Abigail. Everything else faded to a background blur as he crossed the room to greet her. She looked festive and beautiful, wearing a dark green dress and long black apron, and she held out her hands to him.

Nothing seemed so right as laying aside the holly and taking her hands in his own. He knew her for what she was, fragile but incredibly strong, someone to cross the years with and to love for always. . . .

The festivity of the Christmas celebrations resumed after the day of reflection and prayer. The day after Christmas was the usual time to exchange gifts, and Phillip had thought long and hard as to what to give Mercy. He realized, like a dreamer awakening, that Caleb and Abigail spent many whispered moments together, but it didn't bother Phillip in the least. Mercy was his gift in life; he knew it, so he gave out of his feeling of abundance.

He met her as she was carrying a large bowl of scrambled eggs to the breakfast table at John Stolfus's *haus*, where Phillip had been invited to spend the day. He gently took the bowl from her and led her to a corner near the oaken hutch in the kitchen.

"Uh . . . Mercy, I wanted to give you something—something that I feel captures your beauty, both inside and out. And I know that might sound . . . well, like it's not true, but I find you both strong and beautiful." He rummaged in his coat pocket and withdrew a small packet on which he'd painstakingly drawn a mountain and a farm with rows of crops growing. It was as close as he could come to expressing to Mercy how rich and fertile he found her life. He wondered if she would understand.

She carefully opened the packet, and he watched as a smile grew on her face. "*Ach*, Phillip, lavender seeds!" She shook a few of the black seeds out onto her palm.

"What variety is this?" she asked in an excited voice.

"Well, they're an heirloom variety with white frilly petals and light lavender centers, and the flowers fold up at *nacht*." He realized after he said it that the description of the flower sounded rather intimate, and he was about to make an excuse for such talk when he saw Mercy reach into her dark apron front.

"Well, Phillip, I thought that as you are a farmer, you might like a similar gift." She looked around briefly to be sure no one was watching, then slipped a seed packet into his hand.

He looked down and read the words she'd carefully printed on the outside. "'Anyone can count the seeds in an apple but only *Gott* can count the apples in a seed.'" He felt his face flush as he imagined having children with Mercy—dark-haired *sohns* and red-haired *dochders*—all the apples from a seed, a joining of Mercy and himself together. He realized that Mercy was speaking and quickly refocused his attention.

"These apple seeds are heirloom as well. They descend from trees that were first planted in the seventeen-hundreds."

He nodded, then impulsively bent to brush his lips against her cheek. "*Danki*, Mercy," he whispered.

She nodded and then he cleared his throat. "We'd better try to have some breakfast before it's gone."

They bumped into each other, trying to get out of the corner, and then both laughed out loud. It was a promising start to a happy day.

Abigail hid a smile as she watched Abner and Anke insist to Caleb that he take a turn driving the sled—with Abigail for company, of course. Caleb finally agreed and reached out for Abigail's mittened hand. She accepted his invitation, and they had almost cleared the front door when Bishop Kore stopped them to convey his Christmas wishes.

"Well, now—teeter totters and spaghetti, where are you off to?"

"A sleigh ride—unless, um, you'd like to take a turn first?" Abigail hid a smile as Caleb struggled to make sense of the *gut* bishop.

"*Nee, nee, buwe,* I've done my sledding in this life! Manatees and dry roots, I have! *Geh* and have a *gut* day!"

Abigail followed Caleb out onto the porch and laughed once the door was closed behind them. "Poor Caleb, you really can't make tails nor buttons out of Bishop Kore, can you?"

He caught her close and kissed her neck. "Don't you start, miss, or they'll be a kissing fee levied upon you!"

Abigail was still smiling when he lifted her easily into Anke and Abner's sleigh. The sleigh was a deep black and Abigail's artwork scrolling around the top in red and white made for a cheerful sight. Abigail was pleased when she'd gotten seated to find two bright quilts—

Christmas Roses, and a red and green Wedding Ring quilt—nestled on the seat to put over her lap for extra warmth. Not that she needed it with Caleb nearby—his big body radiated warmth, and he snuggled her close as he picked up the reins. Abner's black gelding, Lightning, was in the harness and clearly was ready to run.

Abigail laughed as the black horse dashed through the snow, making light work of the mounds and hills. It was only at the general store that Lightning tossed his head, shaking the sleigh bells but seemingly unwilling to move forward.

"I'll just *geh* and have a talk with him," Caleb said cheerfully.

Abigail looked on in surprise as Caleb indeed seemed to talk to the unhappy horse. When Caleb got back in the sleigh, whatever had been wrong seemed to have been discussed to Lightning's satisfaction because the horse took off at a lively trot.

"Did you just talk to that horse?"

Caleb shrugged and gave her a lopsided grin. "Maybe a little. . . . Birchbark does it, so I've kind of paid attention and here we are!"

Abigail snuggled close to him. "Here we are indeed, Caleb—the place I'd always wanted to be."

Birchbark had made it a point to tell Caleb one *nacht* about the faeries who sometimes sang in the rock space behind Blackberry Falls if two people kissed who were truly in love. Caleb figured it was worth a try and guided the black horse to a low-hanging branch where he could be tied up and given a bag of oats.

Caleb swung Abigail out of the sleigh and swept her up in his arms.

"Caleb." She giggled. "Put me down! I won't mind a little snow on my dress."

"*Jah*, but I mind and—" Caleb took a step into a large, snow-covered hole and fell facedown to land on top of Abigail. He was appalled with himself.

"Abigail, are you hurt? What's wrong? You're shaking!"

"I'm laughing," she gasped. "I haven't had this much fun since I don't know when."

He smiled down at her beautiful face and couldn't stop himself from kissing her, long slow sips of her lips, and then he gently let his tongue touch hers. He felt as if the snow was on fire when she tentatively returned his kiss. *I should get up and run off this warmth*, he thought. But she tasted sweet and womanly, and he couldn't seem to think. . . .

"Hiya!"

Caleb was rudely awakened from his reverie when Birchbark's bellow sounded somewhere nearby.

"Now, then, that's what I like ta see—a man and a woman courting while Lightning watches and longs ta give you some better wooing techniques, *buwe*!"

Caleb groaned and then got up, pulling Abigail to her feet.

"Don't you have someplace to *geh*?" Caleb demanded as he clapped his hat on and proceeded to brush down Abigail's cloak.

Birchbark threw back his head and laughed. "Tryin' ta hear the faeries, were ya?"

"*Jah!*" Abigail called out while Caleb looked at her, his attention diverted from Birchbark.

"Wait—I wanted to kiss you to hear the song, but I didn't know you wanted that as well. . . ." Caleb said in disbelief.

Abigail took his hand, and he soon forgot about Birchbark, who'd moved on in any case. "*Kumme*, Caleb, let me kiss you behind the falls."

And he could do little else but follow her. . . .

Chapter Twenty-Six

The following late afternoon a skating party was planned for all who could attend. One of the farmers, Elijah Raber, had a large pond that had frozen over, and he gladly dedicated his land and home for the afternoon of continued festivities.

The women were to have a cookie exchange in the *haus* and the men were going to build a big bonfire on the level ground near the pond. *Kinner* ran inside and out, playing on the ice and sampling the treats. Little Ruby Raber met Abigail on the back steps. The child's pretty face was swollen with tears.

Abigail sat down on the second step and gathered the child onto her lap. "Ruby, what's wrong?"

"I lost my mitten. It was a pretty red one I got from Mamm. She's sure to be mad at me."

"Well, I was about to put my skates on. What do you say to me going out on the ice with you and finding that naughty mitten? I'm sure it's out there somewhere."

Ruby smiled. "*Danki*, Miss Abigail."

Abigail soon slipped on her skates and gave a demure look to Caleb when he smiled at her as she and Ruby

passed. She took the little *maedel*'s hand and they soon
were skating fast across the pond.

"Do you remember where you lost it?"

Ruby pointed to one edge of the pond. "Up in there."

"All right then! Let's *geh*."

They looked through the brown weeds sticking up
through the ice, and then one of Ruby's skates came
loose.

"*Geh* over on the bank and I'll *kumme* and help you as
soon as I can."

Abigail continued on, weaving in and out of the dried
weeds and brown cattails. Then she stopped still. The
sound of a woman's sobbing came to her and she began
to move again, deeper into the reeds. Finally, she emerged
to see Grace Fisher sitting in the snow on the pond bank.

"Grace?" Abigail called, skating toward the bank where
Grace was.

"*Geh* away, Abigail, *sei se gut*."

Abigail looked up at the leaden winter sky. "Did he hit
you again?"

Grace sobbed softly. "*Nee*, worse."

Abigail wondered, *What could be worse?* "Has he
harmed the *kinner*?"

"*Nee*, but he says he will tell the bishop and the elders
that I am an unfit mother and that if I leave him, I'll never
see the *kinner* again. He claims that when he stole Birchbark's pack, he also stole what he called the magic of the
bag. When he said that, I just ran and ran as far as I could
get and now I'm afraid to *geh* home, but I must. My
kinner are why I *geh* on. . . ."

"Of course, they are! And Bishop Kore surely wouldn't

believe him. Why, everybody knows . . . Everybody would support you. . . ."

"You don't understand. . . . Nobody does. I best *geh* back before he finds me. *Danki* for talking, Abigail, and here's a little mitten one of the *kinner* must have lost."

Grace stood and scrabbled up the snowy bank of the pond, disappearing among the bare trees as Abigail stood helplessly by on her skates. The trouble caused by Sam Fisher and Heather tormented her brain. *I should tell Caleb*, she thought as she skated back to Ruby. She gave the child her mitten, then took her hand and they went back to the large group of *kinner* skating around the pond. Ruby joined the skaters while Abigail headed to the bonfire. When she spotted Caleb, who stood out because of his height, she forgot discretion and waved a mittened hand at him.

He came immediately, searching her face by the light of the fire.

"What is it?" he asked with concern.

She motioned to the outer ring of skaters and spoke low.

"Caleb—I should have told you before. . . . I saw Sam Fisher and Heather kissing the other day while everyone else was eating lunch after worship. And just now I talked with Grace and she's being beaten, Caleb, and Sam is threatening to take away the *kinner*. She feels as though no one would help or understand."

She looked up into Caleb's face and saw his grim expression. "Well, I understand, and I think I'll pay a visit to Herr Fisher and set the record straight."

She caught at his arm. "*Ach*, please don't, Caleb. He said he'd kill both you and Phillip if I told."

He took her hand gently. "Abigail, tell me true—did he threaten you as well?"

She bit her lip, then nodded slowly. "Caleb, listen to me—the *Amisch* are against violence, and you know—"

She was cut off by a woman's horrified scream. "*Kumme* quick! It's Heather—she's hurt bad."

"Keep the women and *kinner* back!" someone else cried.

"Let me *geh* and see," Caleb said, but Abigail grabbed his sleeve.

"I'm going with you, Caleb King. I was just now up in those reeds. The ice was frozen solid as far as I went."

Caleb nodded and they skated on as one. . . .

Mercy pulled a pan of raisin cookies from the cookstove and accidentally dropped an oven mitt. "Ouch!" she exclaimed as she slid the sheet down on the table.

"Did you hurt yourself?" Phillip asked, laying aside the spatula he held and hurrying across the kitchen to take her hand in his own.

"Not much. I simply cannot believe that I am so late for the skating! The cookie swap has bound to have started. . . ." She stopped when he lifted her fingers to his lips.

She watched in fascination as his dark lashes lowered and he kissed the tips of her fingers, gently sucking each one. She forgot the pain of the burn in the heat of his mouth. She'd never experienced such intimacy before— especially not with the *Englischer*. Then, it had been all quick, frantic groping, but *Gott* had blessed that burst of time and she had a *sohn* to love. Tears pricked at the backs of her eyes as she realized that she had not always fully embraced Joshua as she might.

"What's wrong?" Phillip asked tenderly. "Do I presume too much in kissing you?"

"*Nee* . . . oh, *nee*. I was thinking—I should have been more loving to Joshua."

Phillip moved to kiss her cheek softly. "*Gott* doesn't deal in should haves. He allows us to see the past but gives us grace enough not to regret our mistakes as long as we surrender them to Him."

Mercy nodded. "I can surrender—it's easier than trying to carry regrets on my own."

"*Jah*, and I will help you, if you let me." He bent his back and rocked his long legs forward, and she murmured her agreement as he moved to kiss her lips. . . .

Caleb looked down as Abigail pointed to the creek bank. "That is where I sat with Grace only half an hour ago."

Men were bringing lanterns, and soon the sight of blood on the ice looked like some sinister mirror.

Caleb pressed her hand hard and felt her squeeze his fingers in response.

"She must have fallen and hit her head first," he murmured in Abigail's ear. Abigail skated forward and begged the men to stop for a moment as they lifted Heather's limp body from the ice.

"Heather, it's Abigail. Please tell me who hurt you. . . . Was it Sam?"

But Heather was deeply unconscious and Caleb and

Abigail watched as Aenti Fern and Bishop Kore followed with sober faces.

Caleb put his arm around Abigail and tried to turn her from the accident site, but she shook her head and pulled him close. "This was *nee* accident, Caleb. He did it. He wanted to kill her. I don't know why except that Heather seemed nervous when I talked with her the day of the school program. I asked her point-blank if Sam was hurting her as well as Grace."

She nodded. "*Jah.*"

Caleb looked out at the cracked ice and studied it carefully; then he asked Robert Stolis for his lantern. "Stay back," he said quietly to Abigail, but she ignored him, of course, he thought wryly.

"That ice did not crack on its own. Somebody took a hatchet to it." Caleb traced the side of the hole, which was big enough to fit a woman's body.

"We should tell the bishop," Caleb said at last. "Especially given what you know about Sam and Heather."

"I know. Perhaps now before Sam decides to run."

Caleb shook his head. "Sam won't run. Not until he's gotten rid of any person who might bring him before the bishop."

"You mean me, don't you?" Abigail asked.

"*Jah.*" Caleb knew his voice was grim. "I mean you."

Abigail felt Caleb's reassuring hand at the bend in her back as they entered Bishop Kore's cabin. The *gut* bishop nodded patiently as Abigail poured out her experiences with both Heather and Sam Fisher.

"I see." The bishop nodded as she finished. "So, you feel Sam attacked Heather?"

"*Jah*," she said in a low voice.

"Well, anything is possible, but Sam Fisher has a solid alibi." Bishop Kore gestured to the room behind him.

Abigail looked up in bewilderment as Grace Fisher stepped forward. She avoided Abigail's gaze but spoke with determination. "Sam couldn't have done such things. He was with the *kinner* and me all afternoon and *nacht*. We—we were praising *Gott* for the gift an *auld* relative gave me."

Abigail held out her hands. "But Grace, we talked . . . you and I. Don't do this. We'll protect you and the children—"

Bishop Kore held up a hand. "Sam is here, too."

Sam Fisher came to put his hands on Grace's shoulders and smirked at Abigail. "Yep, I've been with Grace all day. And like Grace says, she's *kumme* into a sizable inheritance. So, why should I harm Grace? And Heather— I barely know the girl." He lifted his chin to gesture toward Caleb. "So, you'd best take her home. Seems she's a little *narrisch* right now."

Abigail longed to claw at the man's face, but Caleb whispered in her ear, "Let's *geh*. We'll handle this later."

Abigail nodded and they left the bishop's cabin without speaking. Abigail's thoughts churned, and her fury against Sam Fisher made her grit her teeth.

Caleb gently caressed her hand as they walked. "I think that it would be best if you stayed at Mercy's for a while."

Abigail glared up at him. "And let that murderer drive me from my home and the pottery? *Nee*, I'll not do it."

Caleb sighed. "Well, then, you leave me no choice."

His voice lowered. "I'll have to stay to watch over you at *nacht*."

Abigail frowned. She had no desire to make decisions based on fear, but it was an entirely different proposition to think of Caleb tousled and half-asleep while she kissed the lean line of his throat.

"What are you thinking?" he asked in a husky tone as if he already knew the answer to his question.

"I'm thinking . . . that you can stay. . . ."

Chapter Twenty-Seven

The scream jolted him awake. He'd been lying on top of the quilts, fully dressed and sound asleep when Abigail was plagued once more by a dark dream.

He turned up the lamp and caught her close in his arms. She was shaking and he leaned over and kissed her throat, trying to calm her.

"Was it the same dream, sweetheart?"

Abigail nodded. "*Jah*, I can't help my feelings, but I wish I'd made some sort of peace with Heather before she was hurt. I realized, seeing her on that ice that I've been so wrong to harbor a grudge."

Caleb thought of how he might distract her, but she suddenly sat up. "The blood on the ice and the creek. That place . . . it's near where Heather and Zinnia tried to drown me."

"No wonder you had that dream again. That's two awful things that have happened in the same place."

"*Jah*." She gave him a forced smile. "I just hope I won't have that dream again. But I do believe that *Gott* sometimes speaks to us in dreams and I think that Heather struggled in an attempt to free herself from Sam. And now she's still unconscious, even with the best *Englisch* doctor caring for her."

Caleb watched her face, which looked as if someone had made her sad. "What is it, Abigail?"

"I—I remember struggling, too." Her eyes were full of tears. "I struggled but I was able to pull away from them. . . ."

"And praise *Gott* for that." He caught her close once more and stroked her hair back from her face. He placed the lantern on a nearby table and then sought her lips with an eager mouth. "*Kumme*, sweet. Kiss me please." He lifted her against him until he found that her eagerness matched his own. . . .

Mid-January in Blackberry Falls brought a crystalline world of ice layered over snow. But the men were determined that a clear and safe path should be made to John Stolfus's large cabin for the day of the annual heirloom seed exchange. It felt like a holiday to the *Amisch*, especially with their sadness when Aenti Fern said she could only hope that *Gott* would make a miracle and bring Heather back from the unconscious place where she lingered. Then there was the withdrawal of the Sam Fisher family from community life, though Sam still ran the general store.

Phillip understood Caleb's concerns for Abigail's safety, and he was glad to stay in Mercy's *haus* with the two sisters every few *nachts* so Caleb might get some *gut* sleep at Birchbark's.

Phillip was also glad that not only was his relationship with Mercy developing, but also his friendship with

Joshua. His mentoring of the boy was proving to be a source of joy to Phillip as well.

The Saturday of the seed exchange came, and Phillip enlisted Joshua's and Tad's help as he'd said he would after the Super Ball incident. The *buwes* set up the food tables and chairs around the periphery of the main room and then marked and labeled seeds with their particular details. Soon, folks were pouring in, holding packets and labels of their own.

Bishop Kore had asked Phillip to speak at the opening, and he felt rather nervous until Mercy patted his arm.

"You shall do well," she encouraged. "And I—I promise you a kiss when you've finished."

Phillip smiled at the delightful promise, then made his way to the head table.

"*Gut* morning," he began. "As Adam was steward of the Garden, we too are to be stewards of the seeds that *Gott* provides for us. You'll find today many categories, mainly fruits, berries, and nuts, flowers, vegetables, herbs and spices, and grains. I suggest you take your time and please ask Aenti Fern or myself if you have any questions. *Danki*."

He looked out over the group and smiled, his eyes coming to rest on Mercy's face. "And now, please enjoy the morning with your friends and loved ones."

He stepped away from the front of the room and made straight for Mercy, Abigail, and Caleb. He realized in that moment that *Gott* had blessed him with love and friendship since coming to Blackberry Falls, and he was truly grateful.

"When do I get my kiss?" he asked Mercy huskily.

She looked around, then lifted her seed album to hide their faces from the crowd. She kissed him once and sweet, and it was enough reward for public speaking about an aspect of farming that he loved.

"What do I do with the seed album?" Caleb asked with genuine curiosity as he turned the small booklet over in his hands.

"Heirloom seeds are ones that have been passed down through generations and sometimes communities. So, the varieties are very *auld*. These seeds would be lost to us if seed stewards like Phillip and others did not take the time to collect and preserve. So, you can slide any new seeds that you are given or buy or inherit and keep them in your seed album until it's time to plant."

"*Ach*, I see." Caleb offered his arm and she took it with pleasure. "And do you, Mistress Potter, have any particular seeds that you're looking for?"

He smiled down at her, loving the three freckles on the bridge of her nose.

"*Jah*," she answered promptly. "I'd like to find some Canna Lily seeds. It's a decorative plant but does a heart *gut* to study it in full bloom. It's got big green leaves as well as large, beautiful pink flowers. I'd like to put it in a garden out front of the pottery."

He pressed her fingers on his arm as they made a leisurely walk around the seed tables. "This is beautiful." Caleb stopped to point out a penciled drawing of a hearty lily. "Dutch Iris Golden Harvest. Perhaps we should add a few tubers to this garden you're creating." He paid the

price, then gave her the tubers to put into her apron
pocket.

"This is fun," she said, then waved to someone over his
shoulder. "Look, it's Birchbark."

Caleb stifled the groan that came to his lips as he felt
a heavy hand clap him on the shoulder. He turned and met
Birchbark's long beard. "I thought you were away for a
few days."

"Wanted ta be here fer the fancy seed business."

"Where's your seed album?" Abigail asked with kindness, clearly oblivious to Caleb's dismay.

"They ran outta albums," Birchbark said.

"Wait, I'll be right back. I know where there are some
extra." Abigail hurried away.

"Love her, do ya, *buwe*?"

Caleb sighed. "*Jah*, I truly do."

"I knows it, but there is one thing."

"What?"

"Where'd she *geh* for them albums? Shouldda been
back by now."

Caleb met the keen *auld* eyes, then snapped around,
pushing against the crush of seed stewards. There was no
doubt in his mind that Abigail was in harm's way.

Abigail hurried through the snow, intent on picking up
the seed albums she knew were stored at the pottery from
last year. She knew Caleb would not have wanted her to
geh alone, but she didn't think there was any harm during
daylight hours.

Still, she stopped suddenly when she heard what sounded

like a gunshot echo through the stand of pines that stood near the pottery. Someone was probably hunting, she decided, then moved up the snowy steps and entered her cabin. She quickly found the seed albums in her large rolltop desk and was about to head back out when the sound came again, much closer. She swallowed hard, then turned toward the pottery studio at the back of her cabin.

She tiptoed through the short hall and caught her breath at what she saw. Sam Fisher had a long ax and was systematically destroying the pottery, both the wheels and all the pieces she had made. When he turned toward the kiln, she forgot everything but preserving it.

She stepped from the hall and put her hands on her hips. "Sam Fisher, you'll stop this right now!"

She realized her boldness was a mistake when Sam lifted the ax and began to move toward her. But some intuition, perhaps the Voice of *Derr Herr*, told her not to run, but to stand her ground.

"Think ye're not afraid?" Sam asked her with a wicked grin.

"That's right," she said stoutly.

"You will be. Do you remember what I told you I'd do to you if you told about me and Heather?"

"You hurt her badly, and someday, as *Gott* permits, she will awaken and tell the truth about you."

He laughed. "I told Heather to leave me alone, but she wouldn't listen. Grace is rich now but only so long as she lives and there is no other woman in my life. Heather found out about the money and went to Grace. Lucky I caught her before she could talk. And, *kumme* on. You don't mind so much. You watched Zinnia die. You did nothing, so why worry about Heather?"

Abigail realized that he was using the distraction of his revelations to get closer to her.

"I never wished violence on Heather, and I was wrong to have treated Zinnia the way I did."

"*Ach*, how repentant you are. But I think you deserve justice not mercy." He reached out and struck her delicate jaw with his fist.

She saw stars and felt nauseous, but she realized that she must fight or Sam would hurt her just as he had Heather.

"I'll say one thing for ya. You don't whine like the wife does. Probably because you think you're innocent and undeserving of being beaten."

"No one deserves it, Sam. Not even you. . . ."

She caught up the can of turpentine she knew was on the table beside her and threw it in his face.

He screamed and dropped the ax, then reached out blindly to try to hit her once more, but she reacted too quickly. She was about to pick up the ax handle when she backed into someone. She bit out a sharp cry only to feel Caleb's arms around her.

"You did well, my love. Now let me settle with this beast."

Caleb put her behind him, and she watched as he was about to strike Sam when the grocer suddenly groaned and fell backward to collapse on the floor. He cried out once more and then was still.

The silence was deafening.

"What happened?" she asked as Caleb felt Sam's neck for a pulse.

"I don't know really."

"The man had a bad heart." Birchbark spoke from behind them.

Abigail turned and rushed to hug the big man, who muttered and passed her on to Caleb.

Chapter Twenty-Eight

Mercy tried not to shake with excitement as Bishop Kore opened his door. She and Phillip, Abigail and Caleb had news to tell the *gut* bishop, even though it was only February 1—and Valentine's Day was still two weeks away.

"Well, now, curly-cued pigtails and blue bicycles with rainbow sprinkles—what can I do for you all?"

Mercy bit her lip in anticipation. She thought back to the week before when Phillip had knelt at her feet and asked for a quick courtship but a long marriage. He said the words that Mercy had never thought to hear, and she bared her heart to him as well.

Now Bishop Kore was speaking, and she hurriedly brought her attention back to the moment.

"Since pickled runny noses don't seem to concern you, I say it's wonderful news. But I gave the choosing to Abigail, didn't I? To choose between the mail-order grooms?"

Mercy watched Abigail stand straight and tall, the faint bruising on her jaw nearly gone.

"*Jah*, Bishop Kore," Abigail said. "I am glad to choose. And my choice is Caleb King. I also release Phillip from any obligation as I think my sister has something to say as well."

Mercy felt her face flush but spoke out clearly. "And I choose Phillip—the seed steward, farmer, adoptive *fater* to my *sohn*—he is all in one."

"Well, then"—the bishop smiled—"I suggest we have a double wedding on Valentine's Day. Perhaps it will welcome an early spring and will surely be a splot of joy for the community!"

Mercy found Phillip's arms around her, and he kissed her soundly on the cheek. It was a sweet promise of a life yet to come. . . .

Abigail was ensconced in Tabitha's *auld* bedroom at the Stolfus cabin, planning and laughing with her childhood friend and now attendant. The attendant stood for the bride and a male friend stood for the groom.

"We've got to decorate!" Tabitha said. "Maybe some bowls of crocuses on the tables and especially at the *eck*."

"I know the bridal table is supposed to be decorated. But if we do any more than that, Bishop Kore will have a fit!"

"Not so, my friend. Matthew spoke to the bishop yesterday and we can decorate with lace paper doilies—I want to make hearts out of the white ones, and let's see . . . We'll have to ask Anke to borrow her lace tablecloths, and I've got lace undergarments for you to—"

Abigail covered her face with her hands as she laughed and blushed. "Tabitha . . . I can't believe you sometimes! What about what Mercy may want?"

"I spoke with her as well," Tabitha said airily. "She's fine with what you decide."

"It just seems so amazing that I'm marrying Caleb—he's so kind and loving. But it seems as if you just got married, and now you're pregnant."

Tabitha laughed and rubbed her belly. "You'll be surprised at how quickly it happens to you."

Abigail shook her head. "I can't imagine what it must feel like to be carrying a *boppli*—a gift from *Derr Herr*. *Danki,* Tabitha, for sharing this time with me! And now I must meet Caleb at the pottery. He's been working so hard to clean up the havoc that Sam wrought."

Tabitha reached to hug Abigail. "Praise *Gott* that you are safe!"

"I think about the Fisher family though—Grace and the *kinner*. I wish I could do something to help them."

"Ann Bly has been ministering to Grace who's supposed to open the general store again soon."

Abigail nodded. She had just thought of a gift that she could give to Grace Fisher, and she left her friend bubbling with excitement.

On her way along the beautiful balustrade of smooth oak, she heard voices from below. She finished descending the steps in time for Caleb to *kumme* forward and hold her close. "My love, Heather is awake. She's asking for you . . ."

Abigail grabbed her cloak and made for the big door, with Caleb following her.

But, in the end, she was too late to talk to Heather. As Abigail burst into Aenti Fern's cabin, her eyes went straight to the sick bed where Heather had been lying for the past weeks. Abigail lifted her chin and tears fell from her face as she realized Heather was gone.

"Wanted to tell your sins, make things right, ah, *kind*?" Aenti Fern's voice was as soft as a spring rain.

"*Jah*," Abigail sobbed, allowing Caleb to hold her close.

Aenti Fern came near and whispered, "'Tis the living ya wanted to carry, but *Gott* carries best. It's His time and His timing, not ours. *Jah?* So talk to the One Who lives and do not let the harsh whisper of guilt burden your back. You might grieve, but don't hold sorrow like a stone. Let it *geh*, eh?"

Abigail nodded and sniffed and soon let Caleb lead her from the quiet cabin.

After a day of communal mourning for Heather, Caleb went back to his work tidying up the pottery. He picked the broom up to begin where he'd left off, then abandoned it for the hose. It was better to try to sweep up wet pottery than dusty dry. He had finished the dampening and laid his coat aside so it wouldn't become filled with dust.

A sudden sound made him turn, and he saw Abigail standing in the doorway with a smile on her lips. "You, Caleb King, can make even the most mundane chore look exciting."

He smiled back at her, a secret knowing smile. "I like it when you look excited."

He moved across the room, unpinning his white shirt as he went. He shrugged it off his shoulders and came to stand before her—his arms behind his back.

He bent and kissed her, the fall of his long hair shielding her from the outside world. She knew well how to kiss him now and how to touch. . . . She skimmed her hands down his arms, then back up his rib cage. He closed his eyes, savoring the wash of sensation that ran down his spine to his hip bones, then up again.

"Mmmm," she whispered. "You feel warm."

"I am—burning up inside."

She splayed her hands across his chest, then leaned forward to let her lips follow the touch of her fingers.

He made a choked sound in his throat and spoke hoarsely. "*Ach*, Abigail—I think . . . I want . . . I love you and I . . ."

"Ahem!"

Caleb blew out a breath of frustration and shrugged his shirt on. "Birchbark, can't you see that we—"

"Here now, *buwe*. I need a bit of help with my pack. I have something for your future *frau*."

Abigail clapped her hands like a little girl. "*Ach*, Birchbark, what is it?"

"Well, jest give me an' the *buwe* a minute here."

Caleb moved to help the *auld* man. They half carried, half dragged the pack into the pottery. Then Birchbark reached inside. "It's a mite heavy."

But eventually the two men were able to free the thing from the pack. Abigail jumped a bit in delight as Caleb held the gift out to her for inspection.

"A potter's wheel! *Ach*, Birchbark, it's too much!" She touched the wood with careful fingers, then helped to set it down on the old bench that had somehow avoided destruction.

"There now!" Birchbark said gruffly. "That'll do. I'll leave ya both to yer courtin'."

He was halfway out the door when Caleb stopped him and held out his hand. After a moment, Birchbark shook it and Caleb smiled. "*Danki*, Birchbark."

Birchbark hefted his pack and grunted a farewell. Then Caleb turned back to Abigail. "Now, where were we?"

Chapter Twenty-Nine

Valentine's Day dawned with a breath of spring in the air. True, there was still snow on the ground, but the tiny crocuses and other snow flowers bravely raised their heads.

Caleb had stayed over*nacht* at the Stolfus *haus* with Matthew and Tabitha. Abigail too had stayed, kept hidden in one of the cabin's second-floor rooms while she prepared her hair and dressed with Tabitha's help.

Caleb had promised not to try to see her so he'd gone for a hike up to Birchbark's to make sure that *gut* man was still planning on attending the wedding. Caleb realized that it mattered a great deal to him that Birchbark was at his wedding.

When he got to the cabin, Caleb knocked on Birchbark's door, but it was quiet, as if no one was home. He opened the door and blinked at the changes. He stared about what had been a stark, cramped cabin and found, to his amazement, a faerie wonderland. A sleigh bed of some beautiful wood gleamed with bright white quilts, falling like froth over the sides while stones that looked

like snowdrops glittered everywhere. The fire gleamed
with purple jewel-like coals, low in the grate. Caleb saw
also a rich, rug of white wool that lay under the bed.
Everywhere he looked there seemed to be new signs of
purity and goodness. He touched the skin of a bright
mango and a grapefruit . . . these treats were hard to come
by, yet they were stacked beautifully in a bowl of ice. He
went over, almost on tiptoe, to look where the green curtain had once covered the pantry, but now the curtain was
made of some shimmering fabric that hung like moving
icicles but was not melting in any way. He moved aside
the curtain of ice and saw that the pantry overflowed with
an abundance of all the food needed to feed a family for
many weeks. Then, atop a jar of peaches, he saw a note
and he snatched it and read:

> *Caleb,*
>
> *I've got to say goodbye—never an easy
> proposition, but I wanted to tell you that you
> were close in thinking that I am my cousin Claus.
> But no, not Claus. He gives the tangible gifts, but
> equally valuable are the gifts that you cannot see.
> Love. Peace. Hope. Blackberry Falls is blessed
> with these gifts as are both you and Abigail.
> I leave you my pack to use as* Gott *directs you.
> Look for me once more wherever love abounds.
> And remember—*
>
> > *Love waits for no man.*
> >
> > *Valentine*

* * *

Phillip was glad to have a few minutes to talk with Joshua as the two sat down to a hearty breakfast that John Stolfus had prepared.

"Be you nervous?" Joshua asked after washing down a bite of hotcake with a solid glassful of milk.

"*Jah*, in some ways—but I love your *mamm* and there is no nervousness in that."

Joshua nodded as Phillip went on. "I want you to know, Josh, that I am nervous about you and me. I don't mean to *kumme* in and act like I'm becoming your *fater*. Not until you want that. . . ."

Joshua put down his fork. "But I do want that. Everyone else seems to have a *fater*—even Tad. And I have *kumme* to trust you. . . ."

Phillip smiled. "Then please call me *Fater* or Daed or whatever you wish! And Joshua, I will be glad to call you *sohn*. I should have asked you earlier, but are you—do I have your permission to marry your *mamm*?"

"*Jah!*"

From that moment, Phillip knew he had a relationship with the *buwe* that would hold and grow.

Caleb knocked softly on the upstairs door where he thought Abigail was dressing. Tabitha opened it a crack. "*Nee*—she's getting ready."

"I know," Caleb said in hushed tones. "I only need five minutes."

He could see Tabitha consider.

"Please," he said.

"Five, and not a second more."

"*Jah* . . ." Tabitha slipped past him as he entered the room and looked around in surprise.

Abigail sat in the center of a big, beautiful bed. She was dressed only in a lacy shift and her hair flowed free around her like a waterfall.

"You're so beautiful."

"You're not supposed to see me like this."

"*Ach*, I hope for a lifetime of seeing you like this."

She laughed joyfully and he went over to sit beside her on the large bed. "I have something for you."

"What is it?"

"A valentine." He swallowed. "The kind Birchbark might give." He handed her the heart-shaped white paper that he'd prepared the *nacht* before and watched as she read it.

"They're love promises." He shrugged when she was quiet; then she began to read out loud.

"'I promise to always support you in your art and to always value your work. I promise to always expect the best of you, believing that I will hold naught against you and will promise to end our spats with making love. . . .'" She looked up at him.

"*Ach*, Caleb. I hope we . . . spat a lot."

He smiled and leaned forward to kiss her slowly, then with more intensity, but a knock on the door and Tabitha's entrance made him sigh and pull away.

"Now, out!" Tabitha ordered. "You only have fifteen minutes left to get ready, so hurry. Mercy is already dressed."

He smiled back at Abigail, then hurried to make his own preparations for the day.

* * *

Phillip glanced up and saw Mercy straightening her blue dress and looking nervous. He got to his feet on the hardwood floor and crossed to her. Then he folded her into his arms and rocked her softly.

"You look beautiful." Phillip found the curve of her neck and began to kiss her intently.

"Phillip, stop," she whispered frantically. "Someone will see."

"Mmmm, then I have the perfect solution." He took her hand. "*Kumme* with me, my sweet."

He led her carefully down a side hall away from the mammoth kitchen and opened a tall, slim door. He tried the knob and pulled her inside. Then he closed the door.

"Phillip, what? Where are—"

"In the downstairs linen closet, if you must know."

"Why?"

"Because I love you and want to give you the perfect wedding gift."

"What is it?" Her voice sounded cautious until he found her mouth once more. Then he pressed a piece of rolled paper into her hands.

"I'll tell you what it is. It's a deed, in your sweet name, to a fifty-acre piece of fertile farmland that I pray *Gott* will bless. We can build a new cabin and you will have a room to make your soaps, but only if you want. I can well provide for both you and Joshua."

"*Ach*, Phillip, I know you can even without the deed." She stretched up to kiss his lips and he groaned in response, holding her close.

* * *

Abigail sat facing Caleb with Mercy and Phillip seated next to them. There was a hush over the large community as they listened to the bishop's words of admonition, hope, and most especially, *Gott*.

Abigail barely heard the words of the three-hour service. It was as if there were only she and Caleb in the whole world. And then the bishop asked for their pledges and she spoke clear and true of what she would do to honor both *Gott* and her husband. And then Caleb did the same.

Caleb took her hand and they were led to the *eck*, that corner table so beautifully decorated where both couples could greet their guests and give thanks to each person gathered.

The day went on and they played the usual games and ate. But finally everyone left for home. Abigail had made tentative plans to stay at the Stolfus *haus* for their wedding *nacht*. But Caleb took her hand and spoke gently.

"Are you too tired to *geh* to Birchbark's?"

Abigail looked at him in surprise. "Where?"

"You know, Birchbark's cabin. He's gone now, I think, but I have a feeling he'd be glad to let us stay there."

Abigail reached to feel his head. "Were you drinking moonshine?"

She felt Caleb's bright blue eyes search her face, but he shook his head. "I think you will be surprised, my love, by the changes that have been made there."

"Are you sure?" she asked.

"*Jah*. He left me a note that said, 'Look for me once

more wherever love abounds.' And surely love will overflow on our wedding night." He bent and gently swept her off her feet and up into his arms.

"Caleb!"

"Shhh, do you remember my valentine?" he asked, nuzzling her neck.

"*Jah*." She giggled.

"Then let's pretend that we just had a spat. . . ."

Epilogue

It was high spring, and Blackberry Falls was bursting with an abundance of new life. The *Amisch* knew that *Gott* breathed through every tender shoot or bud or tree.

Abigail sat by Mercy, their bare feet in the creek that ran from the falls. They were taking a moment to cool off after spending all morning planting their kitchen gardens. But soon, talk drifted from heirloom seeds to life and love.

"Phillip is almost done with the cabin," Mercy said. "And I have been spending as much free time as we have with Joshua. He calls Phillip *Fater* and I think we will all continue to grow together."

Abigail nodded.

"You're not listening." Mercy sighed.

"I'm sorry," Abigail said.

She looked out onto the water and saw the ducks and their ducklings. The placid scene was soothing.

"I've been helping Grace Fisher lately," Abigail offered.

"I've heard. Is there anything I can do?"

"*Nee*, but I think she has difficulty running the store

as well as caring for the *kinner*. I've been bringing her pots to paint. I think working on art helps relax her."

"Then I'll take her some seeds. Phillip has a huge collection. Now tell me why you're so quiet?"

Abigail wiggled her toes in the chill water, then looked up to the blue sky to praise *Derr Herr*.

"I'm going to have a *boppli*."

"What?" Mercy cried with excitement. She stretched to hug her sister. "Does Caleb know?"

"*Jah*."

"And what does he say?"

Abigail smiled, a secret smile that spoke of love and trust and passion. She remembered how Caleb's blue eyes had darkened with pleasure when she'd told him about the *boppli*.

"He was . . . full of love." Abigail knew he spoke the truth.

Please read on for a peek at

Marrying Matthew

Book One of
The Amish Mail-Order Groom Series
by Kelly Long

Prologue

Blackberry Falls, PA

WANTED: An Amish Mail-Order Groom. Age 20–35. Must be willing to live in remote Appalachia and build life in said community. Must love books, horses, and possess good teeth. Appearance must be tolerable at least, though bride would favor a *gut* mind over looks. Must understand a woman's sensibilities and not be judgmental. Must realize that *Gott* is the Third in a marriage. Reply to . . .

Twenty-year-old Tabitha Stolfus knew that she was both the sole heir of her *fater*'s company and his sole lament.

"If only you'd been born a *buwe*," he'd wail at times. "Or if only you'd marry! Why can't you marry, Tabby? And why must you be so headstrong?"

Tabitha had heard the words so often, she could almost put them to song. But she had finally had enough and had taken out an ad in the *Renova Record*, a small

Englisch and *Amisch* newspaper far from her home in the Allegheny Mountains.

If I'm to have a husband, she'd considered, *let it be some man who isn't so familiar with what wealth Stolfus Lumber and Woodworking means. Then I will make sure he meets the qualifications that I lay out—not my* fater*'s.*

The idea she'd whispered to herself took root in her mind and grew, and soon a detailed ad was submitted to the far-off *Record*. And, to her surprise, because she'd never actually heard of a mail-order groom, an *Amisch* man responded. . . . Rather coolly, she thought, but nonetheless a response. . . .

She'd kept the letter in the bosom of her shift beneath her carefully pinned collar, and she occasionally slid out the paper to read, trying hard to spot anything suspicious that might lie within the words. But even she had to admit that Matthew King sounded much to her liking. He didn't seem to know about Stolfus Lumber and Woodworking and he didn't seem to possess the self-interest common to some of the local men who'd tried to win her hand . . . and her purse. *Jah*, Matthew King would do just fine. . . .

"Have you lost your mind, big *bruder*?"

Matthew King shot his younger sibling, Caleb, a wry glance, then resumed packing. "I've told you—her da runs one of the best woodworking outfits in the mountains."

Caleb snorted. "Then *geh* and ask to apprentice with him. You don't need to do something *narrisch* like marrying his headstrong *dochder*. I've heard she's as wild as a colt and not exactly marriage material."

"It doesn't matter. I'm sick of pounding out the most basic of furniture. I want to learn what only her *fater* can teach—the art and craftsmanship of woodworking. And Herr Stolfus doesn't favor taking on apprentices. Marrying the girl is incidental. . . ."

As pouring rain thrummed on his back and dripped from the brim of his hat, Matthew recalled the words he'd spoken to his *bruder* with a faint lift of his lips. Then he swiped his arm across his wet face for about the tenth time that morning. It had been raining steadily since he'd left home three days before as he and his hulking guide made their way deep into the Allegheny Mountains, the foothills of Appalachia. During their trek, Matthew had wondered idly if Blackberry Falls was simply a myth. However, there was nothing mythlike about the big-framed *Amisch* man who was leading him. Abner, as he'd introduced himself with a massive paw of a hand, spoke simply.

"I'm Abner Mast. Right-hand man of Herr Stolfus and his *dochder*'s guardian. I've been responsible for ensuring her safety since she was but a child."

Matthew nodded, sensing that there was a test somewhere in the *aulder* man's words, so he kept silent.

Abner grunted after a moment, then growled over the cadence of the rain. "I don't hold with what the maid is doing, marrying blind, and an outsider at that. But I guard her secrets well, so keep that in yer head, *buwe*, for I'll not see her harmed in any way."

Matthew realized that it would be of little use to say that he'd never harmed a woman. He could only imagine what rabbit trails such a comment would produce in *auld* Abner's mind, so once more, he remained quiet.

"Ya don't have much to say fer yerself, *buwe*. Nothing wrong with a man keeping his own counsel—I'll give ya that—but still water runs deep, and Blackberry Falls will not easily welcome a stranger, no matter who he's *kumme* to marry."

"*Danki*," Matthew said lightly; then he was distracted by a stand of virgin sugar maple near the muddy trail. He put out a hand and touched the bark of the nearest tree with something akin to a caress.

Abner grunted in obviously reluctant approval. "Well, ya touch that tree like ya would a woman, so perhaps ya ain't so strange."

Matthew smiled, unconcerned by the other man's dire attitude. *Here was virgin timber, and there would be men who knew how best to work it.* Any thought of Tabitha Stolfus drifted from his mind as he turned his face upward into the rain and thanked *Gott* for bringing him to Blackberry Falls. . . .

Chapter One

"*Nee*, bring me the yellow." Tabitha Stolfus frowned slightly as she gazed into the large, cherrywood-framed mirror in her bedroom. She knew that having such a big mirror might be considered vanity, but she had a good reason for possessing it.

She stood in a light shift, having discarded the blue dress that her faithful housemaid, Anke, had first brought her.

"Yellow?" the *aulder* woman said in a severe but hushed tone. "Ye're not to wear anything but blue to be married. And ya know that . . . Why, if yer *fater* finds out, he'll have a fit."

"As you know, my *fater* is deep in the high timber, looking for red oak. He's not due back until tomorrow, and by then, it'll all be over with." Tabitha took a graceful step away from the mirror and lightly skimmed her trim waistline with her slender hands. Her honey-blond hair hung below her hips in graceful waves and she knew, without conceit, that her face was as comely as her form.

Anke handed her the other dress, yellow as freshly churned butter. "*Jah*, all over with—and you'll be hitched to an *Amischer* ya know nothing about. And just suppose this man doesn't take to marryin' straightaway? Suppose he wants time ta get to know ya? Huh?"

Tabitha slipped on the pretty dress, then eased it over her hips. She stared into the mirror, her sapphire-blue eyes set with determination. "The man is a mail-order groom, Anke. He surely must know that if the roles were reversed, a mail-order bride would be expected to marry upon her arrival."

"Humph, well, I still say it ain't a healthy idea ta marry without knowin' each other. And what will ya do if you suddenly fall in love—true love—with some other fella, but yer forever bound to—what's his name again?"

"Matthew," Tabitha said firmly. "I'm marrying Matthew King, on my own terms, by my own judgment. All will be well. You'll see, Anke. Now, *sei se gut*, help me with my hair and *kapp*; I'm going to *geh* out for a quick walk to clear my mind before I'm due to meet Abner . . . and Matthew . . . in the big clearing."

Anke approached with a light comb, still muttering, and Tabitha caught the *auld* woman's hand and pulled her close for a quick squeeze. "*Danki* for loving me, Anke, and please stop worrying. Things have a way of working out."

"*Jah*, some might say that, *kind*, but you should know better. It's *Gott* Who works things out, and He sometimes sees things a mite different from us."

Tabitha merely smiled in response, certain in her heart that she was acting in accordance with *Gott*'s plans. . . .

Matthew realized that their trek was nearing its end when Abner lowered his bulging knapsack to the ground near a bubbling stream and pool of water.

"Yer filthy and ya smell," Abner said in gloomy tones.

"*Danki*," Matthew returned. "I could remark that you look like a muddy toad, but that wouldn't be quite right, now would it? Not when the thought of soggy vermin might be more the thing."

"Watch yer mouth, *buwe*. . . . She wouldn't want ta see ya lookin' such a mess, so ye'd best git ta bathing."

Matthew needed no further invitation. Turning his back to Abner, he quickly lowered his suspenders, then worked the hook-and-eye closures on his muddy, once-white shirt.

"You need pins," Abner said.

Matthew half turned, his shirt in his hand. "Pins?"

"We use pins here to fasten our clothing."

"That must be painful at times." He undid the waistband of his black pants, then raised an eyebrow at Abner. "I forgot my straight razor. I don't suppose you would . . ."

Abner rooted out a brutal-looking knife from his satchel and tossed it to him.

"Thanks," Matthew said drily as he finished undressing, then plunged into the icy-cold water of the creek's swimming hole. From the creek bank, Abner threw him a rough bar of soap.

"I'd best *geh* and find the *maedel*. You hurry on."

"*Jah*. Got it." Matthew lathered his arms and watched Abner slip away into the forest. It was *gut* to simply draw a deep breath and relax into the cold waters. He stared up at the canopy of green tree branches and began to lather his face. Then he plied the knife against his jaw; the edge could have proven hazardous had he not known well how to manage a blade. He was washing his hair when an abrupt sound caused him to look up at the bank.

"This is private land. What are you doing here?"

Matthew lowered his hands and blinked at the vision of loveliness his inquisitor presented. Honey-gold hair escaped her prayer *kapp* and curled in enticing tendrils against her fair cheeks. Her feminine shape was emphasized by the pristine apron she wore over a butter-yellow dress, and her stance, although she was petite, was one of strength. He knew instinctively, as surely as if she'd shouted her name to him, that this was Tabitha Stolfus—his *frau*-to-be.

He cleared his throat. "I'm bathing, but I don't want to offend your maidenly . . . sensibilities with such an admission." He ran his hands through his soapy hair and pulled until he knew he must surely look like a pointy-headed *narrisch* man.

He watched her pink lips turn down into a slight frown. "My sensibilities are hardly offended, sir, and I doubt you'd cause me much trouble anyway."

"Well—" He splashed at the water in front of him and feigned rising to his feet. "In that case . . ."

He expected her to at least turn away, but she stood her ground until he ducked under the water and hastily rinsed his hair.

Sensibilities . . . Tabitha resisted the urge to take out the letter hidden in her bodice and study it once more, but then she was distracted by the sudden thrumming of her pulse. The stranger was like some big cat, lazily playing in the icy water while she tried to understand why something about him seemed oddly familiar.

She watched as he reemerged from beneath the soap

bubbles on the surface of the water and shook his dark head. His shoulders were broad and his chest finely muscled. And she couldn't resist a hasty glance downward to where dark hair arrowed from his belly into the swirl of the water.

She straightened her shoulders, then snapped her attention back to the situation at hand. "I suggest you make yourself scarce when you've finished your . . . bathing."

"*Danki* for the advice. I'll think on it."

She nodded, then turned away to continue her walk. But her peace of mind had been shaken by the ruffian in the creek. . . .

Abner sighed to himself as he lengthened his strides along the wooded path. His back ached a bit from the recent journey and he felt every one of his forty-seven years. *Not* auld . . . *not yet* . . . He let the truth of his words quicken his steps as his heart gained momentum. He had every intention of seeking out Tabitha, but first he wanted the chance to lay eyes on Anke. He let his mind drift to thoughts of her pleasantly rounded shape, and the way her face flushed with heat when she was working at the laundry outside or canning corn at the cookstove. He longed to be able to help her with her work but knew she was proud and wouldn't appreciate a man interfering—especially the right hand of Herr Stolfus. In truth, he was John Stolfus's half *bruder*, but few knew this *auld*, well-kept secret. He'd been born on the wrong side of the quilt, of an unwanted pregnancy, with no *fater* to help him grow. Still, in the deep backwoods of the Alleghenies, he'd survived to manhood, used to running wild until

John had *kumme* for him and offered him a place, a job, a home.

Now he hurried his steps, knowing he was late meeting Tabitha in the big clearing. But because he understood the *kind*, he wasn't too concerned; he knew she was still probably fussing with her dress. He rounded a corner of the trail, then looked up, amazed as always at the workmanship displayed in the Stolfus *haus*. Truly more than a mere cabin, it rose to three stories, with windows framed by hauled stone from the creek. Abner knew that John Stolfus believed the *Amisch* adage that there is no beauty without purpose, and the purpose of his home was to be a place dedicated to *Gott*, to offer a location for the *Amisch* of Blackberry Falls to gather together in comfort and in times of trouble. And besides, that *narrisch* Bishop Kore had approved the *haus* even though it was much bigger than the small cabins of the other *Amisch*.

Abner mounted the wide, wooden steps and then gave a thundering knock on the heavy wood of the front door. He heard oncoming steps from the other side and whipped off his black hat, hastily running his hand through his thick, graying-blond hair.

Anke opened the door and he smiled down at her. She was obviously busy and gave him a slightly vexed glare as she jerked her apron into tidiness.

"Ye're back, then, with the *buwe?*" she half whispered.

"*Jah*. Is she ready?" He had to resist the urge to reach out and touch one of the brown curls that had slipped the rigorous confines of Anke's work kerchief.

"She's already off to meet ya. She said she wanted ta walk a bit before she went to the clearing."

Abner swallowed hard and nodded. It would be so easy

to bend down and press his mouth to the red of her lips. But . . . his duty waited. "*Danki*." He slipped his hat back on and returned to the steps, walking away without looking back.

Anke watched Abner's broad back as he descended the steps. The man was a giant—plain and simple. She always felt small and delicate around him, even though she knew that her belly and bosom were far too big. But she also knew that she should not be thinking of Abner, not when she could remember all too clearly the horrid touch of her *oncle* when she was ten years *auld*. . . . She sighed to herself as she gently closed the heavy door and laid aside all personal thoughts to go to prepare a bridal supper for Tabitha and her mail-order groom.

Tabitha had devised a menu that Anke felt was less than befitting of an *Amisch* wedding supper. And there would not even be an *eck* or place of honor for the couple to sit. Moreover, there were no guests invited. Tabitha had reassured Anke that there could be a small celebration sometime after her *fater* returned from the deep woods and had accepted the groom of her choosing.

Anke moved about the spacious kitchen, praying that things might *geh* well between Tabitha and her chosen groom. It seemed to Anke that Tabitha was hardly *auld* enough to marry. She clearly recalled Tabitha as a young child, eager to make applesauce or learn to scrape potatoes. Anke had done her best to be a substitute *mamm* to the little *maedel*, but she knew in her heart that Tabitha could be as headstrong as her *fater*.

Chapter Two

Matthew glanced at Abner, who regarded him with the same tense expression he'd worn for the duration of the past three days. "Do you always look like that?" Matthew asked, returning the knife he'd used to shave to the *aulder* man.

"Like what?"

"*Ach*, I don't know. . . . Mad, sad, ambivalent . . ."

Abner shook his hulking frame and grimaced. "Keep a civil tongue in your head, *buwe*. I've told ya who and what I am. Now move. We need to get to the big clearing and then on to Bishop Kore's before—"

The *aulder* man broke off in midsentence, and Matthew glanced at him with open curiosity. "Before what?"

"Never mind. Ya came here to marry, and, if she'll have you, marry ya shall."

Matthew shook his wet head. "Yes, I shall." He extended an arm. "Lead on, grim specter."

Abner glared at him but turned, and Matthew followed, wondering what he'd truly gotten himself into. . . .

* * *

The rushing creek muffled the sounds of the forest and soothed Tabitha's unusually tense mood. It was not that she was anxious about meeting Matthew King; *nee*, her *fater* had paraded at least a dozen men before her eyes, hoping that she would marry someone of his choosing. *Nee*, it was the stranger in the creek who'd unsettled her; there was something about him that tugged at her.

But she thrust away such thoughts and began to pace the pine-needled floor of the clearing in her black shoes, giving a quick tug to the pristine apron at the front of her pale yellow dress. She'd wanted to look her best, planned on it; now she wondered if Matthew King would stand in awe of her beauty—the way many men did. For Tabitha, it wasn't vanity; it was practicality. She wanted to know if the stiffness of his written response would melt beneath her gaze. Would he be smitten? She felt it would give her a measure of control in the relationship, and control was always *gut*.

She flicked absently at a *kapp* string as she moved. She knew that for the Mountain *Amisch*, marriage was a lasting thing and, in truth, she had no desire to be bound to some lout. She swallowed hard when she reflected on her own boldness in creating the ad and then drafting a carefully worded acceptance. *But if he seems ugly in his heart, or a beast of a fellow, I shall simply have Abner drive him off. I've committed to nothing. . . .* She ignored the niggle of doubt she felt, then stopped her pacing as Abner stepped from the laurel bushes with a tall man behind him.

Whatever she'd expected, it was not the handsome man she'd met that morning at the creek. She frowned as she took in his drying hair, now a rich, russet color rather than the dark, soapy strands she remembered. His eyes were an intense green and she felt consumed by his gaze. She was disconcerted and not at all used to the feeling. Then she remembered her resolve to marry on her own terms, and when he held out a large hand, she took it with a direct look. His fingers were warm and enclosed hers for a brisk, businesslike moment, and then he drew away.

She swallowed and spoke clearly. "Herr King. I'm Tabitha Stolfus." *Your wife-to-be . . . Wife. Wife. Wife . . .* She didn't say it, but she felt as if the word hung in the air between them.

"It's a pleasure to meet you . . . properly, I should say." He smiled down at her. "*Sei se gut*, call me Matthew."

His voice was deep and resonant. Strangely, she couldn't help but compare him to other men—*nee, buwes*—in Blackberry Falls. He stood with a commanding presence and was a *gut* head taller than herself.

"At least you are bathed and dressed *properly* for the ceremony." It was a firm declaration, with only the faintest hint of sarcasm, as her gaze took in his white shirt, dark suspenders, and black pants. His damp shirt clung to his chest and shoulders, and she felt herself frown.

But to her surprise, despite her attitude, she sensed a relaxation in him, almost as if his damp shoulders shook with laughter, and she couldn't resist speaking.

"You find something funny, Herr . . . Matthew?"

"*Nee* . . . I'm glad my attire suits you."

Tabitha immediately felt herself flush at his soft teasing but then straightened her spine. "*Jah*, it does. And now we must hurry. Bishop Kore will be waiting."

But once more she felt confused by him when he considered her with a quizzical smile. She had to resist the strange urge to reach up a hand to see if her *kapp* was on straight.

"Your prayer covering is on perfectly, Tabitha. But, I wonder—are we to marry with such haste? Surely you want to see if I fit your needs."

Tabitha stared at him, rallying the driving force inside her—to marry on her own terms. "You seem adequate," she said in deliberate, honeyed tones.

"*Danki.*" He smiled. "But perhaps we could have a few minutes alone to discuss . . . adequacy?" She watched his gaze flick to the silent Abner, and she gave a reluctant nod of assent.

The *aulder* man came forward and stabbed a finger at Matthew's chest. "If ya so much as lay one finger—"

"I understand."

Tabitha watched her soon-to-be husband step away from the accusatory finger and nod his head respectfully. Then Abner grunted and walked away into the forest, and Tabitha readied herself to meet alone with her mail-order groom for the second time that morning.

If Tabitha Stolfus had meant to awe Matthew with her beauty once more, she could not have done a better job. Up close, her *Amisch* dress was the rich color of creamed butter and concealed though still hinted at her fine form and pert bosom. Her slender neck seemed incapable of supporting the mass of honey-blond hair that was mostly hidden beneath her *kapp*. But he hadn't missed the errant tendrils that had escaped to frame her oval face. Wide, sapphire-blue eyes looked up at him with a coolness he supposed was meant to be intimidating to a man, but their depths only made him wonder how blue they'd become when she'd been warmed by kissing.

He blinked, then shook himself mentally. He was here because of her *fater*'s woodworking—*nee* other reason. *As I told my* bruder . . . *she's incidental and only that.* Still, it was difficult to dismiss her beauty, and he watched her perfectly formed lips closely as she prepared to speak.

"According to tradition, a mail-order groom . . . is prepared to marry upon arrival and the meeting of his bride." She lowered her voice. "Now, tell me, do you find me adequate, Herr King?"

Her question sent a rush of warmth down his spine, but he answered with a coolness he didn't feel. "Surely, but there is always more to beauty than the exterior, Tabitha. Like a pine veneer that hides a wealth of burled elm, true beauty lies within."

"That's not what most men think," she muttered.

"What was that?"

"Nothing." She shook her head. "You speak knowledgeably of woodwork."

It was more a question than an observation, but he'd rehearsed this scenario in his mind. He shrugged. "I learned basic furniture making from my *fater*."

"Did you enjoy it?"

Did I enjoy it? Now that's a question I wasn't expecting. . . . On the one hand, he loved every minute he'd worked with wood, but his *fater* had stripped away most of the joy in the process. His *daed* had also limited the family business to making the most basic of furniture, with little-to-no-room for true creative craftsmanship.

He supposed his *daed* was bitter after his *mamm*'s death; he'd certainly been brutal.

Matthew needed to answer her but was saved from having to reply when a tall, gangly man joined them in the clearing. The fellow fixed his beady eyes on Tabitha, and Matthew felt an unfamiliar flare of irritation as he stepped in front of his soon-to-be *frau*.

"Go on with you," he ordered harshly, even as he heard a sigh of frustration from behind him. Clearly, Tabitha had tangled with this beak-nosed *Amischer* in the past.

"Do you think I'd leave this delicate flower alone with some stranger?" The man's squeak of a voice grated on Matthew's nerves. "I happen to have once held the privilege of being betrothed to Tabitha, and I am not so far removed as to think that she is beyond my protection."

Matthew blinked as Tabitha stepped in front of him. "Elam, we were never betrothed; only my *fater* thought so. Now, why don't you just go on your way?"

"And leave you defenseless?"

Matthew thought he could see actual steam coming off Tabitha's head and hid a sudden smile. Clearly, the fellow didn't know what Matthew intuitively understood about the strength of the woman he'd met only that morning. *She's about to blow her stack. . . .*

"I am not defenseless. Now, please. . . . I've got private business with this man."

With his prominent Adam's apple, Elam appeared to gobble, but then Abner came back into the fray. And with one gloomy glare from Tabitha's guardian, Elam wavered away into the woods, leaving Matthew a clear field to tease Tabitha as she turned back to face him.

"A disgruntled man—a broken betrothal?" He reached

out a hand to lightly skim a finger down her rosy cheek. "What am I to think?"

She slapped away his hand, and he laughed.

"You wouldn't be laughing if you knew what a tittering gossip Elam Smucker is!"

"What's there to gossip about?" Matthew asked lightly. "We're only getting married."

He smothered another laugh when she glared up at him and would have said more if Abner hadn't grunted his disapproval.

"Enough of this playin'. Bishop Kore is waiting and we don't have much time."

The *aulder* man's words sobered Matthew's mood as he wondered again about the hurry.

Tabitha turned around on the steps where she stood outside Bishop Kore's cabin; she couldn't deny that Matthew King was more than handsome. He moved with a lithe, pantherlike grace when he walked, and his hair had dried to an even brighter russet color that she couldn't help but find pleasing. As he drew closer, she could see his green eyes and covertly took in his broad shoulders, narrow waist, and long legs.

Something of her thoughts must have shown on her face, though, because he mounted the carved wooden steps behind Abner and stopped to gaze down at her.

"Would you like to examine my teeth?" he asked politely.

"What?"

"My teeth?" He gave her a wolfish grin, baring strong, white teeth. "Wasn't that in the ad? I thought because you were evaluating the rest of me . . ."

She frowned darkly, a sharp retort coming to her lips, but then, she didn't want to give him the satisfaction of knowing that he'd riled her, so she held her tongue.

The opening of the bishop's door reminded her that her wedding was nigh, and she arranged her features into the semblance of a smile. Bishop Kore was an odd, forgetful man until it was time for him to speak during church service; then his voice thundered with certainty. But now he stood with the door open, a congenial if somewhat confused expression on his *auld* face.

"*Ach*, Tabitha and the *gut* Abner. But who else do we have here?"

Tabitha wanted to grit her teeth at the bishop's forgetfulness, but she smiled sweetly instead. "This is Matthew King. We're here to be married. Do you recall that I spoke with you in private some days past?"

"Marriage? *Jah*, a sober state to enter into. Nothing like fruit salad . . . Well, *kumme* in. *Kumme* right in."

Tabitha ignored the strange mention of fruit salad— the bishop's peculiarities were of little concern to her at the moment. She swallowed and followed the *auld* man into his modest cabin, very conscious of Matthew King at her back.

"May we hurry, Herr Bishop?" she asked, frustrated when the man was distracted by Matthew's apparent interest in the carving of one of the key support beams in the cabin.

She watched as he touched the oak beam with strong hands, then smiled at the bishop. "A cabin such as this is built like a rock, sir. No storm could shake it, I think."

Bishop Kore gave a wheezing laugh. "Built *on* a rock, my *buwe*. As sure as sunfish. You're interested in woodworking? Well, *Derr Herr* must surely have made your match with Tabitha. Her *fater* is—"

"Not here!" Tabitha snapped, then amended her tone. "Of course not, Herr Bishop. He's deep in the high timber. Don't you recall? Not here. Not for another day, I hope. . . . I mean . . . surely he'll be returning soon. If we could just proceed . . . right now!"